*Enjoy*
*J. Mullen*

*Dedicated to my Brother's Matthew, Lewis and Chris,*
*Brothers in blood and Bond who I would fight with to the Gates of Hell and Back*

*Please bear in mind as you read this book that I am a solo author and mistakes may be made despite efforts in proof reading*

## Spell translations:

*Ignis – Fire*

*Caelum – Air*

*Unda – Water*

*Terra - Earth*

*Custodire – Protect*

*Incrementum – Growth*

*Revelare – Reveal*

*Sana - Heal*

*Levare – Lift*

*Impediendum - Paralyse*

# Chapter 1
## I'm being Chased again

Yeah, you read that sentence right.

Since I was 10 years old and my foster home burnt to the ground while I narrowly escaped by the skin of my teeth and the flames tickling at my trouser legs I've been constantly running from bad situation to bad situation, or from something that wants to and I quote "Kill me" or "Mayme me" or "Send me to Hell". Take your pick whichever you decide is better in your mind.

But whatever your choice just know that it's not fun to be me.

I don't know why these things want to kill me, I didn't do anything to upset them I don't think … well I mean there was that one guy that I burned his … you know what, never mind it's not that important, but since I was 10 I've been living on the streets fleeing from town to town and eating whenever I can or at least whenever there isn't a flaming fireball coming at my head or an arrow cutting the tip of my ear off (That was really hard to explain at the free clinic) and sleeping with one eye open to protect myself from any threat whether it be from a human or one of the weird things trying to kill me.

So basically, my life sucks, you don't want it, no matter how cool you might think it be that I can run faster than 50mph or hear a person's heartbeat when their three streets away, then there's the ability to see in the dark or see long distances like an owl (Really comes in handy when you want to watch the baseball game but can't get a ticket).

After that there's the super healing as I like to refer to it, basically, my body heals from minor wounds like a cut or a bruise insanely fast and finally I have incredible strength, like stronger than Arnold Schwarzenegger in his prime strong. I remember one time when this guy almost ran me down with his car trying to park, I waited till he went into the coffee shop and lifted his brand-new Mercedes off the ground and moved it into a handicapped spot (the look on his face when he got towed was beyond satisfying).

 Anyway … where was I? oh right, running for my life in Downtown Chicago while being chased on my sixteenth birthday (Hooray for me) and pushing past civilians who moan at me for accidentally spilling their morning lattes all over them (Excuse me for not wanting to get ran through with a spear … trident … sword … what is it this time?) 'SMACK' a gigantic spear sounded as it collided with the brick wall next to my head (Spear, definitely a spear).

 "GET BACK HERE!" the beast yells throwing another spear at me which I promptly dodge resulting in some poor soccer mom's minivan ending up with a spear through her back window piercing the steering wheel sounding at an incredibly loud noise like a foghorn down by the sea (Sorry lady).

Right, I think it lost him, where was I?

Sorry introductions can be tricky when I'm running for my life, so first of all my name is Jason Matthew Parker, (Long name I know). My grandma, before she died, told me my parents had picked the name because my mother loved Greek mythology hence 'Jason' as in the sailor of the Argo and my Father was a devout Christian hence 'Matthew' as in the apostle.

 I have long brown hair that touches the base of my neck and is scraggly and slightly dirty (I know disgusting but when you live on the streets and spend every day of your life running you don't get much time for a shower or a haircut) ocean blue eyes and a tanned complexion (My mom was Columbian).

So now you know everything about me and if you happen to find out why I'm constantly being chased before I do then please give me a call at …. (I don't have a phone, I'm 16 years old and don't have a phone!)

Anyway, this is my story enjoy.

"Found you!" the creature spoke standing at the end of the alleyway grinning at me, "Well damn it" I mutter to myself struggling for breath and facing down the beast, his cold red eyes boring into my very soul, he's currently dressed in centurion armour with black hair, white alabaster skin and an evil smug grin across his face carrying a colossal spear in his right hand and a steel sword in his left (How this guy runs through traffic and doesn't get stopped by the police is beyond me), "I've finally caught you and now I'm going to destroy you" the creature spoke edging towards me grinning his spear griding against the ground and frothing at the mouth.

This is the point when I have three choices, stand my ground and fight and die, scream like a little girl and beg for my life or run for the hills … "BYE!" I yelled turning on my heels and running up the wall two feet and bouncing over to the other side grabbing onto the fire escape (I chose option three, thank you awesome agility gift) "GET BACK HERE!" the creature screamed chasing me up the fire escape jumping from the floor to the metal ladder in one leap almost bringing down the fire escape with me on it (Great another creature than can practically fly, there was one that actually could fly once that ended up burning down an office block … sorry Cleveland) so now I'm running across the rooftops jumping 15 foot gaps like their hurdles and scaring the local pigeon population.

I glanced down as I heard a Hispanic lady scream up at me from her window, luckily being of Latino heritage, I speak fluent Spanish and I would translate it for you but if I do this little tale of my life may become very R-rated, "Sorry" I shout down dodging another flying spear (Where does he keep getting these things?) and scrambling down the fire escape to the street setting off at another sprint in the general direction of the docks hoping for escape by boat (Surely some kind fisherman will give me a lift to the other side of the bay to escape this lunatic …. Yeah, I didn't think so either but a boy can hope).

I'm so close to the dock I can smell the salt water coming off Lake Michigan "Almost there" I think to myself dodging a yellow Taxi that nearly runs me over at 30mph, I can see the fishing boat that can hopefully take me across the lake "Sweet Freedom" I mutter to myself right before I let out a loud agonizing scream and a few words in Spanish that would make a sailor blush and a nun make a cross symbol across her chest as a spear pierces the back of my left calf pinning me to the bridge watching helplessly as my last source of escape pulls away from the dock and onto Lake Michigan.

"Got you" the creature mutters floating over the traffic that has come to a complete standstill, when the spear pierced my leg for some reason I can't explain that was possibly connected to my injury or maybe the scary centurion, everyone around me jumped out of their cars and ran for the nearest shop or anyone who was walking down the sidewalk jumped into a nearby bush covering their heads like a bomb was about to go off, or joining the fleeing drivers into the nearby coffee shop or fashion store leaving me alone with a spear in my leg and a ... I'm just going to say it 'Demonic being' slowly drifting towards me "Damn" I mutter to myself trying to pull the spear out of my calf discovering that surprise, surprise, I'm stuck.

"I've chased you all day across streets, rooftops, alleys and a shopping mall and finally I have you right where I want you" the creature growled twanging the end of the spear vibrating the wooden shaft throughout my muscle causing even more pain (Because you know, the spear in my leg wasn't causing enough pain already) "Look man, I don't know what I did to upset you but just let me go, surely you have better things to do than chase a 16 year old kid across city" I plead twisting my leg slightly ignoring the throbbing pain in my leg (You never know pleading might work) "To wipe you from this earth I would chase you from one side of the planet to the other" the creature replied (Damn you pleading).

"Harsh man, seriously harsh, okay, tell you what, before you kill me let me say a prayer so I can get into a good afterlife and then you can put the next spear through my chest what do you say?" I ask formulating the next stage of my plan, "Very well, I will allow you 30 seconds" the creature replied spinning his sword in his hand and checking its sharpness by slicing through a mailbox like it was made out of paper "Thank you" I replied kneeling down to the ground on my none speared knee (F.Y.I. if you're squeamish about blood you may want to skip this next part), "This is going to suck" I think to myself grabbing the wooden edge of the spear that is stuck in the back of my leg and the part of the shaft closest to the metal arrowhead stuck in the dock.

"Our father who art' in heaven" I mumble (Here it is) before grabbing both parts of the wood and pushing down with all my remaining strength and adrenaline separating the arrowhead section and the staff section from the spear from my calf and leaving a splinter of wood in my muscle, I grabbed the remaining staff section driving it into the creature's stomach and rolling a few feet out of the way whilst letting out another guttural scream "HALLELUJAH!" I scream staring up at the creature who is now staring down at me with an even angrier expression than he already had before I snapped the spear.

"You're going to pay for that" the creature muttered tearing the wooden shaft from his stomach spilling black blood over the grey concrete, "I had a feeling you were going to say that" I replied limping to the chain link fence leaving my bright blue blood trickling on the floor behind me (bright blue blood I know strange right?) "There's nowhere to run, your kind is a thorn in our side to me and my people, we want a simple thing, total and infinite destruction of the earth but you and your people keep stopping us, if I can wipe one of you off this earth then that will at least make me feel a little more confident in my ability to wipe out my enemies" the creature growls confusing me more than I already am on a regular day. "My kind?" I question, "Don't pretend you don't know, I know what you are and so does every being that has chased you over the years, farewell Jason" the creature speaks raising his sword into the air.

That's it, end of story, my life ends laying bleeding on the floor in downtown Chicago with a spear shaft in my leg and a soon to be sword through my heart, game over, I wonder what the next life will hold for me? "Not so fast Eros" a woman's voice speaks as an arrow flies through the air piercing who I now know as Eros through his arm just under his wrist causing him to drop the sword before he can drive it through my chest, I look to my left at a beautiful girl the same age as me I'm guessing with long blonde hair that cascades down the right side of her head onto her shoulder and the left side is shaved with a three lines of braids over her ear in red, blue and pink, she was dressed in a white t-shirt with a red leather jacket, blue jeans, red trainers and a quiver across her back with an ivory bow in her hand.

"YOU!" Eros screams pointing at my saviour with his arrow pierced arm "Yeah, me, step away from the boy and I'll make it quick" the girl speaks drawing another arrow from her quiver faster than I can blink and aiming it directly a Eros' head "I'LL KILL YOU BOTH, YOU AND ALL YOUR KIND, I AM SUPERIOR IN EVERY ..." Eros screams right before an arrow pierces the air landing between his eyes and turning him into a smouldering pile of ash "I hate it when they brag" the girl mumbles as I slowly start to feel myself passing out, "Thank ..." I mumble slumping down onto the ground the world spinning around me, "Woah! Hold on I've got you" the girl speaks running forwards and stopping me from slamming my head against the pavement "Hi" I mumble "Hi, I'm Jennifer Wilson but my friends call me Jen, what's your name?" Jen asks me placing the back of her hand against my forehead "Jason ... my name is ..." I mumble before everything goes black the only sound, I can hear is the roaring of sirens and the panicked shouting of Jen and several other people running down the pavement.

# Chapter 2
## Spoiler: I survived

"Where did you find him?" I heard a voice mumble as my senses slowly started to return, "Downtown Chicago, he'd been running from Eros for an entire day and was about to be run through with a sword if I hadn't shown up" I heard Jen speak as my eyes slowly started to open despite the massive ringing in my ears and the vertigo making me eyes spin in their sockets.
I recognised one of the voices as that of the stunning girl who saved my life (Fine, I'll admit it, she's hot and I think I'm smitten) "Lucky you showed up, you sure he's one of us?" the other voice questioned which I now recognised is a man's voice "Positive, Blue blood, superior speed and agility, combat instincts he's definitely one of us" Jen replied filling me with confidence that my bumbling escape attempt impressed somebody.

"You know it's rude to talk about somebody while they're unconscious" I mumbled slowly sitting upright to find myself surprisingly in what appeared to be an infirmary in a wooden building with whitewashed walls and wooden beams running up the wall and supporting the roof. "You're awake?" Jen spoke shocked "Roughly, nice shot with the arrow by the way" I replied noticing that at some point of being moved from Chicago to this infirmary my shirt was gone along with my trousers leaving me in my boxer shorts covered in a white blanket my skinny body standing at attention (Yes, I'm not your typical macho movie type, I stay this thin for two reasons, my constant running and eating out of dumpsters or leftovers at tables depending on what I can eat while living on the streets).

"Why am I in my underwear?" I asked the first question coming to mind "Your clothes were disgusting, torn and covered in blood so we thought the best thing to do was burn them and give you some new ones" Jen replied passing me a white shirt, blue jeans, white socks and black converse from the table next to me "Where am I?" I asked slipping on my jeans under the covers and then turning out of the bed to slip on my shirt and new shoes and socks, it felt incredibly strange to be wearing freshly laundered and new clothes but a nice welcome change to the lost and found or shelter clothes I usually wore whenever my clothes got torn or set on fire or any other number of things that were beyond comprehension compared to somebody accidentally tearing their jeans when they fell down.

"You're in the infirmary, we brought you here after your fight" Jen replied pointing to the young boy again about my age stood next to her, he was African American with hazel eyes and was dressed in a red shirt with blue jeans and black shoes, "Hi I'm Scott" he replied reaching out to shake my hand which I gladly reciprocated despite the stinging sensation in my ribs "Jason" I replied standing upright and noticing that the spear wound in my calf had slowly begun to heal after being removed by who I hoped was a doctor or medic leaving me with only a slight limp.

"Pleasure to meet you Jason Matthew Parker" Scott replied "How do you know my full name?" I questioned curiously, "We've been trying to find you for a while, you're a hard man, we've been searching for the last two months for you Jason, thirty-four of the fifty states in six years and two states in two months impressive" Scott replied making me even more uncomfortable than I already was. "Not exactly answering my question but okay, why have you been looking for me exactly?" I questioned, "To bring you somewhere safe, a place where you'll no longer be chased constantly, sleeping in alleys or eating whatever you can find in the garbage can" Scott replied with a disgusted look on his face (Smug jerk).

"First off, I've been doing just fine on my own for 6 years, second, I don't always eat from the trash but believe it or not when you're homeless you eat when you can and finally, I'd like to know where I am exactly?" I asked listing out my reasons and limping my way to the entrance to the infirmary doors angrily "Jason wait!" Jen yelled as I pull open the wooden doors and my jaw almost hits the floor in shock.

Outside of the infirmary is a sprawling city that looks like something pulled straight out of the 15th century with wooden whitewashed homes, clay roof's patched with straw, a large square building that looked like the a square version of the Globe that Shakespeare used to do his performances in and unbelievably a large castle at the top of the hill. "I'm definitely not in Chicago anymore" I muttered to myself (Please don't sue me creators of the Wizard of Oz) and looked out at all the people currently staring at me from my sudden appearance "Welcome to the Academy of Protectors" Jen spoke sneaking up behind me and placing a hand on my shoulder consolingly.

## Chapter 3
## Welcome to the Academy

Jen and Scott guided me slowly through the Academy grounds introducing me to the homes of the parents of the students and families that stayed after graduating from the Academy of Protectors, the Coliseum where a group of students were battling each other or shooting arrows at targets or slashing at straw dummies that were somehow striking back at them blocking attacks and striking at them with swords and staffs.

"How long has this been here?" I asked curiously watching a group of small children run through the streets laughing in joy, "Protectors, what you and everyone here is, have been around for millennia and move with the advancement of the Western world, originally we were far across the world protecting the lands as Mercenaries roaming from one town to the next, but eventually a group of elite Protectors met together and established the academy here in the United States three hundred years ago" Jen explained.

"What's a Protector?" I asked curiously, "All will be explained at the end of the tour" Scott interrupted pushing any further questions aside.

Jen and Scott led me to the main hall of the Academy itself from the outside grounds before leading me over to the large square building in the centre of town, "And this is the student halls for the academy where you'll be staying" Scott explains leading me up a large circular staircase where students were leaning against railings chatting to each other and watching my awkwardly limp through the halls.

I stopped abruptly as I noticed a student fly out of a room with a pair of white feathered wings on his back landing in the central courtyard of the student halls, "That guy has wings …" I mutter pointing at the student whose wings had suddenly disappeared as he walked out of the courtyard with a student laughing and smiling. "Yeah, he's not supposed to be in this section but he was probably just visiting" Jen explained "Wings … he has wings … why does he have wings?" I question trying to address the elephant in the room "He's an Angel" Scott explained suddenly.

"Wait a second, an Angel? As in heavenly being, sat on a cloud playing a harp kind of Angel?" I asked looking around for anymore flying students, "That is a stereotype and offensive we don't all play the harp, some of us play the banjo or guitar" Scott replied. "Wait are you an …" I questioned right before Scott flexed his wings and a pair of black feathery wings popped out of his back, "Well that answers that question" I added watching as Scott folded his wings back into his body leaving me staring at his shoulder blades wondering why his shirt hadn't torn and where the wings had gone.

"I know this is a lot to take in but this will all become clearer tonight" Jen spoke stopping at a door that surprisingly had my name on it, thankfully it was just "Jason Parker". "Did you know I was coming?" I questioned "We had this room chosen for you the minute the Diviner found you" Scott replied. "Diviner? As in fortune teller?" I asked drawing on my memory from an old book I had found in a library once (Great refuge if you're homeless by the way, they'll let you stay for a while in the winter to stop you from freezing to death) "Yes, she found you in a vision and we spent the next two months trying to track you down" Jen replied opening the door to my room wide.

If my jaw could have dropped open any wider at that moment I would have turned into a Roger Rabbit cartoon, after months of sleeping on the streets or in shelters (After the 12th attack you basically get blacklisted from all shelters). I was surprised to have an actual room to myself, against the back wall was a large king size bed with Navy blue sheets and pillows with four oak wooden posts on each corner stretching up to a wooden roof that when you laid on the bed and looked up showed the sky above despite being inside.

Against the wall to my left was a 50-inch plasma screen TV with various home gaming systems, an en-suite bathroom with a massive walk in shower and bath at the side of it and a walk in wardrobe with the clothes I had always wanted to wear with various trainers of different styles. "This is a surprise" I mumbled running my hand up and down the smooth wood of the bed post. "The room builds itself according to your deepest desire when it is first built, what you've always wanted all placed into a single room" Jen explained smiling as I struggled to contain my joy at the change from sleeping on the streets to sleeping in a deluxe room.

 "Well, we'll leave you to get settled and see you tonight at the identification ceremony" Jen replied, Scott had disappeared at some point while my back had been turned leaving me and Jen alone (Easy there Perv's it's not that kind of tale) "Identification ceremony?" I questioned completely confused.
"Sorry, I keep forgetting you're not used to this lifestyle, the identification ceremony is a process where your lineage is revealed and you are sorted according to your heritage and DNA depending on what your parents were, do you happen to know what your parents were?"
"My parents died when I was 1 and my grandma didn't talk much about them before I died" I replied.

The truth was, I hadn't known much about my parents other than I had been named according to what my parents liked and what they looked like, but other than that my grandma refused to talk about them and then when she died so did any information about them. "I'm sorry, I didn't know, I can explain a little about your heritage if you like? At least what the Diviner had told us anyway" Jen leaning against the doorway. "Okay" I replied still unsure if I even wanted to know my life had become crazy enough already by this point.

 "Basically, the academy is a place for the Protectors of humanity, Protectors are the children of the realms who are born from a Supernatural parent of a low rank and a mortal. If one of your parents was an angel like Scott then you'll be identified as an Angel and move to the angel's residence to study and learn battle styles, if you are identified as a demon then you'll be moved to the demon halls, if you are identified as a Deinonychus which is a being of Purgatory then you'll be moved to the Deinonychus halls and if you are what I think you are then you'll be staying here" Jen explained making my head hurt with all the information given to me. "Realms? What are those?" I asked curiously "The realms are what we refer to as Heaven, Hell and Purgatory, it's just a shortened term" Jen replied.

"Wait, demons ... aren't they the bad guys?" I questioned choosing one of the many questions running through my head,

"Yes and no, beings directly from Hell do tend to be evil and destructive but Protectors from the academy fight Arch-demons and Arch-angels who both want to see our kind exterminated. Demons fight Arch-Angels, Deinonychus fight both, Angel's fight demons and Hunters fight everything including all magical dangerous creatures" Jen replied.

"Hunters? Is that what I am?" I asked, Jen paused as if trying to dumb down the craziness I had already been told,

"We believe so yes, a Hunter is a being of pure power and balance, all your gifts are the exact same as a Hunter has, we protect humanity from all threats from all the realms and delay the Rapture".

"We? You're a Hunter too?"

"My dad is the mortal of the family, the gene of the superior parent is stronger so everyone will always be what their superior parent is" Jen replied with a hint of sadness in her eyes, the same that I have when I think of my parents.

I wanted to ask more about her parents but I decided that was probably best to leave it at that for now, "The Rapture? Isn't that supposed to happen and be a good thing?" I questioned having a highly devout Christian Grand-mother and seeking refuge in churches whenever possible you definitely learn about the end of the world.

"That's also a common misconception, the Rapture is the worst thing that can happen to the realms. If the Rapture happened then all good mortals would be called to Heaven and the earth and other mortals would be left to the chaos of the forces of Hell.

The angels and our kind would be overwhelmed trying to keep the demons on earth from trying to break through the gates of Heaven, the imbalance would cause purgatory to turn to dust, the ensuing chaos would cause mortals to lose their faith in God which in turn would cause him to slowly lose strength, God's power is based on faith leading to the eventual collapse and destruction of heaven and the end of life as we know it" Jen replied leaving me more terrified than all my days on the street combined "So bad then" I muttered.

"To put it in less words yes, we keep the balance and peace to keep the universe safe. I'll leave you to get settled and see you tonight at the identification ceremony, it starts when you hear the bells ring" Jen spoke grabbing the door handle as she started to leave, "Why because an angel gets his wings?" I joked trying to break the tension, Jen stared at me confused trying to understand my awkward sense of humour.

"I don't get it" Jen replied

"You have seen It's a wonderful life right?"

"Sorry no I've never seen it"

"Oh that's unacceptable, tell you what, tomorrow we'll have a movie night and I'll introduce you to a classic what do you say?" I asked with my arms outstretched. Jen paused for a moment considering my offer "You have a deal" Jen replied smiling at me before closing the door behind her and leaving me alone with my thoughts and the craziness of my new reality "At least I'm not on the streets anymore" I thought to myself as I collapsed onto the cotton sheets and stared up at the clear blue sky above me.

## Chapter 4
## My identification is painful

I relaxed in my room for the next six hours grabbing a hot shower for the first time in years basking in the steam for about thirty minutes before changing into a blue t shirt, black jeans and a fresh pair of underwear and socks. I switched on the TV waiting for the inevitable bells that would signify my identification and welcoming into the academy.

At some point during my relaxation, I had been thinking I missed having books to read (Like I said libraries are a great place to be) a sudden noise interrupted my thought and when I looked to my left, a giant bookcase had appeared along one side of the wall with a few of my favourite fiction novels and a collection of guides about monster fighting and a '*Keeping the balance of the universe for dummies'* book tucked on the non-fiction shelf.

By the time the bells rang at 6pm I had already read through two of my monster fighting guides (I decided to wait for the dummies book till later). I checked my hair glad that all the knots had come out of it after my shower and ran my hands over my freshly shaved face before walking out my door following the other students up to the main academy hall.

Inside I felt like I'd walked straight from a medieval village and into Hogwarts (I know dream come true right) the interior of the hall was full of tables where Angel Protectors were sat with their wings folded in tight, Demon Protectors who were dressed in almost completely black or red (There seemed to be no in-between) were casting fire spells at each other laughing as some would jump up moaning that they had just burnt their favourite shirt.

What I guessed were Deinonychus Protectors, the nerdy looking kids sat blandly eating their meals and struggling to talk to each other about anything were sat apart from the other groups. At the back corner of the hall was a large table occupied by a few students where I spotted Jen sat laughing with a few of her friends.

Overhead was a glowing image of the planet earth and three spaces around it one showing white pearly gates and clouds, another was fiery and dark which was obviously hell and the other looked like static on a television which meant either the vision of Purgatory was broken or just incredibly boring like the students. At the back of the room was a long table with twelve various older adults sat in large wooden chairs, they appeared to be of high status and I noticed that I could see the children of Angels, Demons, Deinonychus and a few average looking people who I guessed must be Hunters between them discussing important matters but my ears couldn't quite pick up what they were talking about over the roar of the crowd.

I spotted a large table that was completely empty and another table that had a few kids sat awkwardly at it so ultimately, I decided to sit with Jen. "Hi" I mumbled walking up behind Jen "Hey, did you settle in okay?" Jen asked turning away from her group of friends who were all staring at me like I had the plague, "Yeah much better change to where I last slept, do you mind if I sit here?" I questioned pointing to the space next to her, Jen looked at the group and then stood up leading to me one side.

"I would honestly but right now you haven't been identified, I know you're a Hunter but the rules are that you can't sit at a table until you've been identified, after that I'll happily save a seat for you but for now do you mind sitting with the other people who are going to be identified today?" Jen asked me. (I know I should be totally offended but I've been excluded before and her reasoning was fair enough for the time being) "Of course not, guess I'll see you after the ceremony" I replied nodding my head and joining the table of candidates.

If I didn't already feel like a bit of an outcast when I first arrived at this place I definitely did now, most of the kids were at least 4 years younger than me some even younger than that leaving me feeling like I'd just been dropped off at kindergarten as a student teacher although I did spot another 16-year-old thankfully so I chose to approach him.

"Mind if I sit here?" I asked the 16-year-old lad next to me, "Sure man feel free, join us" he replied shuffling aside and allowing me to sit down next to him, "Hi I'm William" he spoke, William was what I was guessing was Asian heritage with dark brown almost black eyes, jet black hair that was slicked back like a 1960's greaser and was dressed in a red shirt with black leather jacket, black jeans and large black biker boots with spikes "Jason" I replied shaking William's hand.

I almost yelped in shock as a plate suddenly materialised in front of me along with a chalice and an 18th century ghost floating in mid-air in front of me "For you sir" the ghost spoke bowing slightly although where his voice was coming from I had no idea because he currently didn't have a head. "Umm thanks" I replied trying to form the words as the ghost floated upwards and disappeared into a thin mist "Don't worry the ghosts freak everyone out the first time they're in here but Louis is a nice guy" a girl about 16 years old spoke from across the table from me, she was wearing a white dress with a gold belt around her waist with long brown hair neatly straightened and piercing blue eyes the colour of the sky on a clear day.

"Louis … wait a second … was that King Louis the 14th?" I asked looking around for the king of France who was beheaded a few hundred years ago, "Yeah but don't mention it around him he gets a little bit sore about not having a head anymore, Hi I'm Katie" the girl replied reaching out to shake my hand "Jason" I replied shaking her hand in return, her calloused palm rubbed against mine, clearly she was used to getting her hands dirty (I was afraid to why).

"So, how does this work do I call out for a waiter for a cheeseburger or …" I asked right before looking down at my plate to see a cheeseburger with lettuce, tomato and fries on the plate along with cola in the chalice, "Or I guess I just ask" I added trying the food and savouring the crisp French fry right before wolfing down the rest of the meal at an embarrassingly fast pace (I hadn't eaten fries and a burger in months especially ones that were actually hot).

"Great huh? Anything you want just appears on your plate and in the cup no matter how bizarre" Katie explained as I imagined a large ice cream sundae with hot fudge sauce and a cherry on top smiling as it appeared before me and wolfing that down as well (Bonus about super healing no ice cream headaches) "I love this place" I mumbled resting my hand on my very full stomach.

"Ladies and Gentleman, welcome to the identification ceremony" a man's voice spoke up from the table, he was dressed in a sharp black pinstripe suit with a white shirt and navy-blue tie. His pale complexion stood out behind his brown scraggy hair, I guessed from the utter silence aside from the clapping that this guy was in charge of the academy.
 "Tonight, we welcome 15 new students into the academy" the man spoke pointing down at my table of newbies,
 "Who's the suit?" I whispered to William
"That's Isaac, the head of the council of Protectors and head Hunter" William whispered back to me tapping his steel boots against each other. Isaac kept on with his speech but I barely heard him as I continued my conversation with William.

"So, what are you if you don't mind me asking?" I asked
"Dad's a demon and mom's mortal so I'm definitely a demon"
"You?" William questioned.
 "Didn't know my parents but Jen says I'm a Hunter"
"Jen? As in Jennifer Wilson the most powerful Hunter in the academy and a total babe?" Will pointed over subtly at Jen who was currently sat admiring Isaac.
"Ummm … well I mean … yeah but …" I stammered,
"Dude relax, you can admit she's hot without worrying about her being completely humiliated" William replied materialising a cigar in his hand, "You can't smoke in here" I mumbled "Sure I can, I'm a demon, rules are kind of exempt from us" William replied twisting the cigar in between his teeth.

"WILLIAM SAMSON DON'T YOU DARE LIGHT THAT CIGAR!" a large scary dude dressed all in black with two large scaly black wings protruding from his back shouted from the table, "Sorry Coach Jones" Will mumbled throwing it to the far corner of the room to the muffled laughter of the rest of the hall.

"Anyway, it's time for the identification ceremony to begin, we shall start with Katie Summers" Isaac spoke as Katie approached the stage to the collective clapping of the students, Katie bowed slightly in front of Isaac facing what I recognised as a forest nymph with brown bark skin and pure green eyes with leaves covering her body, she kind of reminded me of nymph's from cartoons (Yes, I know, I should read more but when you recognise something from a cartoon, you recognise it all the time from a cartoon ... don't believe me? Ask a Coyote).

The Nymph was currently holding a golden chalice which she passed to Katie, Katie drank the liquid and stood still for a moment ... in an instant she was surrounded by golden light like the sun making it almost impossible to see her right before two white wings grew out of her back "Behold Katie Summers, child of Angel" Isaac spoke as the angel table let out a loud cheer and Katie bowed before flying over to the angel table joining her fellow students.

"Next up is William Samson" Isaac announced "See you around buddy" William mumbled to me patting me on the shoulder before strolling over to the Nymph dancing cockily as he approached her, Will bowed at Isaac and Coach Jones in respect and took a drink of the chalice, in an instant he was surrounded with dark shadows black as night and two demonic scaly black wings appeared on his back, the demon table let out a loud shout and banged their fists against the table in triumph.

Will winked at the Nymph causing her to blush right before Will disappeared into a veil of shadows and appeared atop the demon table spinning on his heels and finger gunning at the Nymph on the stage causing her to blush a brighter shade of green.

Every other student went ahead of me going to the Angel table, Deinonychus table, Demon table and the Hunter table each with a collective cheer until finally I was the last one sat at the table alone, "And now we ask Jason Matthew Parker to come up for his identification" Isaac announced my full name clearly identifying me as someone already unusual despite being known as the guy who lived on the streets for the past six years. I slowly walked up to the stage feeling my heart pounding in my chest like a drum, sweat was pouring down my back, the clapping of the room faded from my ears until finally I stood before the Nymph and the chalice, I bowed at Isaac noticing the glint of wonder in his eye and turned to face the Nymph taking the golden chalice from her staring at the thick blue liquid swirling in the cup.

I stared deep into the liquid trying to work up the courage to drink it, this would be the most defining moment of my life and the day I was sorted into the group who would affect me for the rest of my days on this earth no matter how many days I had left. I took a drink feeling the cold blue liquid pouring down my throat and waited for the response I was expecting that I had seen from Hunters previously a simple tingling sensation as a H appeared on me signifying me as a Hunter, a book had explained that wherever I willed the symbol to appear on my upper body is where it would appear so I focused on my right pectoral muscle and waited for the tingling sensation … but it never came, what did come instead was a horrible burning pain.

 I collapsed to the ground clutching at my chest and letting out a guttural scream as my body felt like it had been set on fire, everyone in the hall let out a sudden gasp as I knelt holding the burning sensation in my chest. "Jason? Jason, can you hear me?" Isaac asked now knelt in front of me touching my forehead "It burns, why does it burn?" I questioned clutching my heart "What's happening?" Jen questioned who was now stood at my side resting her hand on my shoulder "I have no idea, this shouldn't be happening" Isaac replied casting some sort of spell trying to read what was wrong with me.

"Stand back" I mumbled as I felt my body begin to feel like it was going to explode "What?" Jen asked me, "STAND BACK!" I shouted, the burning sensation intensified in my heart, Jen and Isaac stood aside as I ripped the collar of my shirt revealing a large H in black lettering signifying that I was at least a Hunter but the burning sensation was still there until finally I felt it collect in my back.
 I let out a loud scream raising back up bolt upright, I stretched out my arms breathing heavily at the release of power, the pain subsided and I stared out at the crowd waiting for my welcome at the Hunter's table but everyone was completely silent staring at me in shock "What is it?" I questioned as I felt something moving on my back, I glanced over my right shoulder and saw a flash of white, I looked over my left shoulder and saw another flash of white and I realised why everyone was staring … out of my back were two large feathery wings like an Angel but I had a Hunter engram tattooed on my chest.

"Behold … Jason … child of Hunter and Angel" Isaac mumbled as I stood front and centre at all the staring students.

## Chapter 5
### More of an outcast than I already was

Yeah, you read that right if I wasn't any more of a social outcast when I first arrived being a former 16-year-old homeless kid that had no idea about the crazy world of my family heritage then I definitely was now, (Have you ever had that nightmare where you're in front of everyone in school in your underwear? That's how it feels when you're stood in front of the entire academy with a 'H' tattooed onto my chest and angel wings sprouting out your back). I ran out of the hall trying to escape the awkward looks from the students and stood outside under the night sky having a panic attack struggling in vain to put my wings back into my body.

"Jason!" Jen yelled chasing me out of the academy hall followed quickly by Will and Katie, "I don't know what to do they won't go away, they won't go away" I replied flexing and folding my wings screaming in frustration every time they refused to go back into me "Okay just relax okay, take a deep breath and exhale" Jen replied, taking her on her instruction I breathed in deep and slowly released the air in my lungs instantly feeling a strange tugging sensation on my back and when I looked around my wings were gone.

"Thank you" I spoke smiling at Jen and trying to still hide my horror and shame from how everyone had looked at me in the academy hall, "So, you're a half breed? That's a new one" Will spoke breaking the awkward tension currently building in the atmosphere. "Half breed?" I questioned curiously not remembering seeing that title in the brochure, "Your heritage, you're Half Angel, Half Hunter which is beyond exceptionally rare, you said your dad was a devout Christian?"
"Yeah, so was my grandma"
"Then he must have been an Angel and your mother was the Hunter makes the most sense" Jen spoke pacing back and forth tapping her chin with her index finger.

"Wait ... if my dad's an angel does that mean he could still be alive? I mean he's an angel right and angels can't die, can they?" I questioned hoping for some possible lineage back to my parents. Jen, Will and Katie all looked at each other awkwardly before staring back at me "We're strong and hard to kill but none of us are immortal, I'm sorry" Katie replied crushing any hope that some lineage or connection to my past that could explain this crazy world that I'm now stuck in, "Thanks guys, sorry about running off the whole thing just freaked me out" I replied placing my hand on Jen and Katie's shoulder and then bumping fists with Will "You're always welcome buddy you coming back in?" Will asked pointing towards the door "Actually I think I'm going to head back, it's getting late and I think I need some rest after all that" I replied.

After all the stares I'd got while stood in there and running out, the last thing I wanted to do was walk back into the room and have everyone stare at me once again all I wanted was to lay my head against my pillow and sleep until this whole mess sorted itself out. "Okay, well see you tomorrow then, I'll pop by and knock on your door when it's time for morning classes" Jen replied smiling at me and turning to walk back towards the hall "See you later buddy" Will added smacking me on the back causing me to flinch in fear that my wings might have popped out again "Don't worry your wings aren't showing" Katie spoke from behind me placing a hand consolingly on my shoulder and following Will back up to the academy hall.

After my goodbyes I began my walk back through the academy grounds and towards the Hunter resident halls, "Do I even belong in there anymore? I mean I'm a Half Breed, I'm Half Angel/Half Hunter so where should I actually be staying?" I thought as I slowly climbed the staircase to my room on the 3rd floor (Why did they give me the 3rd floor? Hadn't I done enough running and climbing in my life for one day). I gazed out over the courtyard and watched in awe as small lights flew around the tree in the centre of the courtyard laughing and giggling like they were playing a game at which point I realised that they weren't fancy lights, they were fairies, beating their tiny wings like hummingbirds and covered in a bright colourful glow.

I watched them fly and skitter around with ease and grace "Maybe I can do that, looks easy enough" I thought to myself stretching all the muscles in my body and jumping up and down on the spot readying myself for my first flight attempt. "Here we go" I mumbled to myself as I jumped off the 3rd floor balcony … and plummeted straight down to the courtyard below slamming onto the grass with a heavy 'THUD' leaving a Jason shaped imprint in the dirt.

"Ow" I mumbled to myself right before my wings popped out of my back and sprawled open across the ground around me (If only I had a camera), "Perfect … just perfect" I groaned laying in the dirt ignoring the laughing of the fairies above me. After brushing the dirt off my clothes ignoring the mocking laughter of the fairies, I ascended the stairs one at a time hiding my humiliation and shame thankful that no one had been around to see my first flight attempt. I headed into my room and changed into a pair of blue shorts removing my dirt stained and ripped t-shirt and throwing it into the laundry hamper in the corner before lifting the covers and climbing into bed thankful to finally be going to sleep.

# Chapter 6
## Mr. Sandman don't bring me a dream

Sleeping on the streets you have little time for actual sleep when you're afraid of getting robbed or impaled by an arrow, sword or spear or set on fire or … (Okay, my experience of homelessness may be slightly different to others experiences) you learn that your brain doesn't often give you the chance to dream but right now that is exactly what was happening to me, well I think it was a dream, it felt different like I wasn't so much as creating something with my mind as witnessing something going on right now like I was watching movie.

"A half breed? This is rare Isaac, beyond rare" I heard Coach Jones speak as I felt myself being dragged into a large office in the academy, somehow, I was watching the scene unfold from inside the Isaac's office, the stone walls stood strong and proud along the walls of the room, A large oak desk sat in the back of the room ingrained with images of angels, demons, deinonychus and what appeared to be Hunter's. every scene showed them fighting in combat against different beings around them ranging from a lion to a 10 foot tall scary looking demon to what I can only describe as an evil looking tornado (How does a Tornado look evil you may ask, trust me, you don't want to know) and behind the desk was a wall of floor to ceiling windows showing the valley and lake out behind the academy.

"I know Coach Jones but the boy is clearly identified as one and as such he must receive the necessary training" Isaac replied as I hovered there like a drone watching the conversation unfold,
"Where do we put him? We don't exactly have a half breed section of the academy?"
 "The Diviner says his Hunter gene is strongest so he stays with the Hunter's, I know this is scary Isaac, I'll admit it I'm scared too but the boy is still young, with the right training he could be a great protector of this academy".
"And if this goes wrong, he could be the greatest threat to the realms in millennia" Coach Jones groaned as I felt a force grab a hold of me and drag me into the shadows and away from the academy.

"Great, still not awake yet" I mumbled to myself as I found myself now hovering over a red scarred battlefield with numerous demons fighting each other and preparing weapons on molten hot forges dining and drinking from a large black bubbling cauldron, I don't know much about battle but one thing I knew for sure was that these demons were preparing for war.

"Brothers and Sisters!" a voice shouted from a far corner of the battlefield catching my attention instantly, I moved myself around the space where I was currently hovering and then forwards until I stood floating 10 foot above the source of the shout.

Now, I've met very few demons in my time on this earth, sure, many have tried to kill me long before I knew what they actually were but this demon that I was looking at right now … was like nothing I've ever seen before.

He looked almost human at about maybe nearly 7 foot but he was surrounded by a complete veil of shadows that would occasionally lash out like a viper cracking the ground around him, his eyes pierced through the darkness in a horrifying glow of pure red, his icy voice seemed to resonate around the battlefield as the troops came forward one at a time standing at attention, I don't know how I was here right now but one thing I knew for sure was that this guy was beyond evil.

"Soon our lifelong plan will come into action, the day we have longed for aeons is finally at hand, we will break through into the mortal realm and take it for our own" the demon shouted as the crowd cheered and screamed. "When the planets align our plan will unfold and the gates will be opened, no longer shall we stay trapped here until we are deemed fit to exit and cause mayhem, no longer will we perish in the mortal realm only to find ourselves dragged back here to rebuild in agony and torture until our forms are made whole again, we will burn the earth to the ground and reign down our fury upon it, the mortals will run in fear and their God will bring the worthy to heaven" the demon continued (Was I sweating? Can I sweat in this state?).

"The earth shall be ours and we shall rule upon it with vengeance, demons, succubus and beings of evil alike … our day is soon at hand" the demon finished raising his hand that currently held what I hoped was an animal bone goblet although the fingers around the base of the goblet didn't exactly confirm my hopes as the crowd let out another thunderous cheer so loud the ground shook, I looked behind to me to see for any identifying factors that may help me find this place when I woke up and that's when I saw their way out.

Ahead of me in the distance were two gigantic black obsidian gates with spikes at the top and symbols burned into the metal, skulls were dotted around the frame and pierced on top of some of the spikes. At the base of the gates were 8 large braziers only 1 of which were currently blazing with a hot green flame, the other 7 braziers were full of black logs waiting to burst into flames at a moment's notice. "This can't be good" were the only words that came out of my mouth as I felt my form being dragged upwards through the rocky celling above me, through the earth and back into my room landing back in my body waking up in a hot sweat.

# Chapter 7
## Welcome to Hunter Training, Prepare for your eventual death

 Well after a horrific nightmarish vision of the gates of hell and two leading members of the academy council it was a nice relief to see the inside of my room and not find myself waking up in an alleyway or homeless shelter where I had spent my teenage years sleeping, although the sweat pouring off my back from the panic wasn't exactly comfortable.

 A sudden knocking on my door snapped me out of my panicked trance giving my brain chance to register getting up, I wiped the sweat off my brow before opening the door to my room "Good morning ready for …" Jen spoke standing in the doorway before looking me quickly up and down with a quizzical expression on her face "I see that the identification process went well for you" Jen added "What are you talking about?" I questioned curiously; Jen pointed at my body and then pointed to the mirror against the wall.

Okay, so in my years on this earth I've experienced many shocking things, being chased by a gigantic wolf in North Dakota, set on fire in the New York City rain (Don't ask), stabbed by a spear in Chicago and brought to an academy of supernatural protectors but what I was staring at right now in the reflection took the trophy. My entire physique had transformed overnight, where I had once been a skinny 16-year-old homeless kid, I now found myself with an athletes build, I had a six pack, strong biceps but not insanely big but enough to give me a decent shape, two strong pronounced pectoral muscles and I felt stronger and fitter as well.

"Sleeping gave me abs?" I questioned pressing each individual pack "Courtesy of the identification package, Hunters bodies shape themselves during the night according to the ideal style for that person, clearly for you that involved an athletes' body" Jen replied still staring at me until I looked back at her and she looked away blushing.
 "Sorry, I'll get changed" I mumbled grabbing a blue t-shirt from my walk in wardrobe and changing my shorts for a pair of jeans and black converse before standing back with Jen in the main room.

"So, what's on the agenda for today then?" I questioned running my hand through my hair trying to flatten down the bedhead, "Training newbie, we'll make a fighter out of you yet" Jen replied turning around and heading along the balcony urged by instinct I followed her quickly behind.
When we reached the ground floor, I noticed a group of students staring curiously at the Jason shaped imprint in the dirt in the middle of the courtyard from last night, "What happened?" Jen asked looking at the shape in the floor "No idea maybe somebody fell" I replied trying my best to maintain a poker face, "You tried to fly didn't you?" Jen questioned as we continued our walk towards the fighting arena, (My prayer for the earth to swallow me up at that moment went unanswered) "For the record my wings did come out … just after I landed" I replied causing Jen to burst out laughing running her hand along her braid's.

The training arena was definitely a sight to behold for the first time from the inside and not the outside, around the entire arena was a seating area like the stands in the coliseum, most of the seats were currently occupied by several ghosts just going about their day enjoying the spectacle and chatting amongst each other about the local joys of being dead or the joys of watching new recruits battle it out in the arena for their entertainment, I wasn't quite sure. I scanned the ghosts and noticed a few emperors, roman centurions, playwrights, knights and King Louis the 14th with several pieces of large fruit around him that he kept slipping onto the spot where his head should be.

 "He does that every couple of days, helps him feel whole for a while but he never can decide which fruit is the right fit" Jen explained, Louis picked up a large melon placed it on his neck and then threw it away reaching for a pumpkin. "Alright everyone, today is a practise session for those of you who've been here a while and Hunter training 101 for you newbies" A ghost spoke with a thick British accent dissolving out of thin air and appearing in front of us causing a girl at the end of the row to scream in panic.
The ghost was dressed in full silver knight gear with a helmet visor that showed a pair of white eyes before slamming shut, the ghost opened the visor over his eyes once more only for it to fall back down again and hide his face "Blasted thing" the knight announced ignoring the visor hiding his eyes.

"I am your teacher Sir Galahad" the knight announced (I'll leave it to your imagination what happened to my jaw at that moment in time) "Sir Galahad? As in Knight of the Round table Sir Galahad?" I asked utterly stunned and a little starstruck. Since a young age I had been fascinated with the legend of King Arthur and the knights of the round table and to actually be stood in front of the living legend of heroism and chivalry itself almost made me faint like a girl at a Justin Bieber contest.
 "The very same young man I see you know of me" Sir Galahad replied bowing in response to my comment. "How could I not! Sir Galahad, most noble knight of the round table, searcher and only founder of the Holy Grail, you're the most famous knight in History!" I announced only now realising that there was a group of Hunters, Angels, Demons and Deinonychus watching me fan-girl out in front of our teacher.

"Yes indeed young Jason Parker, I see you're a man of fine calibre, now on with the lesson" Galahad announced removing his helmet and holding it under his arm, Galahad had long blonde hair that reached down to his shoulder blades and his skin was surprisingly full of life for a ghost although his eyes remained a clear white with no pupil.
 "Today class we will be studying your preferred forms of combat, for some it is the bow and arrow a weapon of range and power, for others it is the Axe a weapon with a strong hit but difficult to swing, for some of you it may be the spear close combat but also useful to keep a distance from you and your enemy and for many of you I imagine you will choose is the sword" Galahad announced drawing a large silver broadsword from his sheathe holding it aloft. "Is that?" I questioned "The sword of David correct" Galahad replied swinging the blade in his hand in a circle before returning it to its sheathe.

"Students choose your weapons, those of you who will be practising archery today the range is over there and Miss Jennifer Wilson will be leading you in this practise session, she is a master in it after all" Galahad spoke turning and bowing at Jen "Thank you Galahad, those of you interested in Archery follow me" Jen spoke signalling and turning to see five of the fifteen students following her.
I stayed back for two reasons, one, I wanted to spend more time with Galahad and two because archery didn't seem like the right choice for me at least at this moment in time; three students left and grabbed spears, two grabbed axes and five including me stayed with Galahad for our training session. "Okay students, choose your sword of choice" Galahad spoke pointing over to a weapons cabinet filled with various swords, some students chose Katana's or great swords, some chose a cutlass so they could and I quote "Be Pirates" but my eyes instantly locked onto a steel arming sword or as it's otherwise known a 'Knightly Sword'.

"Interesting choice Mr. Parker, why did you choose this sword when your classmates chose differently?" Galahad asked me "I don't know … it just felt right" I replied feeling the weight of the sword in my hand, it felt … natural, like I should have wielded a sword my whole life. My body went into overdrive and my fighting instincts heightened, my focus which was usually occupied by a hundred things around me (My first foster parents had gotten me diagnosed with ADHD but I never really paid attention to it) was now solely focused on the sword in my hand, "Clearly you were meant to wield a blade of this calibre" Galahad announced guiding us onto the training area.

"Okay students, I want you each to choose a partner to train with, just simple fighting for now a clash of blades but no stabbing, the medical department has enough problems without patching up bleeding students, Mr. Parker as there is an odd number you will train with me" Galahad instructed making me feel like a spotlight was shining down on me along with a neon sign pointing at me screaming "TEACHERS PET" (To be fair I was but it's nice not to be known as one).

"Okay students begin your training" Galahad spoke drawing his sword from its sheathe and turning to face me while the other students began locking blades battling cautiously, one student produced black wings from his back and his partner drew two white feathery wings from his "Angel against demon … awesome" I thought as they took flight and began to battle in the air, the other two students stood blankly occasionally tapping swords when teacher was looking (Deinonychus, I know right). "Are you ready young Parker?" Galahad asked me "I was born ready" I replied confidently twirling the sword in my hand, me and Galahad stood facing each other waiting for the other to strike and make the first move, I could see the look in his eyes despite he didn't have pupils and I knew that he would never make the first move, he was the embodiment of chivalry and it was in his nature to only begin combat when his opponent struck first so I chose my moment.

I stepped forwards and jabbed at Galahad who quickly deflected my strike like he was swatting away a fly, "Too slow Jason I saw your attack coming a mile away, watch your footwork" Galahad spoke stepping forwards and slashing his blade down at me but instead of blocking I decided to use my flight instincts and dodged, the blade passed through the ground never making contact with it.

 "I presume being dead you can choose what the blade hits and what it doesn't" I asked circling Galahad, "You presume correctly, a precaution so that I don't accidentally hit you" Galahad replied lunging at me again, I deflected the blade and staggered backwards from the impact. "Good block Jason but remember your footwork, do not hold back, use all your gifts to fight me, you are not only of one world Jason do not forget that" Galahad instructed, (Don't ask me how I knew how to do this next part I just did) I felt my blood begin to course through my body, generations of instincts passed through my mind as I felt my muscles tighten and my strength surge "You're right Galahad … I am of two worlds" I replied stretching my back and releasing my wings.

Galahad stood back stunned slightly at the sudden reveal of my white feathered wings and I took my chance in that moment lunging forwards connecting my blade with Galahads upper arm, his chainmail shredded and revealed the skin ghostly skin underneath. "Excellent work Jason!" Galahad announced touching the damaged part of his armour, "Thanks Galahad but are we going to complement each other like little girls or are we going to fight?" I replied twirling the sword in my hand and stretching my wings out "I like your confidence" Galahad spoke stabbing at me.

I knelt and span closing my wings in together creating a shield that deflected the blade away and my brain clicked, the battle instincts kicking in … Galahad's sword was the Sword of David! It was a divine weapon which meant it had no effect on other angels or those with angel blood. I stood back up and smiled at Galahad "Interesting, why the smile?" Galahad asked "Because … I know exactly how to fight you now" I replied spinning and flexing my wings, Galahad slashed his blade downwards at me but the blade bounced off my wings uselessly while I slid on my knees and slashed Galahad across the back of his knees, Galahad let out a shout of pain grabbing the attention of the other students who had now stopped to watch.

 "Galahad! I'm sorry are you okay?" I asked stepping forwards only to receive an elbow to the nose from the noble knight "I'm a ghost Jason, I can't be killed and rule one, never underestimate an opponent" Galahad replied as I pressed my fingers to my now broken nose ignoring the blue blood, "Good lesson, now to finish this" I replied dashing forwards using my wings as a shield, Galahad tried to slash at my legs but at the last moment I jumped and corkscrewed through the air my blade outstretched knocking the Sword of David from Galahads hand and sending him flying backwards a few feet.

Galahad stood back up and I thought that he was completely furious with me until he started to clap, "Bravo young Jason, Bravo" Galahad spoke placing his sword back into its sheathe "I proudly concede the fight to you" Galahad added bowing and standing back up, the students around me clapped at my fine battling style and victory over our teacher including Jen who stood nodding her head at my battling style "Thank you Sir Galahad" I replied bowing in respect to a great master and realising that for the first time in my life ... I felt right at home.

# Chapter 8
## Welcome to Defence against the dark arts (Wait … wrong book, don't sue me J.K.)

After finishing our session with Sir Galahad who promptly disappeared into thin air once again into whatever existence of afterlife that he had, Jen and I walked back into the academy grounds before separating for our different classes for the day she headed for History of the Realms and I headed for Magic practising 101.

The classroom was under the main academy compound down a series of staircases so deep that for a brief moment I wondered if I was descending down into Hell, "Don't worry buddy, that's just where they keep the dragon" one of the students commented as I nervously passed by a steel door that seemed to be smoking. Finally, we reached the bottom of the staircase and entered into Magic 101. The room was massive compared to the doorway entrance, yet again another pleasant surprise of the academy was that rooms tended to be bigger on the inside, on the left side of the room was a standard classroom with several wooden desks facing a chalkboard that was floating in mid-air surrounded by a white veil, on the right side of the room was a large what appeared to be a firing range with a long stretch of space leading to several cardboard shapes at the end including a cartoon demon, a wolf and a dragon "This is … different" I mumbled to myself.

"Hey buddy glad to see we've got at least one class together" Will spoke from behind me approaching me and slapping his hand against my back "Will! It's good to see you man" I replied turning to face Will and embracing him in a bro hug, "Good to see you too, how did your first class go?" Will questioned walking with me into the classroom sitting down at a desk placing his heavy steel boots on top and leaning back in his chair.
I proceeded to tell Will all about my class with Galahad and battling him including using my wings in combat as Divine weapon deterrence, "Clever, you struck me as a sword fighter when I first met you, I prefer a great sword myself, I like to be able to swing the blade in a wide circle and take down as many bad guys as I can" Will replied (I know! Demons, right?).

Will protruded another cigar from mid-air once again and set it between his teeth chewing on the end "Where do you keep getting those?" I questioned looking back and forth for the teacher, "Illusion magic my friend, best gift being a child of a demon can give you, I can make simple things appear in my hands when I need them, weapons, medicine, a bunch of other boring stuff and my favourite cigars" Will replied swirling the cigar around his cheek "But you don't light it?" I asked "Of course not! Do you have any idea how bad smoking is for your health" Will replied with a wicked grin on his face.

"Ladies and Gentleman welcome to Magic 101 or as I prefer to call it How to kill monsters" a voice came from the front of the classroom right before a ghost materialised once again out of thin air in a thick cloak of shadows. The ghost was dressed in a long purple cloak over a black suit with a red shirt and purple tie the same colour as his cloak, thankfully this ghost did have a head with wild purple hair that stuck up in every possible direction that made him look like he'd been struck by lightning and solid green eyes with a giant smile spread across his face (Truthfully, he reminded me a little of the Joker from Batman).

"Are all the teachers' ghosts?" I whispered to Will "Don't have to pay them I suppose" Will replied tapping his unlit cigar against the desk, "I am Nicholas Flamel or Nick if you prefer, your teacher for the foreseeable future of your time at the academy" Nick called out "Wait, Flamel? As in the discoverer of the Philosophers stone?" I questioned raising my hand. "That bloody rock, you find one strange stone that kills you and turns you into a ghost and you spend the rest of eternity getting questioned 'Did you find the Philosophers stone'" Nick replied annoyingly using air quotations when he described the stone.

"Sorry I asked" I replied "And that is your first mistake Mr.?" Nick questioned his hair moving frantically from left to right like it was trying to escape his head, "Parker, Jason Parker" I replied swallowing the remaining saliva in my mouth in nervousness.

"Parker? My god … you look just like your Father" Nick replied as I felt my mouth almost slam against the desk,
"You knew my Father?"
"I knew both your parents, I taught them both, I was horrified when I found out about their deaths, I never even knew they had a child" Nick replied floating over and placing his ghostly hand against my cheek, the whole situation was beyond awkward but I didn't care, for the first time in my life I felt like I had an actual connection to my past.

"They passed when I was so young I never got a chance to know them, my Grandmother raised me" I mumbled the classroom now focused on me and my tragic life story like a night time dateline show. Nick let out a snuff noise from his nose and floated back a few inches
"You poor soul, I knew your Grandmother as well, a fine woman but a fire in her heart that would burn me if she got mad enough"
"Yeah, she was like that, I'm sorry to be the one to tell you that she's gone too"
"I'm so sorry, how long?"
"10 years ago"
"Wait … but you would have been 6, where did you go after she died?" Nick asked me.

I looked around at the students who were following my story with every word and wondered if I should stop here but when I saw Will who nodded at me I knew that I should continue and tell them everything. "My first two years I spent in a foster home with 6 other kids but one day the house collapsed, no one was inside thankfully but I got moved into another home and then another, and then another until finally when I was 10 and in my 12<sup>th</sup> Foster house one day the house burst into flames which the fire department could never explain … after that I lived on the streets until I was found and brought here" I explained noticing a few students in the corner dabbing at the corner of their eyes and one angel making the sign of the cross while mumbling in Latin.

"I'm so sorry Jason, you should have had someone there to teach you the skills you needed to know but now at least we can start teaching you how to truly fight" Nick spoke placing his hand on my shoulder consolingly before floating back over to the chalkboard and started writing down various words in English and their translation into Latin. "Okay, so on with the lesson, there are many types of magic but there are four major ones that we focus on allowing students to excel at other magic themselves through the use of their choice in this class, the four major types are Elemental, Healing, Nature and Combat magic" Nick explained pointing at the various symbols drawn on the board.

"Why do we have to speak in Latin to cast spells?" I asked curiously,
"Excellent question, the mortals believe Latin to be a dead language and therefore of no use for the modern world. Magic is powered by Latin being one of the first languages ever spoken when it was discovered, since then mankind has left Latin behind and therefore the magic that connects them to it which is why we no longer see many mortal witches or wizards" Nick explained.

"It is your choice which magic you may choose to focus on but it will highly depend on your heritage, for those of you who are Angels" Nick continued as several students in white clothes seemed to hover out their seats in anticipation "You will likely find Nature and Healing magic more comfortable to use" Nick added, several of the students frantically noted down what their choices would be.
"For those of you who are demons or Deinonychus, you will likely depend on Elemental magic as it will link to your realms Fire, Ice, Air etcetera, etcetera" Nick spoke gesturing with his hands.
"And you Hunters" Nick added looking directly at me, "Will benefit from Combat Magic, you will use offence and defence regularly on your assignments and as such will be the skills you need to survive" Nick finished occasionally scrawling on the chalkboard.

The class continued on as Nick explained the fundamentals of magic, the history of magic, the warnings of using escape magic in public and how it can go wrong resulting in the death of the caster "I remember warning Houdini that one of those tricks would kill him one day" Nick added (Surprise! Houdini was a demon in the sense of magic and who his heritage was), "Okay, I think I've talked enough and learning practically is always better than from a book so let's begin on the training course" Nick finished waving his hand causing the chalkboard to disappear into a fine mist.

## Chapter 9
## Warning! Don't use fire magic, Fire magic bad

We all moved our way over to the firing range and training area ready for the next section of our session gathering in a line in front of a desk ready for Nick to begin his lesson, "Okay folks, time to begin our session today, the magic you use will be best suited to your abilities so first let's try something simple and safe, Nature magic" Nick commanded snapping his fingers causing a flower pot filled with soil to appear in front of each of us.

"Your first task is simple, grow the plant from its seed as far as your abilities will allow" Nick added showing us the Latin word for Growth "*Incrementum*". A few of the angel students in an instant began to grow small plant life from the pot spiralling up from the soil till they bloomed into blossoming flowers of various sizes depending on the skill level of the student while my flower pot remained nothing but a useless pile of dirt. "Yeah … I don't think Nature magic is for me" Will mumbled whose flower pot was gone, "Where did your plant go?" I asked following Will's finger to the soil trail that led from one side of the room to the other disappearing into a crack in the wall, "It just got up and ran away" Will replied shrugging his shoulder making another cigar appear in his hand and placing it between his teeth.

"Well, after Mr. Samson's apparent creation of sentient life that is still being chased by the academy security" Nick spoke "**THERE ON THE CEILING! IT'S COMING TOWARD US … OH GOD!!! IT HAS TEETH!! WE NEED …."** The security guard shouted through the intercom system right before a loud roar was heard and the intercom went to static before cutting off completely, "Why does it have teeth?" I whispered to Will who had now chewed his way through three cigars his nerves in overdrive "I don't know … oh wait … I was casting the spell and remembered watching a film with my mom about something called … the Triffids I think?" Will replied tapping his finger against his chin in thought.

"*IT HAS LEGS NOW!! WAIT … IS THAT ANOTHER ONE? … OH GOD, THEY'RE MULTIPLYING!*" A different guard screamed into the intercom right before the intercom went static again (Never, ever, think of the triffids when casting a nature spell). "I think we'll move onto Elemental magic" Nick mumbled keeping a close eye on the gap in the wall in case Will's plants decided they wanted to come back to daddy.

"This form of magic will allow you to manipulate the four elements to your advantage Air, Water, Earth and Fire or as they are used when casting" Nick continued showing the Latin elements on the chalkboard "*Caelum, Unda, Terra and Ignis*", "Alright … now we're in my forte" Will spoke walking over to the firing range "Will?" I questioned watching as Will took in a deep breath and focused on his target, for a brief moment his eyes seemed to go completely black "*IGNIS*" Will shouted stretching out his arm towards the target, in an instant a ball of fire shot from Will's hand and down the firing range colliding with the Wolf target and turning it to ash.

"Excellent work Mr. Samson" Nick applauded admiring the burning cardboard cut out "Too bad for the wolf" I joked clapping Will on his shoulder, "Thanks man, fire is my specialty" Will replied turning to face me his eyes thankfully back to normal … except for his hand that was still currently on fire "WILL, YOUR HAND!" I shouted jumping back as Will frantically screamed and jumped up and down shaking his hand trying to put the flame out (Being a demon he was fireproof but the majority of the rest of us were not) "Mr. Samson calm down please, take a breath" Nick pleaded trying to guide Will away from the rest of us, Will took a deep breath and released the air from his lungs … igniting his other hand in flames.

"Damn it!" Will shouted as the fireballs now decided it was their turn to go where they wanted firing frantically around the room "DUCK!" Nick shouted as a fireball passed through him and he breathed a sigh of relief. "Thank the realms I'm dead" Nick added tapping his purple suit while the rest of us jumped and ducked and dodged and dived (Hey! new motivational poster for a gym idea, if you can dodge a flaming fire-ball, you can do anything!) "Guys run!" Will screamed right before his whole body was engulfed by flames, I knew one thing for certain … Will was about to explode.

My Hunter instincts went into overdrive at that moment and time slowed down, I scanned for every exit but seen as we were in the deepest part of the academy and the only way out was a door that currently had a strange looking vine growing across it that I guessed was from Will's latest experiment there was no other way out. Will was still getting hotter in intensity singing the hairs on my arms and reddening the cheeks of everyone in the room, "Okay, so no way out, that we means we have to fight but we can't hurt Will it's not his fault, he's building in heat which means he needs to explode soon which means our best bet is …" I thought as Will began to glow as bright as the sun and my mind drifted and combined with my instincts.
 A word drifted into the recesses of my mind, it glowed and shifted its way through my mind colliding with my synapses sending my instincts into overdrive (Don't ask me to describe any more of what happened next I gave you enough right there). I cast out my hand and focused on the space around myself and the other students imagining a solid wall between us and Will, the pressure built up as my arm began to pulsate and I focused feeling the intensity burning behind my eyes "COMPADIRE!" I screamed right at the moment that Will detonated.

I waited for the heat to hit us and for us to be vaporised into a million little pieces but it never came, the heat stopped around us, "By the realms" I heard Nick mumble as I finally dared to open my eyes. Between us and Will was an orange barrier spreading from one wall to the other like a shield holding back the flames that continuously encircled a screaming Will, in my hand was a small magical orange glowing ball that floated and turned as I moved my hand keeping the shield in place, the word *Compadire* flooded back into my mind as I realised what I'd called "To Protect" I mumbled right before the flames stopped and my shield disappeared leaving a very burned room, crying students, a shocked teacher, my arm feeling like it was on fire and Will stood in the middle of the blackened room wearing only his boxer shorts.

"Dude" Will mumbled right before his head lolled to one side and he passed out. The angel students who had been practising healing cautiously approached Will and began to wave their hands over him muttering incoherently in Latin "Jason, that was … incredible" Nick mumbled right before I felt a burning sensation on my chest where my tattoo was "Not again!" I mumbled but the pain wasn't as intense this time, it was almost pleasant, I pulled down the collar of my shirt till I could see the tattoo noticing a shield symbol growing onto my skin in black ink slowly behind the large 'H' "Incredible" Nick muttered examining my new tattoo,

 "What does it mean?"

"Congratulations Jason … you are officially assigned as a specialist in combat magic" Nick replied as my vision started to blur and I collapsed to the ground on one knee struggling for breath.

## Chapter 10
## Welcome to Blacksmith 101, hope you didn't wear anything nice

After an awkward conversation with the teachers and security who had come pounding through the door shortly after the explosion to see what was happening leaving me to explain most of the details along with Nick while Will materialised a fresh pair of clothes onto his body in his usual style, we were finally admitted to leave and go to our next class so that the pixie's could clean the soot off the walls and the servant trolls could fix the furniture.

"You okay buddy? I asked Will walking with him towards the back of the academy and towards the large crystal blue lake that sat behind it stretching out onto the horizon, "Yeah better now, thanks for saving everyone with the spell man ... I just couldn't stop, I tried my best, I can't help but think what would have happened if you weren't there" Will replied his face wracked with guilt.

"It's not your fault man, you heard what Nick said, magic can be tricky and dangerous that's why we have to learn so we don't destroy everything all the time, honestly, I have no idea how I created the protection spell I just did, but if it had gone wrong, then I could have squashed us like bug before you turned us into ash" I replied grinning at him "You're a good friend Jason" Will spoke tapping his hand against my shoulder.

Our next class, blacksmithing, was on an island in the centre of the vast lake accessed by a long wooden gangway from the shore with a wooden fence to stop us from falling into the lake, "Hey look!" one student announced leaning against the railing and pointing into the water below grabbing every student's attention including myself. We looked down into the lake and after all the crazy things I'd seen so far, I half expected to see the Loch Ness Monster floating around underneath us but instead what I saw were beyond beautiful women swimming through the water, their various hair colours shining despite the colour of the lake propelling themselves forwards using their long fish tails to swim gracefully through the water.

"Mermaids" I mumbled as one of the mermaids spotted me and floated slowly upwards till she emerged gracefully from the top of the lake. The mermaid had scarlet red hair that cascaded down her back almost to her waist where her tail began and the most sparkling blue eyes imaginable leaving me utterly entranced and almost making me want to dive into the lake with her, "Hi there, I'm Alexa" the mermaid spoke almost singing as several other mermaids appeared and began to converse with the students "Hi ... I'm Jason" I mumbled utterly smitten and unable to look away,

"Hi Jason, are you ready for your class today?"

"So, do you always hang around the lake or can you come onto land?" I heard Will ask his mermaid came so close that he was practically in the water with her, I rolled my eyes and chuckled at his sudden change in attitude.

"Should I be worried? You're not going to drag me down to my demise are you like the sailors of old, I mean it would be worth it but …"  I joked,

"You have nothing to fear Jason, mermaids are peaceful calming creatures who only wish to protect our oceans and lakes, sirens are the dangerous ones that sing and lure men to their doom" Alexa pushed a stand of hair away that had fallen in front of her face.

"Glad to hear that, you are truly beautiful though" Alexa giggled and blushed smiling her perfect white teeth back to me.

 "Come here" Alexa replied twitching her finger at me in the worldwide known symbol for "*Come here*", I leaned flat on the boardwalk on my stomach and looked deep into her eyes inches away from her face.

 I couldn't explain it but I was utterly entranced by Alexa, I could feel a connection with her unlike any other (Yeah, she was beautiful but that wasn't the reason why) "Why am I so drawn in by you?" I questioned,

"Your half angel, we mermaids are basically the angels of the sea, our connection is strong and you're a man if there's one thing, we mermaids know what to do …" Alexa replied pulling in so close to me that her lips were inches away from mine "It's how to trick men into coming too close to the water" Alex added splashing water in my face drenching my head before disappearing beneath the surface laughing and smiling.

I spat out a trickle of water that had been splashed into my mouth and stood back upright wiping the water off my brow and looked over to Will who had lipstick all over his face from the top of his head to his chin and his neck, "You have serious charm with girls dude" Will spoke laughing at my drenched hair "Looks like you had better luck at least" I replied pointing at his face causing him to look at his reflection in the water, "Worth it" Will spoke splashing his face with lake water washing away the lipstick off his face before standing back upright "Come on, we better get to class" I said leading the way with Will at my side heading towards the large hexagon shaped wooden platform in the centre of the lake.

The platform had a series of furnaces around the permitter alongside wooden workbenches fitted with tools, in the centre of the platform was a series of benches facing a large chalkboard written with various instructions along with "Blacksmithing 101" written along the top. "Where do you think the teacher is?" I questioned sitting on one of the benches facing the chalkboard with Will at my side, "No idea, you think it's another ghost?" Will replied, "There are no ghosts upon my lake William Samson" a heavenly voice sang, I glanced around rapidly searching for the source of the voice but there was no one around. Suddenly to my right, slowly and gracefully from a pier that edged off the platform, a beyond beautiful woman floated up from the water and landed delicately onto the wooden platform.

I've already described to you the beauty of mermaids and how much I liked Jen (Don't judge me, I'm 16! I can think more than one girl is beautiful) but this woman was beyond imagination when it came to levels of beauty. Her long blonde hair cascaded down her head sitting just below her shoulder blades almost to her waist perfectly straightened and dry despite having just emerged from the lake, she was wearing a long ice blue gown that trailed behind her as she walked, her bare feet tapped softly against the ground almost as if she was floating across the platform, her eyes were her most dazzling feature the same colour as the lake but seemed to ripple and shimmer every time she looked at you almost as if the lake itself was alive in her eyes.

"Wow" Will mumbled his jaw practically set on the ground. "My name is Nimue and I am your teacher" the lady replied settling herself in front of the chalkboard, "Nimue? Why does that name sound familiar" Will whispered almost silently, "Excellent question Mr. Samson" Nimue said, apparently, she had phenomenal hearing along with her phenomenal beauty, "Not many know me by name, usually I am simply referred to by the world as The Lady of the Lake" Nimue replied.
"As in King Arthur and Excalibur?" Will asked utterly stunned, "Yes Mr. Samson, I was the one who gifted the sword to Merlin so that he could place the sword into the stone" Nimue replied with a hint of sadness in her eyes, "Merlin was your betrothed I seem to remember wasn't he?" I questioned, a single tear rolled down Nimue's cheek and I felt like the biggest idiot in the world "Merlin was my love yes ... I miss him deeply" Nimue replied brushing the tear off her cheek.
"It has been a long time since I last saw him, he disappeared many aeons ago, I am tied to the lake so I cannot search for him" Nimue added, "Merlin's still alive?" I asked shocked "Merlin was a powerful magician, the rules of life and aging did not apply to him" Nimue replied turning to the chalkboard hiding her sadness from us and I knew for one thing for certain at that moment ... when I had the chance ... I was going to find Merlin for Nimue.

"Okay class let us begin, today you will be forging the weapons that you will use for the rest of your days, once you have chosen which weapon you wish to forge you will choose your rare material which is collected from across the western world and will be either Divine steel, Purgatorium Bronze, Demonic Obsidian or Hunter Silver" Nimue explained pointing to various metals laid out before us.
"Once you have done this, we will begin to forge your weapon" Nimue explained "Once the weapon is shaped you will lower the weapon of your choice into my lake securing it's magical properties and then you will choose which form you wish the weapon to take while it is out of use" Nimue added, "Which form? How do you mean?" I asked raising my hand "Good question Jason, while you are out in the mortal world your weapons will take a form so as not to attract attention although the haze will hide your activities, swords and bows do tend to attract attention, so we disguise our weapons in various forms whether that be a necklace, a ring, a watch or anything your heart desires" Nimue replied.

(I won't bore you with the rest of the class describing how to forge and how to bind the weapon together and all the other details involved in making weapons, Do you want to know how to? Then google it) "Okay class take your position at a forge and we will begin" Nimue commanded. We each had to share a forge so me and Will took up position together and began to craft the hilts to our weapons, I grabbed a Hunter silver handle and cross guard for my sword that I would be making and began to bind them together whilst Will grabbed an obsidian black handle and cross guard and began to hammer them together binding the hilt in a leather wrap.

Will took position first at the forge and began to blow heat onto the coals in the furnace melting the obsidian ingots ready to be poured into the Great sword mould that would create his weapon for the foreseeable future. "Nimue?" I asked looking over at the lady of the lake who turned her attention away from an angel who was beginning to forge a divine steel bow and quiver and walked delicately over to me,

"Yes Jason, do you need any help?"

"I was just wondering, would it be possible to create a weapon that uses two of the minerals instead of one?",

"It is possible yes, although it hasn't been done in a long time, what did you have in mind?" Nimue asked.

After his obsidian ingots had melted, Will poured the mineral into the Great sword mould hardening it and then began beating the sword with a heavy hammer forging it into perfect shape before lowering it into a hole in the floor where the lake could be seen, the water let out a loud hiss as steam rose from the surface and glowed slightly before will removed the blade and bound it with a spell Nimue had taught him to the cross guard, "Excellent Mr. Samson, what is the disguise for your weapon?" Nimue asked while I waited for my two bowls of ingots to melt, "A watch" Will replied, Nimue tapped her hand on the sword and it instantly shrank down to a black metal watch that rested comfortably on Will's wrist.

Will smiled at the watch and pressed the wind-up knob, in an instant the watch formed into the Great sword that he had spent the better part of the afternoon forging. I glanced at the blade and noticed the lettering written along the blade near the cross guard *"Tenebris"* or in English "Darkness". Several other students had also finished forging their weapons and were beginning to test their strength and weight admiring the disguises that they had chosen.

One angel had turned her bow into a silver necklace with a gold pendant that when she removed the pendant the bow would grow in her hand and the quiver would form on her back, another demon had hidden two daggers as spiked wrist cuffs, a deinonychus had forged his katana into a pair of glasses that surprised no one (Like I said Deinonychus equal dull) and I was stood at the furnace removing the jar that held Hunter silver liquid from the furnace pouring it into the mould, the liquid slowly trickled onto the left side of the mould until the jar was empty and I grabbed the second jar pouring it into the right side of the mould forming the shape of a knightly sword.

Once the blade had begun to harden, I removed it with a set of tongues and transferred it to the anvil smashing the metal with a hammer, the embers from the blade licked at the hem of my shirt burning it slightly before dying out but I continued to work until the blade was forged into the shape I desired.

I lifted the heavy metal from the anvil and dipped it into the lake, the lake bubbled and hissed letting out a cloud of steam and glowed before I removed the blade and placed it onto the table binding it to the cross guard, a few of the students stared at my weapon as I held it aloft the words inscribed into the flat of the blade *"Divinus Furor"* or for those of you who don't speak Latin "Divine Fury".

"Bravo Jason and your chosen disguise?" Nimue asked "A ring" I replied, Nimue tapped the end of the blade twice and the sword shrank down to a golden ring on my middle finger in the shape of a 'H' with two wings growing out of either side of it. I clenched my hand and Divine Fury sprung to life in my hand, my plan had worked perfectly, one side of the blade was Divine steel and the other was Hunter silver, like me it was of two worlds perfectly balanced and capable of destroying any threat that I would face "Dude" Will spoke touching the blade "OUCH!" Will shouted as the instant his hand touched the blade a small cut ran along his fingertip, being half demon, the blade was lethal to him "Don't touch" I replied shrinking the blade back into its ring form, in the distance towards the academy several bells rang "Excellent work everyone, class dismissed" Nimue replied clapping her hands and walked over to the pier.

The crowd dispersed walking towards the castle ready for lunch rubbing their stomachs in hunger, I ignored the growling of my stomach (Blacksmithing is hard work) and looked over at Nimue, "You coming?" Will asked me "I'll catch up" I replied walking over to The Lady of the Lake. "Nimue?" I asked the lady of the lake who turned to face me at the edge of the pier,

"Is everything okay Jason?"

"I just wanted to say thank you and to ask you something",

"Ask away"

"I was wondering, do you have any clue or idea where Merlin is?" Nimue looked to the ground and shed a silent tear before reaching into the lining of her dress. "This washed up on my shores many years ago, I have no idea where he is now but this is the only thing I have" Nimue replied passing me a photo of a postcard from Dallas, Texas, on the back was a message for Nimue:

> *"Thinking of you always my love,*
> *I pray that one day we may be reunited*
> *All my love and care,*
> *Merlin"*

"Thank you, Nimue," I replied passing the postcard back to Nimue

"Why did you ask Jason?"

"I spent half my life living on the streets after having everything taken away from me, my parents died when I was young and my grandma died when I was six so I know what it's like to lose someone you love and because when I can, I'm going to find Merlin and bring him back to you, I give you my word" I promised. Nimue placed her hand over her chest and passed the postcard back to me "Thank you" Nimue mumbled holding back her tears placing her hand on my cheek. "I'll bring him back" I promised one last time, "Your courage reminds me of Arthur he was a Hunter like you but your heart is exactly like Merlin's, you are a good man Jason and I have no doubt you will be an amazing Protector" Nimue replied stepping away from me and dissolving into a pool of water draining back into the lake, the information that the great King Arthur was a Hunter was definitely a surprise but I knew one thing for certain.

With my friends at my side and Divine Fury in my hand, I would find Merlin and bring him back to the academy and I would keep my word to the Lady of the Lake.

# Chapter 11
## Jen and I discuss dreams

After a long walk from the lake back up to the academy grounds I was happy to see the inside of hall where we would have lunch finally after forging for hours straining my newfound muscles and breathing in the noxious soot from the furnace. The hall was already packed full of students by the time I had arrived of all different cultures and protectors, Angels chatted and glowed sharing each other's activities during the day and the newbies showing off their weapons to the students that they had forged earlier.
Demons threw food at each other and fought (Seriously it was like Mad Max at that table) Will had already joined his fellow Protector kind and was currently laughing about his plant that had come to life and was likely still running around the academy somewhere.

Deinonychus sat idly chatting and discussing their classes and everything they had learned about maintaining balance throughout the day and at the far side of the room was the table of Hunter's where Jen was sat smiling and laughing with her classmates. When I'd first entered this hall, I'd sat at the table with the other students who were waiting to be identified but now I had no idea where I should technically sit, should I sit with the angels and swap stories with them or should I join Jen and the Hunters considering that apparently was the strongest gene in my body, seen as Jen was the first person I had met and one of my favourite friends I decided to choose the latter.

"Room for one more?" I questioned leaning over Jen's shoulder catching her by surprise "Of course move aside guys" Jen replied as the classmates next to her shuffled over slightly so I could squeeze in next to her, out of the corner of my eye I spotted a few of the Hunter's staring at me intensely and whispering lightly "Is everything okay with them?" I asked Jen taking a drink of the orange juice that had appeared in my chalice (Magical chalices are great aren't they?). "It's okay, it's just that some Hunters are a bit uncomfortable with ... Half breeds, they think that they should sit at the Half breed table" Jen replied pointing over at the long empty table.
 "Seriously? That's a bit racist against Half Breed's, isn't it?" I asked forgetting the fact that I was probably the first Half breed in hundreds of years "It's just how it is, Angels sit with Angels, Demons sit with demons, Deinonychus sit with Deinonychus, Hunters sit with Hunters and Half breeds sit with their own kind, although you're the first Half breed in five hundred years so it isn't exactly fair to make you sit alone" Jen explained, a part of me wanted to storm off and sit at the Half breed table on my own but I also knew that the Hunters would never respect me if I did, I was already the Half breed that had been homeless till he came to the academy I didn't want to appear any more of an outcast than that so I decided to stay where I was and stand my ground.

"How was History and astrology?" I asked Jen after pausing deep in thought for what had been several minutes, "Same as usual, a lot of information about things I already knew but I did learn that the planets are going to align soon for the first time in two thousand years so I can't wait for that" Jen replied igniting the memory in my brain from the dream I had had last night. "Huh, I had a dream the other night about the planets aligning but I had no idea they really did until you just said" I replied, "That's a thing that happens to us all, we sometimes have visions in our sleeps of things that are happening, will happen or have already happened, curse of being the child of a supernatural being I'm afraid, last night I dreamt that I was watching a pack of werewolves descend on a small town in Canada luckily I saw a few angels ready to fight them off, still didn't make it any more comfortable though" Jen replied causing me to flinch and shiver slightly (I have bad memories when it comes to wolves but that's not something I like to discuss).

"Wait a second, our dreams could be things that are happening right now?" I asked "Yeah, why what did you dream?" Jen asked me. I started to tell her everything about my dream last night from the conversation between Isaac and Coach Jones to the vision of the Gates of Hell, when I finished Jen had gone white as a sheet (I'd say ghost but so far the ghosts I'd seen had been bright and colourful). "Are you sure that's what you saw?" Jen whispered looking at the other Hunter's "Yeah one hundred percent ... I have a feeling this is bad, isn't it?" I replied, Jen wiped her face with a napkin and grabbed my hand "We need to go talk to Isaac, now" Jen replied pulling me away from the table.

We climbed up several flights of stairs together higher and higher up to the top of the academy until we finally reached Isaac's office, Jen knocked twice on the heavy wooden door and stood with me trying to catch our breath "Come in" Isaac shouted from the other side of the door, Jen pulled down on the iron handle and led me inside the office closing the door behind her. "Jennifer, what can I do for you?" Isaac asked while I stared around the office, behind us were four large floating images of what I guessed were Heaven with clouds and bright sunlight, Hell with geysers of molten magma and red rocky terrain, Purgatory which was static like a broken television (Either Purgatory was still broken or it was more boring than I already guessed it was) and an image of an open valley with mountains and forests which clearly symbolised the earth which we were destined to protect.

Behind a large wooden desk sat Isaac scribbling away at documents spread across his table that once he'd finished writing on flew through the air and sorted themselves into the filing cabinets or sealed themselves in envelopes and climbed into a tube similar to the ones in old post offices before firing off to somewhere into the universe. Today Isaac was dressed in a sharp blue suit with a white shirt and a red tie, "Council head Isaac, we came to talk to you about something that Jason dreamed about last night" Jen replied pushing me forwards making me feel like I'd just been placed in front of a bullseye with an apple on my head, "A dream?" Isaac questioned, I turned to face Jen who nodded and then proceeded to tell Isaac everything I had already told Jen watching as the same reaction that Jen had shown now showed up on Isaac's face.

Isaac stood up from his desk and began pacing back and forth in the room scratching at the stubble on his chin, "This is bad, beyond bad" Isaac mumbled "Does this mean what I think it does?" Jen asked "Yes Jennifer, I think it does, we must assemble the council immediately" Isaac replied pressing a button on his desk "All students please proceed to leave the hall for an emergency council meeting, all members of the council please proceed to the main hall" Isaac spoke his voice echoing through the intercom system in his room.

"Jen, Jason come with me, I hope you're ready to tell your story once more Jason" Isaac spoke leading me and Jen out of his office and down the staircase back to the hall "Why do I always cause trouble everywhere I go?" I thought to myself continuing down the stairs.

By the time we had reached the back to the hall, all of the students had left and the council was sat waiting in their respective chairs arguing with each other about the disturbance, "Isaac what is the meaning of this?" Coach Jones asked noticing us as we entered the room "I'm sorry for the sudden call for this meeting but this is a matter of utmost importance, Jason please tell us what you saw in your dream last night" Isaac replied taking his seat at the centre of the table (I really hate recounting stories). I stood before the council and took a deep breath before telling them everything for the third time today, the council all looked at each other and whispered before turning back to face me (Ever seen those nature documentaries where a gazelle realises its surrounded by Lions? That was me at that moment).

"I'm afraid we all know what this means" Isaac spoke to the council who all nodded their heads in agreement "Can someone please explain what is happening?" I asked finally getting to ask the questions, "Jason, your vision is of a great danger to the world as we know it, this demon that you witnessed, the one surrounded by shadows. Is the Devils most valued warrior, his name is Galadriel and he is the vessel of darkness and shadow in the world, when the planets align a week from now a great change will affect the earth, the magical energy released throughout the planet will allow the gates to open and for the rapture to begin" Isaac replied filling me with utter dread.

"If we do not stop him before the gates open fully then the armies of hell will break from their prison and wreak havoc on the earth, it will be the beginning of the end of life as we know it" Isaac added (Now I really was shaking), "There must be something we can do to stop it" I said looking at each member of the council in turn.

"There is nothing we can do to stop the gates from opening but if a team can get there before they are fully opened then the gates can be closed and the attack stopped before it comes into effect, unfortunately we will need our armies will be spread thin to fight the attacks on the earth on Sunday which means that no one is left to close the gates" Isaac replied, "I'll go" I spoke not realising the words that I was speaking before they left my mouth.

"Jason, while we appreciate your bravery you are still new to this world, we cannot allow you to go forth on this assignment without the proper knowledge" Isaac replied, "He won't be alone, I'll go with him" Jen interjected suddenly standing by my side "Jennifer, you are one of our fiercest warriors but even with just two of you this task ..." Isaac spoke "You can count me in too" a voice spoke from the back of the hall "And me" another voice shouted, I turned to see Will and Katie who were now walking up the aisle.

"My parent is a being of hell, if anyone can handle the gates and any demonic threats it's me" Will spoke up, "I first met Jason when were in the identification ceremony together, he's new to this world and if he's going then I'm going too" Katie added standing at our sides along with Will. Each member of the council examined us and then looked back at each other "This vision was Jason's which means that by rule he has the right to claim this assignment as his own and choose his team" Coach Jones spoke looking at Isaac, "We must take this as a vote it is the only way" Isaac replied looking at each member of the council "All those in favour" Isaac asked, the vote was unanimous, "The motion carries and the assignment is confirmed" Isaac added banging a gavel against the desk.

"You will have until Sunset on Sunday, the most sacred and dangerous day of the week before the Gates will open" Isaac explained "This task will be carried out by you four together, your task is to find the gates, seal them before they open and prevent the rapture, you will be provided with supplies and transport to the nearby mortal transportation for your quest to begin" Isaac commanded, "How do we find the gates?" I asked "You must assemble Dante's compass, this will guide you to the Gates of Hell, each piece was separated years ago but if you can find the first piece the others will become easier to locate. The case for the compass is in St. Louis, we will reach out to a contact who will meet you at the station and guide you to the case but from there you will be on your own, are you absolutely sure you want this?" Isaac asked.

"I spent my life running away from the threats who chased me, no more, it's time to fight, the vision came to me so it is my responsibility to stop it and with my friends at my side, I know we will succeed" I replied (Where the confidence came from I have no idea so don't judge me too harshly on the classic hero command). "Very well, you leave at sunrise tomorrow, rest up" Isaac replied dismissing the council and walking towards us, "Good luck, I believe in you all" Isaac added tapping us on the shoulder before heading back to the staircase to his office.
 "Where did you guys come from?" I asked turning to face Katie and Will, "We saw you head up to Isaac's office and when the message came through we knew it must be serious so we hid until the right moment" Will replied "You guys are insane, this assignment or whatever you want to call it is dangerous" I spoke, "Which is exactly why we aren't letting you two do it alone, if you're going then we're going" Katie replied.
My heart warmed at that moment, here we were, three new students to an academy of protectors already given a task beyond danger and we were ready to fight it to the end and these newfound strangers I had known for just over a day were willing to literally follow me to the gates of Hell and hopefully back, "Thank you" I spoke placing my hands on Will and Katies shoulder who in turn placed their hand on mine and Jennifer's forming a circle.

"Looks like we're going on an adventure then, I better pack my things" Will replied folding the shadows around him and disappearing with a wicked grin on his face "I hate it when he does that" Katie replied turning and walking out the door, "Looks like I'm going to have to take a reign check on that movie night" Jen spoke as we started to walk together out of the academy "Well, I guess I'll just have to watch it when we stop the end of the world" I replied smiling at Jen and wondering how I had gone from homeless to living in an academy to going on a dangerous assignment in two days … "Such is the life of a protector I guess" I thought to myself staring at the setting sun over the lake.

# Chapter 12
## Off on the assignment we go

After an actual peaceful night's sleep whether that was due to some excitement of my journey and assignment that I would soon be facing or utter fear of what would happen next I wasn't sure but I was glad to sleep the full 8 hours. The next morning I packed my bag with a few changes of clothes and underwear, an extra pair of trainers in case I ended up standing on a bear trap or falling into a burning pit narrowly escaping with my life (I swore I'd never again go back to Los Angeles after that incident), Divine Fury on my finger in its ring form and the supplies provided by the academy. I dressed in a leather jacket, white shirt, blue jeans and black converse and headed down to the courtyard ready for the assignment.

Jen was already waiting for me down in the courtyard with her blue backpack on her back tapping her feet in anticipation, she was currently wearing a white t-shirt with a blue hoodie, grey jeans and red converse with her hair neatly combed the red, blue and pink braids neatly aligned. "About time you woke up" Jen spoke as I descended the stairs tugging on the collar of my brown leather jacket, "Well excuse me for being prepared for my first assignment ever" I replied not appreciating her tone (clearly neither of us was a morning person).

We headed down through the academy grounds under the watchful gaze of the other students who seemed to be staring at us in either jealousy or in nervous anticipation I wasn't quite sure, the parents of the students and adults who had chosen to live on the academy grounds also watched as we passed until we found ourselves stood at the entrance where Katie and Will were waiting for us along with the council leaving me feeling like I was walking into the lion's den covered in barbecue sauce.

"Hey you two, ready for some fun?" Will asked tugging on his small backpack slung over his shoulder the strap stretched across his torso, his outfit today was the same as pretty much every day a black leather jacket, red shirt, black jeans and black biker boots and a cigar perched in between his lips. "I know I am" Katie added checking the weight of her backpack and straightening the folds of her black t-shirt, today she had switched out her long white dress for a white leather jacket, white shirt, blue jeans and white converse "Last chance to back out guys" I said looking at Will, Katie and Jen "Not on your life" Jen replied "With you to the end brother" Will added "And you know I can't let you two idiots go alone with Jen, someone needs to help keep you in line" Katie spoke smiling.
I walked with my group over to the council who were stood ready to bid us goodbye "Madam Wilson will be driving you to the train station where your quest will begin, I think I speak for all of us when I wish you the best of luck on your assignment and rest assured, we will do everything we can on our end to ease your assignment" Isaac spoke gesturing over to the elderly Madam Wilson who we could never decide was either 80 or 800 years old … although the latter was unlikely.

I nodded at the council and Coach Jones who appeared to be smiling at us on our assignment a change from his usual scowl or miserable grin, "Thank you members of the council" I spoke bowing in respect followed by Jen, Will and Katie before walking towards the red ford focus that Madam Wilson would be driving us in to the train station, although judging on the old style of the academy I had no idea where they had gotten a ford focus from. "Shotgun" Will shouted at the last moment jumping into the passenger side of the car "This is going to be a long quest" Jen spoke climbing into the right side of the car in the back seat, "I'm sure it will" I mumbled climbing into the left side seat of the car after Katie had sat down in the middle ready for my first assignment ever and the journey to prevent the rapture. "The fate of the universe is in your hands" Madam Wilson told us when she started the car its old engine growling in protest, "No pressure" I thought to myself as the car pulled onto the long bridge that led away from the academy.

An Angel, a Hunter, a Demon and a Half breed on a quest to save the world (What could possibly go wrong?).

After a surprising 3-hour drive into town driving through miles of countryside and passing a sign to Chicago on the freeway although where the road that led to the academy had come from I had no idea, Jen had told me that the Haze (the thing that hides the supernatural world from mortals) obscured the academy from all beings aside from Protectors to allow safer lives for the students and all residents of the academy. We finally arrived at the train station and climbed onto the Amtrak train to St. Louis after bidding a goodbye to Madam Wilson who wished us luck before driving off back into the distance towards the academy.

The landscape flew past as the train sped down the tracks towards our destination and the future of our assignment, Jen had kindly volunteered to head to the dining car and had returned with four hot dogs and soda's which were gone in a matter of minutes (What can I say being a Protector is hard work). "Okay so apparently the base of the compass is hidden somewhere in St. Louis guarded by a fallen angel" Jen spoke opening a document from her backpack that Isaac had given her shortly before we left describing everything we needed to know about the compass (Although we only knew where the base was, the rest we would have to find on our own) "A fallen angel? Why would he have the base of the compass?" I asked, "Apparently the compass is the reason he fell, the compass doesn't just lead to the Gates of Hell it also leads to your heart's deepest desire, when the angel found the base he became obsessed with finding the other pieces but in the process he ended up killing a fellow angel who was trying to stop him, he broke a golden rule of the realm of Heaven and was banished because of it" Jen replied.

"Any idea where this fallen angel is?" Will asked rolling up his napkin and throwing it through the air in the direction of the bin missing completely, "Don't litter! Go pick that up" Katie commanded slapping Will on his upper arm, "Make me angel!" Will replied (Never turn down a command from an angel). Katie opened her wings suddenly catching Will of guard sending him crashing face first into the table "Ow" Will mumbled rubbing his forehead, "Katie! Are you crazy? Put those away" I spoke looking frantically around at the mortals around us, "Relax Jason, the haze remember? They can't see the wings" Katie replied standing up and spinning on the spot with her wings unfurled, nobody even reacted to her instead they stared at her as if she was that weird girl who just burst into dance for no reason.

"I like it when you dance, what do you say want to go to the bar section of the train and fool the bartender into thinking we're 21?" Will questioned flirting with Katie like he did any female being with a heartbeat, "Thanks for the offer, but you're not really my type" Katie replied folding her wings back in and sitting down next to him, "Why because I'm a demon? That's racist on so many levels and offensive" Will asked throwing his arms around frantically. "No genius, it's because I'm gay" Katie replied, I think it was safe to say that I was as surprised as Jen and Will were at this sudden confession of information "Fair enough" Will replied leaning back in his chair and conjuring a cigar in his hand.

"No smoking on the train" the conductor told Will who quickly made the cigar turn to mist and disappear, the conductor nodded his head and continued his inspection with the other passengers "Oh sure, that they see" Will complained conjuring a deck of playing cards out of thin air "Poker anyone?" Will asked, "Yeah this is going to be a fun trip" I thought to myself taking my dealt cards from the table (I lost to Will who had three of a kind, damn cheating demons).

"Isaac said that we had till Sunday to find the Gates of Hell, why is that?" I asked curiously losing another round of Poker, "Sunday is the last and most dangerous day of the week for Protectors, on the Seventh Day God rests and supernatural threats spread onto the Earth even faster, Protectors are spread thin to all corners of the United States to keep the supernatural beings at bay, it's been like this since the Day of Black Sun" Jen replied beating Will with a Royal Flush (Jen has got a great poker face).

"Black Sun?" I asked curiously, "The day of Black sun is when the sky went dark and Supernatural threats poured onto the earth in full, it was also the day that twelve Protectors united and formed the first council of Protectors, a unique day, 33 C.E. or as mortals know it ..." Jen added, "The Crucifixion of Jesus Christ" I interrupted remembering the brief time I had sought sanctuary in a Church. "Seven is a sacred number for the realms, the universe was created in seven days, there are Seven deadly sins, Seven angels in the book of revelation for the apocalypse, so if something involves the Divine, chances are it involves the number Seven" Katie spoke filling my brain with more information about a heritage I had only just learnt about.

# Chapter 13
## Eat me in St. Louis

Well, after a very uneventful train trip across country towards St. Louis with no attacks or fights (A rarity for me) we finally arrived and disembarked our Amtrak train at Union Station in downtown St. Louis, we were completely surrounded by the sprawling skyscrapers and the mortals going about their day to day to and from the office carrying their briefcases without a care or worry in the world. I used to be just like them aside from the constant running from dangers and threats but now my eyes had been fully opened and I was fighting to prevent the end of the world with my ragtag group of friends before the planets aligned and the Gates of Hell opened in 6 days (God, pressure much).

"Okay so where do we start?" I asked looking to my left and spotting the famous Gateway Arch next to the Mississippi river something that I'd always wanted to visit although now it seemed less exciting, "First we have to meet our contact who has information for us about the case although I don't see him anywhere" Jen replied staring around at the crowd, I searched for any sign of someone searching for us, maybe a guy with a suit on stood next to a limo or a man with a placard sign reading "Protectors" or just any sign of someone who could help us but the only people who appeared to be around were mortals (And one demon with red skin and a beard but he was talking on his phone and on his way to work so I suppose he didn't count).

"You must be Jason, Katie, Will and Jen" a voice spoke from behind me, I jumped a foot into the air bringing Divine Fury to life in my hand ready for a fight, Jen had apparently had the same instinct and was stood holding her ivory bow aimed directly at the voice an arrow pressed against the string, Katie had unfurled her wings and materialised two Sai (an ancient Chinese form of three pronged dagger) like an angel Elektra ready in her hands and Will had unleased Tenebris holding it high in the air ready to bring it down and slice our surprise in half. "Easy there! I'm here to help, Isaac called for me to meet you here" the man replied currently hanging his head towards the ground hiding his face from us under his black fedora hat, he was dressed in a long black trench coat, black boots and black gloves along with an umbrella he was using as a shield despite it being 30 degrees outside and clear blue skies.

"Who are you?!" I demanded ready to drive my sword through this stranger just in case, "My name is Adrian, I'm your informant and I'm here to help you find the fallen angel" the stranger replied in a thick what I guessed was Romanian accent, "Why are you hiding your face?" Katie asked.

"Because my dear, I do not respond well to the sun" Adrian replied raising the umbrella above him and looking directly at us, he had pale white skin brighter than Jen's ivory bow, pink eyes almost as if he was albino and red lips with two fangs poking out near the corner "You're a ..." I mumbled "A vampire, yes, now can we continue our conversation in the café across the street please?" Adrian asked pointing to Union station cookies and cupcakes, I retracted Divine fury back into its ring form followed by everyone else withdrawing their weapons still cautious and following Adrian to the seating area outside Union station cookies and cupcakes.

So, to add to my top 10 list of weird things I've experienced in life along with being chased by rabid hounds, thundersnow in Boston and discovering that I'm a Half Breed warrior Protector I could now add cupcakes and tea with a vampire to the list (You mortals have it so easy). Adrian retracted his umbrella once he was under the safe canopy of the café and sat before us drinking his herbal peppermint tea from the blue floral cup with his pinkie raised, I could feel everyone else's legs around me tapping as we sat readied for battle including myself sat grinding my fingernails into the oak table (Protectors don't do well when it comes to waiting).

"Alright Adrian I'll bite …" Will spoke stopping when he realised the words that he'd just said to a vampire "How can you help us with the fallen angel?" I asked saving Will from completely falling into the hole he'd just dug himself, "The fallen angel you are looking for is called Dagon although now he goes by Nathaniel Markson you know, modern day adaptation and all" Adrian replied spreading jam onto a scone "Please god let it be jam" I thought to myself, "How do you know where he is?" Jen questioned "I'm a vampire my dear, when you've been on earth as long as I have, then you meet a person or two" Adrian replied sarcastically with jam dripping from his fangs (Not a pleasant experience).

"So how do we find him?" Will asked tapping his knuckles against the table creating a steady beat like a drum, "Nathaniel lives in an apartment complex in Tower Grove South, 2100, Fairview Avenue, Penthouse, the complex is called Heavenly heights" Adrian explained glancing up at the sun overhead which was slowly creeping its way across the table, "Heavenly heights? Seriously?" Katie questioned chuckling "Apparently Dagon appreciates the irony" Adrian replied retracting his hand an inch away from a stray sunbeam.

"Scared you're going to start shining?" I joked,
 "That damned movie, the book too, ruined life for vampires alike, if the sun hits a vampire we don't shine, we turn to dust and we're not dreamy and handsome like that Robert fellow either" (Sorry twilight fans, I'll make it up to you) Adrian replied slamming his hand against the table attracting the attention of a nearby elderly couple. Clearly the haze was doing its work or the elderly lady may have called the police on the four teenagers having tea with a vampire, "So, we go to the downtown, break into the apartment, steal the case of the compass and run away as fast as we can" I spoke trying to form some sense of a plan "That won't work" Adrian said stirring his fourth sugar cube into his new cup of tea.

"Why not?" Jen asked "Dagon has traps built in everywhere, you won't get one toe through the door before you get set on fire or dropped down to hell or …" Adrian listed "We get the picture" Jen interrupted,
"So how do we get into trap central?" Will asked, Dagon glanced behind me as if something had disturbed him but when I turned around all I saw was a crowd of people complaining over the mass delay of train services. "That I cannot tell you, I will accompany you to the building the best I can and then from there …" Adrian continued glancing behind us again at the mortals who kept complaining before storming their way out of the station.

"You may want to get your weapons ready" Adrian spoke (Stress levels up much?) "What's going on?" I asked staring around at the mortals fleeing up the stairs of the lower underground area of the station in terror. "My guess is that the train's aren't going to be running out of Union station for a while" Will spoke tapping the knob on his watch causing Tenebris to form in his hand, a loud deafening roar sounded from the below the stairs (Cue danger music here) "That doesn't sound friendly" Katie spoke flicking both her wrists causing the silver bracelets on her wrists to shake before her two Shui daggers appeared in her hands, Jen pulled the hairpin out of her hair and clutched it tight turning it into her ivory bow and drawing an arrow from the quiver that appeared on her back.

"Perhaps I should …" Adrian began to speak right before a green acidic glob flew through the air missing my head by a few inches and landing on Adrian's chest, Adrian gasped and detonated into dust leaving his fedora hat collapsing to the ground and a pool of acid eating away at the floor, "ADRIAN!" I shouted (Ayyy! I finally did a Rocky reference). "LION!" a woman screamed right before diving into the nearby flower stand, another roar shook the metal rafters of the station sending every delayed sign to "CANCELLED".

"Ladies and Gentleman, we apologise for any delays or cancellations you may be facing at this moment" the lady over the intercom announced (Did she really exist or is it automated now I wonder), the ground underneath us shook and vibrated as the beast ascended the stairs. The first thing we saw was a giant Goat head (Bet you didn't see that coming) it let out a loud "BAAA" and a shockwave detonated across the station nearly launching us off our feet, next we saw the snake twisting and writhing in the air sticking out its forked tongue from behind the goat and baring it's fangs, another loud roar made my ears vibrate (Stupid superior Hunter hearing) and a lion's head and mane appeared at the front of the beast.

"Lion, Goat and a snake all in the same body … that's a new one" I mumbled clenching my fist bringing Divine Fury to life, "Any idea what that thing is?" Will questioned ready to leap into battle with the (Ligoake?) "It's a Chimera" Jen replied destroying my hope of identifying a new species of monster, "So, how do we kill it?" I questioned as the Lion stared at me hungrily his gaze fixed on my soul and the snake gurgling green acidic venom up from its throat "Usually we die, but seen as I have no intention of dying today … I say we hack and slice till it dies" Jen replied "Sounds like a plan to me" I spoke not exactly thrilled of our plan but it was the best we had, the Chimera roared and simultaneously we charged into battle.

## Chapter 14
## I perform for the Chimera

Our heroism and Protector DNA kicked in at that very moment, we charged bravely at the beast and fought it with all our ferocity till it lay dead at our feet, the city cheered and we were revered as heroes, the slayer of the chimera (Did you believe that? … yeah, me neither).

What actually happened was more like something you would see out of a looney tunes cartoon, five feet into running towards the Chimera I tripped over a piece of luggage and slid under a row of seats, Will spread his scaly wings and flew through the air before being smacked aside by a shockwave from the goat head, Katie spread her wings and corkscrewed towards the chimera which quickly dodged sending her spiralling down the stairs towards the underground section of the Union station and Jen dodged two venom attacks and then tripped over another small pink backpack with my little pony stickers on it (Damn mortals and their tiny backpacks) and fell into a subway sandwich prep area.

 "Well, that was heroic" I thought to myself banging my head on the seats when I tried to stand up, I crawled out of my comfy position of lying in a sticky puddle of soda (Please God let it be soda) and stood back up prepared for battle. "Alright ugly open wide" Will shouted charging at the beast with Tenerbis pointed directly at the lion head which was currently baring its fangs, I tried to recall a story I'd read about the Chimera in Greek mythology and how it was slain by some hero, "I think he used lead but what was the Chimera's most dangerous feature?" I thought to myself right before my brain seemed to click (If life had been a cartoon a lightbulb would have appeared above my head in that moment) "WILL, NO!!" I shouted as the Chimera began to growl/gurgle and let out a loud billowing roar of fire (Surprise, Chimera breathe fire too).

After the flames subsided Will was still stood the tips of his spiky black hair burning slightly and smoking, his face was covered in soot and the top of his shirt was burned away, Will let out a cough sending a pocket of smoke into the air "Good thing he's fireproof" I thought. The chimera swung around lashing out with the snake head which Will quickly rolled under and stabbed the beast in its side striking the first blow a small cut in its side no bigger than a spot, "If it bleeds we can kill it" I thought to myself cursing my stupid memory that remembered useless lines in dangerous situations.

I ran over from my covered position and met Jen at the subway stand "You, okay?" I asked her as she stood up with a lettuce leaf and a tomato slice stuck to her shoulders leaving her one ingredient away from being a B.L.T "I've been better" Jen replied brushing the food off her shoulders and jumping over the stand. Will landed next to us keeping his demonic wings unfurled and Katie appeared behind me making me jump out of my skin "Any ideas?" I asked her "We kill it one section at a time, cut off the snake so it can't spit venom on us, cut off the goat head so it can't use magic spells and then finally stab the beast in the heart" Jen explained "Sounds like a plan" Will replied.

Aside from the my utter uselessness up until this point I was glad that at least one of our merry bunch knew what we were doing "Will, you go for the snake use the shadows to get close" Jen spoke pointing at Will who nodded in agreement "Katie use your wings to get in close and use heavenly light to blind it and then cut off the goat head" Jen added placing her hand on Katie's shoulder, "I'll attack from the side at the right moment and stab it in the heart once you guys are out of the way" Katie finished staring at the beast who was currently smashing an intercom speaker finally stopping the annoying announcer woman.

"What do you want me to do?" I questioned feeling a little left out, "You have the most important job of all Jason" Jen replied staring directly at me "Act like your goofy self and distract it" Jen added, "Okay, but ..." I muttered "Good, now that we're all on the same page let's do this" Jen interrupted before Will disappeared into the shadows under the stand, Katie took flight leaving me with Jen who was currently staring at me "Distraction, I'm on it" I replied running over to the centre of the station "Hey tigger!" I shouted (I know, wrong animal but you try thinking of the correct animal when you're facing a fire breathing monster).

The chimera turned to face me and growled its eyes baring into my very soul, the beast swung out its paw knocking a coffee trolley across the station directly at me, coffee beans spilled over the floor as the trolley bounced three times letting out a deafening metal clang sending my instincts into overdrive, I quickly slid along the floor dodging the tumbling trolley by inches and stood back upright with Divine fury by my side "Clang, clang, clang went the trolley!" I shouted dancing from left to right looking over at a crouched down Jen who was staring at me like I was a complete and utter idiot.

The Chimera blasted a fireball upwards striking the bell above him with a deafening bong. "Ding, Ding, ding went the bell" I sang spinning in a circle dodging a fireball and continuing my best Judy Garland impression, Will let out a scream as he appeared in the shadows underneath the Chimera swinging his blade and severing the snake head from the chimera at the base of its tail "YEAH!" I yelled as the snake head hit the ground and melted into dust. The Chimera roared in anger and pain right before Katie descended from the roof and glowed as bright as the sun blinding the beast and stabbed the goat in both sides of its neck with her daggers before twisting them removing the goats head from the Chimera's body, the goat bellowed and vanished into dust leaving only a lion body with black blood trailing down its back.

I decided to join in the fight and cause a distraction much closer turning Divine Fury back to its ring form and grabbing an abandoned guitar from its case strumming the guitar strings in a random tone (I had no idea to play the guitar so you can imagine how bad it sounded) "Zing, Zing, Zing, went my heart strings" I sang as Jen slid on her knees underneath the Chimera and fired three rapid shots into its chest, the beast looked at me in shock and exploded into dust leaving no trace of the beast only the damage it had caused to Union station, "From the moment I saw him I fell" I sang to the confused looks of Katie, Will and Jen.

 "Seriously?" Will asked wiping the gunk off his blade with a t-shirt he stole from the gift shop "Judy Garland, an amazing singer and an appropriate distraction" I replied placing the guitar back into its case. The sirens of various emergency vehicles sounded in the distance finally arriving once the danger was over, "We should go" Jen spoke returning her bow back into her hair as a clip "Yeah, I don't want to try and explain to the cops where the lion went" Will added his sword returning to its position as a wristwatch "Heavenly heights here we come" I muttered following Jen, Will and Katie out the emergency exit door just in time right before the police officers and animal control burst into the train station from the main entrance.

## Chapter 15
### Welcome to Heavenly heights, please leave your souls at the door

We ran 5 blocks from Union station desperate to escape any new danger or threat including the police who were currently searching Union station and the surrounding area for any sign of the 'Lion' which was currently advertised on numerous news stations, the zoo's in the area had accounted for every lion in their collection so now the news were trying to guess where it had come from (I was waiting for the news reports saying a lion cub had been left in the sewer). Finally, we reached the bus station and climbed aboard heading downtown towards heavenly heights.

The number 10 was more than welcoming to us, although the six demons, a snake headed creature and what appeared to be woman with bird wings which Jen whispered and informed me that it was a harpy and that I shouldn't stare (although I did begin to wonder why she wasn't using her wings instead of catching the bus), her death stare including the rest of our fellow bus travellers who seemed to be ready to tear us apart still made the ride less than comfortable, thankfully they ignored us and we disembarked on Fairview Avenue.

"Was it just me or was the bus driver missing his right eye?" I asked glancing back at the bus continuing its way down the road billowing out thick black smoke, "Oh yeah definitely, he was a ghoul, most of them work menial jobs that don't require a great deal of human interaction you know, bag boys, cinema workers, construction crew etcetera" Will replied changing my viewpoint on all the workers who refused me access to supermarkets when I had spare change laying around, "Here we are, 2100 Heavenly heights" Katie spoke after we'd walked 2 blocks from the bus stop.

Heavenly heights was a sight to behold, it stretched high up above the surrounding neighbourhood by at least 20 storeys possibly more, the entire building was white limestone with multiple windows reflecting the blue sky and sun overhead and a private security guard sat behind a desk in the lobby which we could see from the outside through the floor to ceiling glass windows. "So how do we do this?" I asked twisting my ring on my finger "My guess is we go in and talk to the security guard, Adrian told us that we can't enter without permission and there might be booby traps, maybe we can convince him we're friends or family of Nathaniel" Katie replied using an air quotation gesture when she mentioned him by name.

"I say we bust down the door, rush up the stairs, break into the penthouse and steal the case and then fly off the balcony" Will argued bouncing on his heels and punching the air like a boxer, "Ummm … hello, I'm a Hunter, I can't fly" Jen spoke raising her hand "Jason will carry you" Will replied pointing at me, "Yeah, I can't fly either" I admitted "But you have wings? Your half angel" Will replied. "I'm sorry, excuse me if I spent so many years running for my life that I never learnt how to fly with the wings I didn't know I'd ever have" I spoke sarcastically mocking Will.

"Okay, let's call it Plan B, for now we talk our way in" Jen said putting an end to the discussion of the most likely way to get us killed, we headed inside pushing our way in through the revolving door and walked across the white tiled lobby towards the security guard. "Hi we're here to see Nathaniel Markson, we're his nieces and nephews" Katie spoke smiling at the security guard who looked up at us turning his attention away from the football game currently playing on his mini TV, I nearly leapt out of my skin the moment he turned to face us (I miss when I used to only jump out of my skin when something attacked).

The guard who had appeared normal from the outside now showed his appearance in his true form, he had no skin from head to toe instead being completely skeletonised, his cold black holes where his eyes should have been were boring into my soul and making me feel empty, his blue security guard uniform was in tatters and his skeletal fingers were clutched around a Big gulp soda cup, the guard took a drink although where the liquid was going considering he didn't have a stomach I had no idea and I had no desire to find out.

 "Sure, Penthouse suite, I'll open the elevator for you now" the guard replied smiling (Can skeletons smile you ask? Yes, they can, although it's terrifying) and pressing a button on the dashboard of his console. "Thank you, glad you could be so helpful" I replied ignoring the fly that flew through one eye socket and exited the other, "I always like to help, plus the guy's a Jackass so even if you're here to kill him, I really don't care" the guard replied turning his attention back to the football game and placing his boots onto the desk crossing his legs at the ankle. "I guess in we go?" I spoke walking over to the open elevator door "I guess so, although that seemed too easy" Jen replied following me into the elevator followed by Will and Katie "Which means whatever we're facing next is very likely to kill us" Will added sending a shiver up all our spines in anticipation as the elevator doors closed and the grinding of motors began as the elevator ascended.

## Chapter 16
## We walk into (You guessed it … a trap)

After an uneventful elevator ride up 20 floors to the Penthouse Suite being tortured to the Rap stylings of Kanye or 50 cent or some other type of rap artist (Who chooses this music for an elevator anyway?) we finally arrived at the Penthouse Suite to the familiar 'DING' of arrival, the gold doors in front of us opened wide to a spacious penthouse so spectacular that my jaw almost hit the while tile slabs underneath my feet.

The walls were painted a mixture of Robin egg blue in the hallway and pearly white in the living room leading to large floor to ceiling windows that stretched out over the St. Louis skyline with a clear view to the Mississippi river and the St. Louis arch, the blue skies and white clouds up above almost giving the sensation that you were walking straight up to heaven. To our right was a kitchen so big that a family of twelve could live and sleep in it and still have room, it had a large steel grey oven with 8 hobs and a double fridge with an ice dispenser (Always wanted one of those fridges) and a living garden over the kitchen island where various herbs and a tomato plant were growing blasted with a soft mist of water to keep them alive.

"Damn this guy knows how to live!" Will shouted spotting the 75-inch plasma TV on the wall facing a round white sofa and mahogany table and the spacious bedroom at the end of the hall with a bed that could sleep 8, "Real stealthy Will" I mumbled sarcastically noticing Katie who was also rolling her eyes at him "My bad" Will whispered.
 "Okay does anyone know anything about magic traps that we should watch out for?" I asked watching every step I took "A little, the ground will be okay to walk on all the traps are likely on the valuable objects so don't touch anything" Jen replied looking over at Will "Why does everyone keep looking at me?" Will asked his hand currently outstretched about to touch a glass case containing a baseball signed by Babe Ruth.

We decided to split up on our search for the case checking every corner of the room without touching anything just in case anything decided to blow up in our face or set off an alarm or drop us into a pit of doom (Damn you Indiana Jones for teaching me nothing about robbing fallen angel apartments). "Hey guys over here" Jen shouted from the living room taking me away from my valuable time of pressing every shower tile just in case one of them lead to a secret room.

We met up together in the Living room where Jen was currently stood in front of a painting by Peter Paul Rubens of St. Michael casting Lucifer and the fallen angels out of heaven, the angels eyes were full of passion and seemed to follow you around the room whilst the demon eyes seemed to shake you to your very core and looked full of rage and jealousy making me wonder if that's what angels really looked like, if maybe my father had once looked something like that. When you're the child of a supernatural being you wonder what your supernatural parents are actually like living or dead, I'd never met mine but I did wonder how the other protectors at the academy felt about their parents, "I guess that's a question I'll have to ask everyone later" I thought to myself.

"If I was going to hide something that I didn't want anyone to find, I'd hide it behind a painting like this" Katie spoke creating a ball of energy in her hand that flew around the edge of the painting frame and blinked once in front of Katie before disappearing "No traps, we're all good" Katie added pulling back on the frame. The painting and its frame swung outwards revealing a large black obsidian vault with a keypad and a thumb recognition pad, "Yeah that's definitely somewhere I'd lay traps and valuable objects" I joked (Nobody laughed, depressing for someone as funny as me).

"So how do we open it?" Katie asked, "OPEN SESAME!" Will shouted spreading his arms out wide, the vault didn't budge, "Nice try but I think it's a bit more complicated than that, lucky for us I'm an expert on this sort of thing" Jen replied approaching the keypad *"Revelare"* Jen mumbled, a green orb grew in her hand and her eyes seemed to change to a luminous green colour "WOAH!" Will shouted causing me and Katie to jump out of our skin as a ghostly figure edged its way into the room approached the keypad and pressed "3,5,2,9" before disappearing into a veil of smoke.
 Jen collapsed to the ground on one knee and breathed heavily as I rushed to her side to help her up, "I'm okay, just took a lot out of me, thanks" Jen replied steadying herself against my shoulder.

"Well, that's the combination sorted all we need now is a thumb print, any ideas?" Will spoke up "I've got one" I replied passing Jen over to Katie who was still hanging limply gasping for breath watching me run around the room like a headless chicken, "I saw this in a movie once" (It was in a homeless shelter and in Spanish but it was easy enough to remember) I replied grabbing a role of Sellotape from a drawer in the spacious kitchen and pressing it against various items that were likely to be used by Dagon often. I tried his lamp with no result, his bar trying the shakers and the glasses with only partial of what I needed so I discarded the piece in my hand and tried my last item hoping it would be the one "Bingo" I replied placing the TV remote back onto the table and holding up a piece of Sellotape with a thumb print on it "What kind of magic is that?" Katie asked "Mission impossible action my friend" I replied placing the Sellotape onto the safe scan pad.

"I'll open it, you guys let me know if it's going to explode in my face okay" I spoke looking over at my shoulder who were now stood primed and in battle stance ready to fight or flee at a moment's notice, "We've got your back buddy" Will replied as I reached up and punched in the combination the same as the spectral had and pressed my thumb against the thumb pad and Sellotape.

A red light appeared scanning the adopted fingerprint, when the red light stopped at the bottom it blinked twice and turned green sounding out a heavy "CLUNK' from inside the safe. A large sigh of relief left my lungs as I slowly pulled open the vault door "DUCK!" Will shouted sending my instincts into overdrive and allowing me just enough time to drop to the floor before a massive fireball blasted outwards to the back wall, the once pristine white wall now had a big black scorch mark on it from the flame impact and Will, Katie and Jen were all staring at it and me "Too close" I mumbled slowly rising to my feet cautiously looking inside the safe.

The safe was filled with various other treasures including a golden goblet, precious jewels, a few bags of gold and in the middle ledge protected by a glass case, was the compass case. The case itself was completely black with marks etched into it of what appeared to be tiny demons fighting with angels and flames erupting from the ground all around them, "Found you" I whispered, I looked around the room and grabbed a small bronze artifact resting on a table nearby "Here we go" I thought.

I reached in with my left arm and slowly wrapped my fingers around the glass case and quickly lifted it up resting the bronze artifact on top where the compass had been and holding it in place while looking around the room for any sudden traps.

"What? You expecting a boulder or something to come crashing down?" Jen asked "You can't be too careful" I replied smiling and turning the case in my hand. "I don't know how to open it" I mumbled turning the glass case searching for secret latches, a combination, a thumbprint or anything else that might open it "Let me take a look" Jen spoke taking the case from my hands and inspecting it intensely, I looked back into the safe and spotted something in the corner, a manilla envelope stashed amongst various white paper documents making it seem clearly out of place, I removed the envelope and looked at the wax seal and the symbol imprinted on it; a shield with three golden crowns.

It seemed familiar somehow to me, I don't know why but it just did, I broke the seal and pulled out a white sheet of paper, my jaw would have hit the floor had I not clamped my hand over my mouth in shock "What is it?" Katie asked approaching me "This picture, I've only seen him in drawings but if this is correct then it means …" I replied before a loud crash interrupted our conversation. "GOT IT!" Jen shouted holding the compass in her hand and stood atop shards of glass from the smashed case (Plan B was always an option), "Good now let's get out of here" Will added.

 I quickly folded the paper and stuffed it into my back pocket for later (Sorry everyone, you're going to have to continue reading if you want to know what was on the paper). Will, Jen, Katie and I began our walk back to the door of the apartment ready to leave until a shadowy form suddenly appeared in the corridor in front of us and three other shadows appeared on our left, right and behind us in a full circle, the form in front of us slowly took shape. It was a man with white pale hair, a ripped faded white shirt and blue jeans with black trainers, his skin looked as if it had once glowed but was now falling off his body leaving behind only a black hollow skeleton in parts, his right eye (the only one he had) was watching each of us intently and locking his gaze on the compass in Jen's hand, "I think you have something that belongs to me" Dagon growled unfurling his wings one a bright glistening white that was slowly fading and the other a skeletal wing with chunks of flesh hanging off the bones "Damn" I mumbled.

# Chapter 17
## We ruin a perfectly good apartment

Well, if things couldn't have possibly gone any more from bad to worse in that particular moment confronted by a fallen angel that looked like an extra in the Walking Dead, his minions suddenly protruding giant swords in their hands that looked as if they were on fire it definitely became bad. "Sorry, we're just borrowing this for a while but we'll bring it back" I lied hoping that he might be dumb enough to fall for it "I can't allow you to take Dante's compass I'm afraid, it is necessary for my future" Dagon replied (Well it was worth a try).

"Why do you need the compass?" Katie questioned curiously bouncing on her heels ready for battle, "The gates of hell must open my dear that is why, I have no interest in the compass itself merely it's protection from the likes of Protectors like you" Dagon mumbled his one good eye spinning its gaze onto Katie "You want the gates to open?" I asked dreading the battle that I knew would be coming soon, "My boy, the gates are the only way I can earn back what was taken from me" Dagon spoke staring straight into my very soul and then looking at his one functioning wing.

"You want to go back to heaven" Jen spoke reaching for her hairpin slowly, "I was cast out for choosing a side, but this … this is beyond unreasonable" Dagon replied as a feather fell off his angelic wing turning to ash as it hit the ground. "Every day I awaken in utter agony as more of me falls apart, soon I will be nothing more than a skeleton with wings, many of my brothers have already become these creatures, they lose their mind and become feral monsters slaughtering anything in their path, once we were cast out of heaven the Devil rejected us, told us that we were no longer of any use to him now that we were slowly going mad" Dagon added making me kind of feel bad for him.

"So, I am going to allow the gates to open and for the rapture to begin, I will fight the demons when they arrive on earth and earn my place back in heaven" Dagon finished his shadow friends never removing their ghostly gaze from us, "You honestly think God will let you back in?" Katie asked trying to suppress her laughter. "He won't have a choice, he will be weak from the lack of faith in him from humanity and I will use that weakness to get through the golden gates" Dagon growled fixing his gaze on Katie, "If the Rapture happens the whole world will be destroyed, the entire fabric of reality, you won't be able to return to heaven because there won't be a heaven to return to" Jen argued.

"Enough of this nonsense!" Dagon screamed "Hand over the compass and I may allow you to live" Dagon added stretching out his hand, a chunk of flesh fell from his palm and hit the rug turning slowly to ash, I looked at Jen, Will and Katie and we all gave a quick nod in confirmation of what we were going to do. "Sorry, but we aren't leaving without that compass" I replied watching Jen who quickly snuck the compass into her backpack, Dagon sighed and put his hand by his side, "Then you have sealed your own fate … kill them all" Dagon replied looking at his shadows who began their attack "Here we go" I thought to myself bringing Divine Fury to life in my hand and striking out at the shadow to my right.

Will and Katie were fighting in different rooms battling their shadow enemy and occasionally smashing any nearby objects that got in the way including the giant plasma tv that came crashing down with a heart wrenching 'CRUNCH' as it shattered against the rug (I know, I felt that too). Jen was currently locked in battle with her shadow creature firing arrows at it and using Bojutsu (Martial arts with a bow in case you were wondering) to use when the shadow got too close for comfort while I fought my shadow creature in the kitchen and let me tell you, I'm thankful that I was born with battle instincts otherwise you would not be reading my tale.

The shadow blocked almost every swing that I made and the ones that he didn't block he managed to shift and dodge leaving me with a sword implanted in the marble countertop, "Knock it off!" I shouted at the shadow swinging my blade in an arc and destroying the sink behind him, a jet of water from the tap fired into the air soaking me and then slowly trickled to a small fountain, the shadow struck out at me again slicing a small cut on my arm as I tried to dodge out of the way. "Ouch" I mumbled my blue blood leaking onto the white tiled floor, "Alright If that's how you want to play, let's play" I replied tensing the muscles in my back and releasing my wings.

Despite not having a face the shadow seemed to look surprised when my wings unfurled smashing the blender and the coffee maker at the same time (Yes, they were expensive and yes it was a shame to smash a pot of perfectly good coffee). I lunged forwards slicing downwards at the shadows leg, sensing my movement the shadow jumped upwards "Got you" I thought as I swung my left wing upwards and uppercutted the shadow sending him smacking into the ceiling leaving a small crater in the roof, the shadow crashed back down onto the floor face first and I brought Divine Fury down driving it through the shadows back while he was stunned, the shadow let out a loud squeal like a boiling tea pot and burst into ash.

It felt good to know that I'd actually killed a genuine threat for once rather than wounding it or distracting it with my phenomenal Judy Garland impression (Hey don't judge me I could be a great singer for all you know) "That was fun" I muttered looking back into the living room where Jen had just brought down her shadow creature with an arrow to the eye and where Will and Katie had smashed a window and thrown the shadow creatures out into the sunlight introducing them to the 20 storey drop "Well … that was disappointing" Dagon mumbled, "We're leaving, you can either let us go and we'll spare you or stand your ground and we'll make sure you don't get the chance to rot away" I spoke pointing my blade directly at Dagon's chest.

Dagon mulled the thought for a brief moment and then brought two short swords to life in either hand that looked almost like a roman sword in a way "I'll take that as a no then" I added preparing for another battle "You should have left when you had the chance" Dagon growled taking one step forwards before bursting into ash with an arrow in his skull, I looked over to Jen who was holding her bow steady. Myself, Katie and Will all stood staring at her in shock "What? I already fought his shadow friend so I thought why not finish him while he's monologuing" Jen replied shrugging her shoulders and returning her bow back to its position as a hair pin "That's fair" Katie spoke smiling and returning her dagger's back to bracelet form.

"Well, I don't think the landlord is going to be happy" I mumbled looking around at the utter carnage and destruction of what had once been a beautiful penthouse apartment, Jen's battleground in the living room now consisted of a white couch with multiple cuts and arrows protruding from it and a shattered fireplace mantle, the room where Will and Katie had been fighting aside from the two smashed windows letting in the cool St. Louis air now also had several scratch marks in the paintwork and one crater showing the insulation in the wall of the apartment and of course the kitchen where I'd been fighting was now slowly beginning to flood from the damaged tap. "I don't think so either, so I suggest we get out of here before he shows up" I replied walking back over to the elevator.

We descended back down to the lobby after our battle listening to the torturous elevator music and ran back through the lobby heading for the door, "HOLD IT!" we heard a voice shout as we were five feet away from the door, we turned around to see the guard who had let us in was now looking over his shoulder having never even moved from his spot with his feet on the desk. "Is something wrong?" I asked twirling my ring on my finger and preparing for another battle, "Dagon … is he dead?" the guard asked "Yes" Will replied causing us all to fear that the guard may decide to have a fight as well "Disappointing, now I have to get used to whatever neighbour moves in next, here's hoping it's a sexy single succubus" the guard replied crossing his skeletal fingers "Well, why are you still here? Don't you have somewhere to be?" the guard asked waving us off, still shocked by the guard's attitude we looked at each other, shrugged and headed back out onto the street to catch our bus.

## Chapter 18
### One down, three to go

After an uneventful bus ride back to the train station again which thankfully was only full of mortals and nothing that was trying to eat us this time, we managed to board our delayed train heading North West to Nebraska. "So, the next piece of the compass is in Nebraska? How did you find that out?" I asked Jen who was currently studying a map with several pieces of paper around her all of us trying our best to ignore Will who was currently swallowing a burrito so fast that his jaw looked as if it had unhinged like a python.

"When we were at Dagon's apartment I found a bunch of notes in his desk, apparently he'd been looking for the other pieces of the compass so that he could unite them and destroy it so no one would ever be able to stop his plan" Jen replied flicking away a piece of cheese that had landed on the map over Wisconsin. "Any idea where to start? I mean Nebraska is a big state" Katie asked studying the various pieces of paper on the desk, "I don't know yet, the next piece of Dante's compass that we need is the magnet" Jen replied tossing aside a stack of papers "Maybe it's to the north of Nebraska, the highest point" Will spoke occasionally sending a spit chunk of meat or cheese flying across the table "Don't talk when you're eating" Katie replied throwing a pen at Will smacking him directly between the eyes.

"Why North?" I questioned looking over at Will who had finally finished his burrito, I tried my best not to laugh at the blue ink spot between his eyes, "A compass always points to true north right? That's how magnets work, so if we're looking for a magnet then wouldn't it make sense that it would be to the highest northern point, we know it's not in anyone's possession from Dagon's notes so it must be hidden somewhere high up" Will explained. His logic seemed sound but it still left us with a few hundred miles of territory to search for something the size of a fun size candy bar.

"There must be some way to find it, some disturbance in the mortal world" Katie spoke tapping her chin "Breaking news!" we heard an announcement come from a mortal's computer from the seat in front of our table, "Welcome to channel 52 news I'm your anchorman Tommy Watt's" we heard come from the computer, leaning over slightly to catch a glimpse of the screen which had a middle aged reporter with a face beyond full of Botox sat in a news conference room with large red lettering behind him announcing the 'BREAKING NEWS'.

"*There have been reports of an 6.9 earthquake in the town of Valentine in Nebraska, as of now there have been no reported deaths but many are injured and the authorities are still searching through the remains of some buildings, the earthquake hit the town two hours ago causing mass hysteria and panic amongst the town people*" Watt's announced as we all looked at each other sharing an equal understanding that the earthquake would have hit at roughly the same time as when we had liberated the compass case from Dagon. "*We go live to Diana who is on scene, over to you Diana*" Watt's announced as the camera changed suddenly showing an attractive 40 year old red headed woman smiling at the camera with impossibly white teeth.

"Thanks Tom, I'm here with Isaiah Williams who is one of the townspeople of Valentine least affected by the earthquake" Diana explained as the camera extended showing an overweight gentleman in blue overalls and a white shirt and trucker cap (Think old school farmer from when you were a kid and you'll know what Isaiah looks like). "Thanks for agreeing to this interview Isaiah, could you explain what happened when the earthquake struck please?" Diana asked holding the microphone out closer to Isaiah's mouth. "Why yes I can miss, it was the strangest thing, I was out in the barn when I hear this loud rumbling and I look over to the town which you can see from the upper part of my barn" Isaiah replied with a strong country accent pointing to a square gap on the second floor of a large red and white barn "And I look over at the town and all the buildings are shaking from left to right and collapsing and such … it was freaky" Isaiah continued using his hands to describe the scene.

"And how do you mean it was freaky?" Diana asked using air quotation marks with her fingers, "Well, there wasn't an earthquake where I was stood, no shaking nothing, my house was rocking a little but nothing as bad as the folks' down there" Isaiah replied pointing in what we guessed was the direction of the town "How far out of town are we Isaiah?" Diana questioned "About five miles, close enough that my whole house should have been shaking, guess when the preacher blessed my crops, he made my land earthquake proof" Isaiah joked and right at that moment his shirt untucked slightly and a square piece of metal the size of a fun size candy bar popped out of his collar attached to a golden chain.

"No way" Katie mumbled catching the attention of the mortal who now looked over at us curiously wondering why four teenagers were staring at his computer screen and watching the news, we quickly ducked down and leant close to the table away from prying ears. "You think that's it?" Will questioned as the news report continued talking about the area before handing over to "Johnny Markson with weather", "It's possible, I mean it's a divine substance, the guy probably doesn't even know what it really is" Jen replied tapping her finger against her chin.

"The magnet really made his land earthquake proof?" I asked, "No, the magnet acts as kind of a northern point and an earthquake is a rappelling force of two tectonic plates rubbing together. When we took the case from Dagon the magnet reacted to the experience and let out a wave of energy but because the magnet was already in the north then anything nearby south of the area was affected by the wave" Jen replied. "I get it, it's like when you try to put two northern ends of a magnet together and they keep pushing each other apart, the magnet literally collided with the northern part of the world and caused a ripple effect in Valentine to the south of his farm" Katie spoke marking on the map with a red sharpie.

I'd never been gladder to have friends who actually knew what they were doing because I was lost beyond all measure (If you understood any of that then consider yourself as smart as the child of an Angel, Hunter or demon). "Okay so we head to the farm, ask him nicely for his necklace and unite the pieces, should be easy right?" I asked, Will, Katie and Jen all looked at me with one eyebrow raised "Right, when is it ever easy for us" I added staring out the window at the passing landscape.

"It's going to be a long ride, let's try and get some sleep and recharge ready for tomorrow" Jen spoke folding the maps and pages shoving them into her backpack before resting her head against the seat, "Sounds good to me, that burrito really tired me out" Will replied letting out a phenomenally loud belch before leaning back and shutting his eyes slowly beginning to snore. "You going to try and get some sleep?" Katie asked me settling herself into her chair and placing her head against the window, "Yeah, just going to enjoy the scenery for a while first" I replied looking out the window and watching Katie drift off out of the corner of my eye.

My world had changed so much in the course of the past few weeks, I'd found out I was a protector and the child of supernatural beings, I'd gained three amazing friends who I hoped would have my back for the rest of my life and I'd been sent on an assignment with them to save the world as we know it. My life had definitely gotten more interesting but with every passing day I remembered what my life used to be like, the highs and the lows, the places I'd slept never knowing if I was safe or where my next meal was coming from and the things I'd done to survive, as my mind drifted to an old memory of a time long since passed and a person I wondered if I would ever see again my eyes began to feel heavy and the world turned black.

## Chapter 19
## Dreams really suck when you're a protector

Surprise, surprise, I got taken on a little adventure once again when my eyes shut, my body now long behind sleeping peacefully on a train I found myself floating in front of the gates of hell once again where I had been before although this time two of the braziers were lit instead of one and it appears that the army had also grown in amount and ugliness.

"My Lord, I bring grave news" a demon spoke bowing before Galadriel who was sat on a large throne made of various bones high above his army with steps leading up to it like an Aztec temple, the small demon pressed one clawed hand against his chest and kept his gaze on the floor, "Speak" Galadriel replied dismissing a small winged demon that had just brought him a silver chalice moulded to look like a skull and completely black obsidian with two ruby eyes.

"Dagon is dead" the demon mumbled hiding his eyes from Galadriel's intense stare who had now after taking a drink from his chalice set it down to the side of his throne, "How?" Galadriel asked calmly fixing his gaze on the demon "An arrow to the head sire, it appears that Protectors were involved" the demon spoke barely above a whisper and literally shaking in his cloven hooves.

"When?" Galadriel asked taking another drink from his chalice and setting it down once again next to him, "Early this morning sire" the demon spoke scanning around the open valley as though looking for the nearest exit "This morning" Galadriel mumbled pausing and wrapping his dull grey fingers around the cup. Galadriel picked up the cup and downed the last of whatever liquid was in it (I didn't get any closer because I had absolutely no desire to find out what) "And why am I only finding out about this now?" Galadriel asked holding the chalice in front of his face examining the craftsmanship of the cup.

"Well, sire, my lord, we have been preparing for the coming day and …" the demon replied daring to look into Galadriel's red eyes before returning his stare to the floor. "I understand completely" Galadriel replied gripping the chalice and throwing it at the demon with impossible speed striking him in the forehead and knocking him over and down several steps behind him.

"This plan has been in the making for centuries and you" Galadriel added standing up from his throne approaching the demon before kicking him in the ribs sending him sprawling down another few steps catching the attention of the demons below him who were now staring up at the beating that the small demon was receiving. "Only tell me about it hours after it has taken place!" Galadriel shouted kicking the demon with each word that came out of his mouth harder and harder each time.

"Sire please" the demon begged spitting out a puddle of black blood trying his best to flap his small wings that had just protruded out of his back, the demon managed to get a few feet off the ground before Galadriel grabbed him by the wings and (Get ready for it) ripped both wings off the demon, the Demon let out a loud blood curdling scream, Galadriel dropped the demon to the floor black blood began oozing down his back (Warned you).

Galadriel spun the demon around with his foot and grabbed him by his throat lifting him high off the ground. The demons' legs kicked repeatedly as he tried to escape Galadriel's grasp but his efforts were in vain due to Galadriel's immense strength as an Arch-Demon. "You should have told me sooner" Galadriel growled bringing up his right hand wrapping it around the back of the demons' head and with one quick spin with both hands simultaneously, broke the demons' neck and turned him to a pile of ash (So much for don't shoot the messenger).

The rest of the demons and monsters in the valley below stood staring up at the cruel torture and murder that they had just witnessed by their glorious leader's hand, "Let this be a message to all of you" Galadriel shouted using the shadows around him to cause fear to everyone in the crowd and even a little to me despite the fact that I didn't technically have a body right now to even feel fear. "This plan must come to fruition if you ever want to leave this cursed place all at once rather than one at a time as we have been doing for the past several thousand years!" Galadriel boomed his voice echoing around the valley and bouncing off the gigantic gates of Hell causing them to rattle slightly on their hinges.

"I will not tolerate any failure, if there are any more reports of what these Protectors are doing" Galadriel announced spitting at the word "Protectors" coming out of his mouth as though it was poison for him to say it. "Then I want to know, if there is so much as a whisper then I want it reported to me immediately, no more failures, no more late notice, immediately!" Galadriel shouted once more walking back towards his throne and sitting down on it one leg angled to the right, "Or next time I will not be so merciful" Galadriel mumbled gesturing at the pile of ash in front of him where the demon had once stood.

I looked back over at the gate once more as the third Brazier ignited and I was dragged back to my body.

# Chapter 20
## My funny Valentine

My horrific nightmarish vision of Galadriel caused me to jolt awake with a sudden yelp of fear causing Jen and Katie to jump out of their slumber in shock staring around the train searching for any threats that had suddenly appeared. "Sorry, sorry, I didn't mean to wake you" I mumbled running my hands over my sleep deprived eyes trying to regain my focus and determine where exactly where we were.

Outside the train window was nothing but open countryside for what seemed like eternity, the peace and serenity of the valley made me long to be out there relaxing under the midday sun and not on a journey to stop a terrifying arch demon by collecting several pieces of a compass to point our way to the gates of hell that were apparently guarded by several beings that highly likely wanted to kill us and one mortal who we would have to liberate his necklace from (My life is really complicated).

"It's alright, nightmare?" Jen asked me taking a deep breath and staring around the empty cabin, "Yeah, I think you guys should hear this" I replied looking over at the seat next to me which was surprisingly empty. "Where's Will?" I asked looking over the back of my chair and spotting him flirting with what appeared to be a young attractive college student several seats behind us "WILL!" I shouted causing Will to take his attention away from the college student for a moment, Will bidding her farewell kissed her on the back of her hand and joining us back at our table.

"Sorry guys, too hard to resist" Will replied winking causing Katie to roll her eyes in disgust and annoyance at Will's constant flirting with anything that has a heartbeat, "Anyway as I was saying" I mumbled beginning my tale of Galadriel and the beating of the messenger, my friends listened and hung on every word until I finished with a deep and heavy sigh "Well … that sucks" Will spoke summing up a 5 minute story in one sentence.

"If Galadriel knows that a bunch of Protectors are trying to stop him then he's going to send everything he's got at his disposal to stop us" Jen mumbled staring out the window as though an attack was about to come flying through the window at any moment, although considering that we were the children of supernatural beings that wasn't exactly unlikely to happen.

"The third brazier is lit which means we're running out of time, if we don't get all the pieces and find the gates before they open fully then we won't be able to stop them and the rapture will happen" Katie added just to highlight how screwed we were just in case we thought that things might be going well. "When we reach Valentine we need to head straight for the farm, grab the necklace and try and figure out where the next piece of Dante's compass is" I spoke and oddly enough right at that exact moment the conductor shouted through the intercom *"Ladies and Gentleman we are now arriving in Valentine, all passengers who are disembarking here please make sure you have all your belongings with you"* the conductor finished by cutting off the intercom to the protest of the speakers which let out a loud fizz noise that burned my already sensitive ear drums, "Here we go" I added as the brakes cried out and we pulled into the station.

Okay mortals this is a description of the town of Valentine for you in one simple sentence, if you've ever seen a Christmas romance movie on Netflix then you've seen the town of Valentine.

The whole city was tiny when we disembarked off the train and frankly very peaceful, even as we walked down the street heading in the general direction of the farm that we had seen people were waving and tipping their hats to us despite the lower section of the town that had been completely flatted by the earthquake leaving rubble where buildings used to be and gigantic cracks in the tarmac ruining the whole home feeling vibe for us at that moment.

We began our five mile walk out of the city under the hot mid-day sun admiring the open landscape around us, the cows bellowed and chomped at the grass around us, birds sang and flew over our heads and the air seemed to flow around us it was peaceful, too peaceful (When you're a Protector peaceful only means one thing, that you're likely to be attacked very soon). A loud honk from a car horn caused us to stand at the ready for an attack almost bringing our weapons to life in our hands which would have been unfortunate for the poor farmer pulling up next to us in his green dodge pick-up truck with a humongous smile on his face.

"Howdy, you kids lost?" the middle aged farmer asked leaning out of his pick-up truck and flashing us a kind smile with his yellowed teeth tipping his white Stetson at us, Katie approached the vehicle being the only one of us not terrified that this was some demon or monster here to kill us, "No, we're just trying to reach our Uncle Isaiah's farm a few miles from here" Katie replied pointing up to the hills in the distance.
"Well shoot" the farmer replied sounding genuinely like a cowboy from an old western (I swear to God I'm not making this up), "That's miles away, I'm heading up that way anyway, why don't you hop in the back and I'll drive you as close as I can" the farmer added making me even more suspicious that he was about to kill us.

"Thank you so much" Katie replied at which point did I only just realise that she'd had one of her daggers out this whole time hidden behind her back which she promptly turned back into one of her silver bracelets before hopping up first into the open space of the pick-up truck trunk. Jen, Will and I quickly followed as I found myself face to face with a panting Border collie with two different colour eyes one blue and the other a light brown, "What are you? Hell hound? Demon? Vicious nightmarish creature that's going to rip my throat out as soon as my back is turned?" I thought right before the dog proceeded to rub its wet tongue on the side of my face in affection "Nope, just a regular old dog" I thought stroking the collie behind his ears and pushing him playfully away from my already saliva covered face before it could end up covered anymore.

After a short 30 minute drive that would have been a 2 hour walk had it not been for Jameson our driver and Bud the border Collie we arrived at Isaiah William's ranch, despite the fact that every other ranch that we had passed on the way over here Isaiah's was entirely different in so many ways. The crops out in the field were lush and abundant as if the drought that had only stopped last month according to Jameson hadn't affected the crops at all, the house was well built and perfectly painted down to the finest detail even on the banister and a flock of chickens aimlessly wandered around the lush grass garden pecking mindlessly at the tiny bugs that lived there.

"This is weird" Will spoke as we walked slowly towards the house disturbing the chicken's pecking routine, "Everything is so alive" I muttered preparing for the likely event that we would be attacked soon. "We need to be ready, if he isn't mortal then we may need to fight, if he is mortal and doesn't hand the necklace over then we'll have to do it by force" Jen added as we slowly began our climb up the stairs to the front door. The oak wooden door made my adrenaline begin to go into overdrive as I prepared for any possible upcoming battle (You may think I'm being dramatic but you try being chased for six years and having things try to kill you constantly you'd be paranoid too).

Jen knocked on the door in the classic four tap and two tap tone "Just a second" Isaiah announced from somewhere inside the house as we stood primed and ready to fight, the sound of Isaiah's footsteps as he walked down the hallway towards us clearly visible through the glass window on the front of the door seemed to echo like thunder making my heartbeat impossibly fast and causing me to bounce on my heels.
The door opened wide to reveal the kind smile of the farmer we had seen earlier on the news broadcast "Hi there, can I help you?" Isaiah asked with a kind beaming smile on his face. I looked at Katie and Will who both seemed to relax and felt the adrenaline begin to wind down in my own body, I felt a strong feeling in my gut that this guy was nothing more than your average mortal and not some kind of monster or demonic threat that wanted to kill us. "Hi, my name is Jen and these are my friends Jason, Katie and Will" Jen spoke pointing to each of us in turn "We were hiking and trying to find our campsite and we seem to have gotten a little lost, do you happen to have a map or something so we can find our way back?" Jen lied perfectly with a smile on her face "Damn she's good" I thought to myself nodding my head at her statement in agreement.

Isaiah studied us for a brief moment and then smiled the same kind way that he had when he had first seen us on the porch of his house, "Of course come on in, you can use the computer I'm sure that will be more useful to you than the paper maps I got in the truck" Isaiah spoke stepping aside and welcoming us in "Thank you so much" Jen replied fluttering her eyelashes and entering the household first before we quickly followed smiling and nodding at the kind mortal farmer willing to help us lost campers.

Jen and Will began their search on the computer for the "campsite" while me and Katie stood with Isaiah in his kitchen drinking the lemonade that his wife Angelina had made earlier this morning. "So where is your wife?" I asked glancing at a picture on the wall of Isaiah and a woman about the same age as him with greying hair and a giant smile on her face as she stood holding hands with Isaiah like a couple of newly wed kids, "She's in town helping the folks with the rebuilding project, surprised you guys aren't back home after an earthquake like that I bet your parents are worried sick about you" Isaiah spoke placing his empty glass on a wooden coaster on the kitchen countertop.

"We called them on a satellite phone that they gave us for emergencies, they were glad we were okay but didn't want us to call off our trip just because of a shake that we were nowhere near" I lied although where this sudden lie had come from I had absolutely no idea, maybe Jen was rubbing off on me making me a great liar too (Don't tell her I said that either, she'll never let me live it down). "Ah that's alright then, where you folks from?" Isaiah asked shifting to the left and causing his necklace to fall out of his shirt bringing the magnet of Dante's compass into clear view.

The small black piece of metal seemed to be calling out to me and I guessed so was Katie considering the way she was staring at it practically ready to rip it off his neck, "Los Angeles, we all are, we're college students" Katie spoke looking over at me and nodding subtly "Well that explains why a little earthquake wouldn't both you none" Isaiah replied.
"That's an interesting necklace you have their Isaiah" I spoke pointing to the piece of metal around his neck "Do you mind if I ask where you got it from?" I added ready to take the necklace by force if I had to.
"This old thing?" Isaiah asked twirling the rock in his fingers "Found it out in the yard one day when I was turning the soil, back in those days nothing grew on this land but when I found this the whole farm just seemed to come to life, Angelina calls it our good luck charm although I don't believe in none of that nonsense" Isaiah continued letting go of the magnet now letting it hang clearly in view, "I'm actually a geology major at U.C.L.A back home, do you mind if I have a look?" I asked flawlessly lying once again, Isaiah studied me for a moment and then pressed the rock into his palm.

"I don't know, I mean I know I said luck isn't something I believe in but I haven't taken this off since the day I found it" Isaiah spoke holding the magnet close to his chest, a part of me didn't want to take the magnet by force but judging on how Isaiah was acting I guessed that we wouldn't get that luxury. "Please Isaiah?" I asked as I heard Jen and Will edge into the room behind us, "Hey there, find the campground?" Isaiah asked looking over our shoulders at Jen and Will "Yes thank you, it's really close so we should be okay" Jen replied spotting the chain around Isaiah's neck.

 "Good, I want to make sure you get back home okay, where are you all from again?" Isaiah asked looking directly at Jen. "Chicago" Jen replied without a second thought (Never lie kids because it will usually come back and bite you in the butt just like right now), "Funny because this one here said you're from Los Angeles" Isaiah announced pointing at Katie. "Sorry yes, I'm from Chicago originally but now we live in Los Angeles together" Jen replied panic in her eyes "Right, your college students at Cal. State, right?" Isaiah asked once again "That's right" Will spoke before I could silently tell him no.

Isaiah studied us all and then smiled "Nice try kids, but do you think I wouldn't notice four Protectors walking up here?" Isaiah questioned with a smug expression on his face, we all knew at this moment that not only were we absolutely screwed but that we had also completely underestimated Isaiah.

 "I'm sorry what?" Jen asked running her hand through her hair subtly removing her hairclip, "Don't play fool girl I knew straight away what you all were, after all, there's two high bounties on this one here" Isaiah spoke pointing at me. I looked at Isaiah totally and utterly shocked "Me? Who would put a bounty on me?" I asked readying myself for battle, "That's for me to know and you to never find out, the higher bounty is for alive for you kid, but I'm going to kill the rest of your friends" Isaiah replied removing any hope that he may let us go, "You don't have to do this, just give us the magnet and we'll go" Katie replied bringing her two Shui daggers to life in her hands "Sorry sweetheart but if I give you this then you're going to go after the faceplate and then the guy who put the bounty on you will be real unhappy" Isaiah announced.

"So, the faceplate is with the client huh?" I asked a smug expression on my face "Damn, me and my big mouth, oh well, he wanted you alive but he never said how alive" Isaiah announced swinging his right arm backwards, I brought Divine Fury to life in my hands right before Isaiah's now transformed massive fist collided with my face sending me flying through the living room and out into the front of the garden terrifying the chickens who now ran at full speed for their coop.

"Ow" I groaned right as Katie was sent flying out the side window of the house, Jen flew out the front of the spot where I had been sent through landing her directly on top of me so her face was practically inches away from mine, "Sorry" Jen mumbled pushing herself up slightly "No problem" I mumbled sitting upright once Jen had climbed off of me spotting Will who was currently sprawled out in the rose garden.

"Foolish Protectors, you never should have come here" Isaiah announced walking out onto his porch through the giant hole in his wall. Isaiah had changed from a kindly farmer to a nine foot demon with black skin and horns, fists the size of basketballs with sharp claws attached and hair that was on fire (I mean literally on fire, like Ghost rider) "Well damn it" I mumbled bouncing onto my feet and standing with Jen who had her bow drawn with an arrow at the ready.

# Chapter 21
## We bring the house down


Jen was the first to attack Demon Isaiah firing two of her arrows directly at his head and I really wish I could tell you that it killed Isaiah instantly and we went on our merry way, unfortunately, Isaiah caught both of the arrow's mid-flight and snapped them like twigs "That's unfortunate" I muttered as Jen drew another arrow and knocked it into her bow, I unfurled my wings and charged directly at Isaiah as he brought a large black sword to life in his hands. Isaiah brought his sword down on top of me and I used the precious few seconds I had to block the sword before it could split me in half, Isaiah's blade collided with Divine fury with a deafening clang and I knelt to the ground grinding my toes in the ground trying to prevent myself from being driven further into it.

"I really don't want to hurt you Jason, stand down and I'll allow you to leave with your limbs attached" Isaiah announced as the sweat poured down my back from the pressure, "I'm going to have to turn down that offer, you made two mistakes starting this fight Isaiah" I replied spotting Katie and Will climbing up from their where they had crashed. "And what are they exactly?" Isaiah asked me a smug grin grew across my face as I watched my friends move in close to each other (You're going to love this next part).

 "Your first mistake was taking on four Protectors all by yourself" I spoke shifting my weight and strength into my wings. "I am an arch-demon and a powerful being, four Protectors are nothing more than a minor annoyance" Isaiah laughed glancing over at Will, Katie and Jen, "Would you like to know your second mistake?" I asked pressing my left palm against the flat side of Divine fury's blade, "Enlighten me" Isaiah growled his fiery hair flaring even fiercer than it already was "Your second mistake was letting me get too close" I replied with a smile on my face (Here we go kids).

I quickly unfurled my wings outwards colliding the tip of my divine wings against Isaiah's strong demonic ankles with the same impact as hitting him with a metal baseball bat (If you've never been hit with one of those before ... it hurts). Isaiah let out a loud bellow right before I pushed upwards with all my strength against the flat edge of Divine fury slamming the flat of the blade against Isaiah's chin knocking him back a few feet, I performed an awesome backflip and landed with a superhero landing between my friends who were all stood in battle stance (Epic right?!).
 Isaiah reached up his demonic hand and wiped away some of the black blood that was oozing from his now very broken nose, "Ouch" Isaiah remarked his flaming orange hair now turning to an impossibly hot bright blue (That's science kids, look it up) "You guys ready for this?" I asked raising onto both of my feet spinning Diving fury in my hand "Born ready man" Will replied with a wicked grin as we charged directly at Isaiah as a team.

Jen fired two arrows into the crook of Isaiah's arm piercing his thick demonic hide before he had a chance to catch them, Katie let out a small flash of Divine light stunning Isaiah like a flashbang causing him to stagger back a few feet onto the porch of his now ruined farmhouse, Will jumped into the shadows caused from the nearby shed and disappeared before reappearing at Isaiah's left side from the shadow of the house and jumping through the air removing one of Isaiah's horns from his head and I slid along the floor on my knees spinning Divine fury in an arc and slicing the Achilles tendon on Isaiah's left leg.

Isaiah let out a loud bellow and collapsed onto the knee of his now utterly useless left leg. "YOU DAMNED PROTECTORS!" Isaiah bellowed trying to stand back upright (If anyone reading this knows anything about the human body then you'd know how much pain this would cause). Isaiah stood on both his legs grinding his teeth together from the pain and putting all his weight onto his right leg "Stand down Isaiah and we may let you live" I spoke pointing the tip of my blade directly at Isaiah's chest, "Never" Isaiah replied slamming the point of his blade into the ground.

The ground shook with a loud rumble and cracked like an earthquake shaking the area around us and the trees causing several of them to come crashing down to the earth disturbing the local animal forest population within a 3-mile radius. A rock suddenly protruded from the ground on my side and struck me directly in the ribs launching me back and slamming me against a small oak wood tree (Why me right?).
I slid down the rough bark of the tree and slumped against the floor "Broken … definitely broken" I thought pressing my hand against several broken ribs, I'd broken bones before and they usually healed within a day or two but when you're in a battle with a nine foot demon then broken bones aren't exactly helpful. "Jason, are you okay?" Jen questioned kneeling by my side while Will and Katie continued to do battle with Isaiah keeping him distracted, "I've been better" I joked standing back up resting my hand against Jen's shoulder, "Do you want to sit this out?" Jen asked me "Not a chance" I replied smiling at Jen, Jen smiled back at me and we charged back into battle with Isaiah.

Jen fired another two arrows into Isaiah's shoulder blade's when his back was turned causing another loud bellow to erupt from the demon, "Nice shot" I spoke winking at Jen following her into battle glancing over at Katie and Will who were now recovering after being slammed against the house leaving a Will and Katie shaped hole in the wall. I charged forwards and spiralled in a corkscrew with my wings launching myself forwards and driving my sword into Isaiah's thigh causing a bellow so loud that I thought my eardrums might burst.
"That looked like it hurt" I joked sliding across the ground and standing mantis style with Divine fury outstretched in my right hand, "Forget the first bounty, the Commander wants you dead then so be it!" Isaiah shouted launching himself at me, I wondered who Isaiah was talking about before spotting that in his attack he had left himself totally exposed, "Big mistake" I replied waiting until he was inches away from me before stepping to the side using my Hunter speed and bringing my sword down on Isaiah's legs cutting both of them off at the knee, Isaiah crumpled to the ground screaming in agony and trying in vain to crawl away.

Jen, Will and Katie stood by my side as Isaiah propped himself against a tree gasping for breath as black blood oozed from the corners of his mouth and his legs turned to dust, "I must say, that was fun" Isaiah joked coughing up a cloud of blood and spitting it out onto the earth causing the green grass on the spot to suddenly turn yellow and die. I edged forwards and reached out ripping the chain and magnet away from Isaiah's neck, the magnet felt warm in my hand and vibrated almost as if it was calling out begging to be reunited with the case and become whole once more, I passed the magnet over to Jen who quickly followed through on the magnet's request and united it with the case.

The compass glowed slightly before dimming and sealing itself shut, "You said the client has the faceplate of the compass, who is he?" Will asked pressing the tip of his blade against Isaiah's neck, "No need for violence, I'll happily tell you if only to see the expression on your face" Isaiah replied pushing the blade away from his neck. "Where is it?" Jen asked tucking the compass into her backpack, Isaiah looked at Will, Katie and Jen before locking eyes with me, his cold black eyes seemed to lock on mine draining the warmth from my heart "Why don't you go ask your boss?" Isaiah growled at me.

An ice-cold shiver ran throughout my entire body (You know the feeling, some people reference it as someone just walked over your grave which I always found really bizarre I mean, how are you supposed to know what someone walking over your grave feels like? You'd be dead right?).
 "You're lying" I mumbled feeling my heart thunder in my chest impossibly fast, "Look into my eyes Half Breed and ask yourself this" Isaiah gargled locking his gaze with mine "Do you honestly think I'd lie about this?" Isaiah added.

My body seemed to shake with fear and I questioned whether my heart was still beating fast or whether it had stopped completely, I swung Divine fury around and severed Isaiah's head from his neck turning him to dust and sending him back into the pits of hell "JASON!" Jen shouted.
 "We needed him alive to know where to go" Katie added, I turned Divine fury back into ring form and ran my hand through my hair, "No we don't, I know where we're going" I replied grabbing my backpack from the wreckage of the house and slinging it onto my back "How?" Jen asked me as I started the leading walk back to the town of Valentine "Because of what Isaiah told us" I replied "We're going to Dallas" I added as the remains of Isaiah's home crumbled to rubble behind me and I started my walk towards the station and my past.

# Chapter 22
## A long and awkward train ride

For the one hour long walk back into town, the 20-minute wait for the train to Wichita and the first one hour of the train ride I didn't speak a word to my friends, I sat in our shared booth across from Will and Katie with Jen on my side clenching my still broken ribs and staring blankly out the window at the passing environment.
The battle with Isaiah had hit me deep, not in the physical sense as in my broken bones and numerous bruises but as in an emotional sense, memories bubbled to the surface, memories that I had spent years trying to forget.

"Rib's still hurt?" Katie asked me being the first to break the silence and snap me out of my trance, "Yeah, not as bad as before but still sting" I replied my gaze never leaving the window, Katie reached into her bag and withdrew a small plastic green canteen like you would see soldiers drink from, "Here, take a small sip of this" Katie added passed me the canteen "Thanks" I replied utterly confused as to why Katie thought that a canteen of water would be suitable for broken ribs.

I took a small sip feeling the cold liquid flow down my throat and the strange sensation of sour sweets on my tongue, I'd loved anything sour since I was a kid but it did make me question what I was drinking but what was truly surprising was that the stinging sensation in my ribs was gone, in fact, I could feel my ribs stitching themselves back together faster than normal.
 "What is this?" I asked wiping my lips and passing the canteen back to Katie who quickly took a drink herself before placing the canteen back into her backpack. "It's Holy water" Katie replied "Holy water? Why did I just drink Holy water that tasted like sour sweets?" I questioned utterly confused watching Will take a drink from a metal flask with a loud satisfied gasp after he had a small sip and Jen took a drink from her plastic water bottle, "For mortals, nothing, but for the children of angels a small amount works as a cure all for our injuries, it won't instantly heal you or fix major injuries but it does speed up the healing process" Katie replied providing me with new information that I had never heard before.

"Is that what you guys drank?" I asked looking over at Will and Jen, "God no, if I touched that stuff it'd make me sick for weeks" Will replied disgusted. "My dad's a demon so we drink liquid sulphur" Will added belching out a cloud of yellow vapour, "Okay … what about you Jen?" I asked turning to face her, "For us Hunters it's concoction called Robur Elixir, your part Hunter so you should be able to drink it too" Jen replied my brain loosely translating the Latin word *Robur* as the word for strength "Cool" I replied struggling to decide on any other word.

Will and Katie both stared at me and each other "You feeling up to talking about what Isaiah said?" Will asked me sending another cold shiver down my spine, I took a deep heavy sigh and looked at all my friends. I'd only known them for such a short time and we'd already come so far, Will was the brother I never had and my closest friend I knew that much, Katie was like my sister and I felt an overwhelming urge to protect her at all costs, Jen to me would always be the one who took me in and taught me all about my heritage, she was my friend and mentor, if I was a Padawan then she was the Jedi master, my Qui Gon-Jinn to Kenobi (Respect to the great George Lucas) and if there was one thing I knew at that moment … it was that I could trust each and every one of them.

"You guys deserve to know the truth" I mumbled staring at my feet, "It's not easy for me to talk about my past, You guys may not know but since I was 10 years old, I'd lived on the streets running for my life until Jen found me" I added smiling at Jen while Katie and Will looked at me with pitiful eyes. "Dude … I had no idea, I'm so sorry" Will replied a look of shock spreading across his face, "Thanks, see the thing is … it's not the whole truth" I spoke looking over at Jen whose face had now changed to one of absolute confusion.

"What do you mean?" Katie asked me, if my soul didn't already feel like a lead weight when I'd first heard Isaiah mention to return to my boss then now it felt like an anchor that had just been dropped overboard. "From the age of thirteen to fourteen I lived in a warm home with three meals a day and a steady pay, I went from living on the streets to an apartment on the upper west side of Dallas" I replied, you could feel the tension in the room as I remembered the fateful day when my life had changed forever …

"You guys should know everything" I added.

## Chapter 23
## Back to the past

*Another night in Dallas, Texas, it was my fifth city in one year but I hadn't moved for over two week, I was in too much pain after all, my last meal had been just over a week ago and my stomach growled at me every few hours reminding me of the crippling agony of starvation.*

*I'd never gone this far without food before even if it was something as small as some left over food on the top of a trash can but lately I hadn't been able to find anything edible and I couldn't go begging around restaurants or I might find myself grabbed by the cops and thrown into a home for troubled teens so I had to survive however I could.*

*The rain was beating down heavy on my shoulders as I sat wrapped up in the old and torn coat that I had stolen from the local libraries lost and found when I spotted the Bentley speeding past me and pulling up outside the five-star restaurant downtown. "Can I really do this? I mean I've never done anything like this before but …" I thought right before clenching my stomach at its loud growl "I don't have a choice" I added edging myself slowly towards the Bentley.*

*The valet for the restaurant hurried over to the car with an umbrella over his head and a man in the driver's side of the car climbed out with a black umbrella raised over his head, for a chauffeur the guy was absolutely huge, he could have been a professional wrestler or body builder from the size of his muscles. His bald head shone under the moonlight and reflection of the few raindrops that had hit his head whilst he had climbed out of the car, the titan approached the back of the Bentley and opened the passenger door holding the umbrella over it.*

*"We're here sir" the man mumbled in a rough gravelly tone as another man climbed out of the backseat of the car. He was dressed in a sharp black suit that just screamed "I'm filthy stinking rich!" and tugged his sleeve over his solid gold Rolex as he stood upright and straightened his smooth black hair that hung like a mullet down the back of his neck, "Thank you Julius" the tycoon replied straightening his Scarlett red tie and walking around the back of the car with his loyal lap dog in tow holding the umbrella high above him so that not a single drop of rain touched his boss' precious suit. "Be gentle with her" the man announced as he slipped the valet a fifty dollar bill, the eager young valet bowed his head and ran around to the driver's side of the car protecting himself with his umbrella before climbing into the driver's side and gently pulling off into the parking lot at the side of the restaurant.*

I'd never seen so much money handed over so easily as if it was nothing more than pocket change, "It's now or never" I mumbled edging my way slowly over to the tycoon tugging the fabric of my coat impossibly tight against my body. I'd rehearsed this a hundred times in case I ever needed to use it but had never actually done it until now against a living person "Here we go" I thought to myself stumbling slightly and brushing up slightly against the tycoon.

In the brief second of contact we shared I slipped my hand into the tycoon's jacket and stole his leather wallet sneaking it into my own and spinning on my heels as the hulking gorilla bodyguard grabbed me by my collar. "I'm sorry sir, I'm so sorry, please excuse me" I stuttered locking eyes with the tycoon and trying my best to enhance the fear that was already showing in my eyes.

I thought I was a goner as Julius turned to look at his boss and clenched his right fist ready to collide it with my nose, the tycoon studied me for a moment with his cold almost black eyes and then smiled "It's okay son, accidents happen" the tycoon replied dismissing Julius who promptly let me loose shoving me down the street. "Thank you" I muttered rushing my way down the street and ducking into a nearby alley sheltering under a fire escape that protected me slightly from the rain.

I opened the stolen leather wallet and glanced inside, inside were several credit cards that I knew to leave alone lest I find myself handcuffed in a police station for credit card fraud but in the back was over a hundred dollars in cash "Thank you God" I announced crying with relief. This could feed me for a month or if I rationed it maybe even two months, I had finally caught a break and was ready to stuff my face and fill my stomach with whatever fast food joint I arrived at first, my stomach growled in anticipation of its upcoming meal and I almost jumped up from my seated position in glee "Nice lift kid" a voice spoke snapping me out of my trance.

I looked up and stared into the same cold dark eyes that I had seen outside the restaurant, the eyes that belonged to the rich tycoon, his gorilla bodyguard Julius stood by his side cracking his knuckles against the palm of each hand. The tycoon was holding on tight now to the umbrella that had a minute ago been carried by his loyal servant, I was totally screwed, at best I'd end up in a police station in handcuffs, at worst I'd find myself beaten to a bloody pulp by the gorilla bodyguard.

"I'm so sorry! Please here take it" I begged passing the wallet back to the tycoon and tucking my legs in tight against my body, the tycoon checked the inside of his wallet and nodded at the credit cards before opening the back section of the wallet.

"Last time I checked there was over a hundred dollars in here" the tycoon spoke shaking his head from left to right and making a "Tut, tut, tut" sound. "Damn it" I thought as I removed the crumpled bills from my pocket and passed them back to the tycoon "I'm sorry" I mumbled feeling the tears pouring down my cheeks combined with the rain dropping from my scraggly brown hair.

The tycoon stared down at me studying me and held the crumpled bills tight in his hand, "When was the last time you had something to eat?" the tycoon asked standing by my side and leaning his back against the wall. "A week or so" I replied wiping away the tears and daring to look up at the tycoon, the tycoon looked at me with pity in his deep dark eyes and let out a loud heavy sigh, "Why aren't you at home?" the tycoon asked looking over at his bodyguard who returned back to standing position from attack position and clasped his hands behind his back.

"I don't have one" I replied, I couldn't explain it but I felt comfortable around him, like a wave of ease was emanating from him and calming me down, my guard was totally lowered and I felt like I could tell him anything and everything. "No parents? No family at all?" he asked, I shook my head from left to right and returned my gaze back to my shoes "No, it's just me" I replied "I see" the tycoon replied staring over at his bodyguard.

"That truly was an impressive lift you know? If I hadn't gone to tip the maître D' I wouldn't have known until after my dinner" the tycoon added a smile spreading across his face. "Thanks" I mumbled trying to smile through the fear of when this guy was going to call the police, "Here" the tycoon spoke passing me the crumpled bills back, I took the bills cautiously from his hand and held them tight as though I had just been passed the holy grail.

"Consider it an advance" the tycoon added "An advance?" I asked utterly confused "I could use a man like you working for me if you're interested, I'll start you on two hundred dollars a week, I've got a spare room in my apartment complex and you'll have full use of any service that you need plus three meals a day from top chefs" the tycoon replied offering me what could be the literal holy grail but there was the back part of my mind that screamed "STRANGER DANGER".

"Don't worry this isn't some sort of creepy tactic to pick up young men I'm not that kind of guy, I just see potential in you and I think that with the right training and help you can be a great man" the tycoon added pushing that cool wave of comfort back into my soul. "If I refuse are you going to call the police?" I asked, "No of course not, if you decline my offer then you'll simply continue your life on the streets and walk away with the money you have now ... but I think I already know what your answer will be" the tycoon spoke holding out his hand towards me.

I thought for a moment at the danger I may be facing and where it may take me if I follow this stranger but I knew deep in my soul that he was right, it was too good an offer and I knew what my answer would be "Okay" I replied taking his hand in mine. The tycoon clenched my hand and lifted me back upright, I looked into those same cold black eyes that seemed to stare at me with admiration and the smile spreading across his face showing his pearly white teeth "Glad to hear it, welcome umm ..." the tycoon spoke grinding his teeth together.

"Jason, Jason Matthew Parker" I replied using my full and very embarrassing name, "Pleasure to make your acquaintance Jason, shall we?" the tycoon asked me holding out his hand gesturing towards the entrance to the alleyway I had ducked into as a poor homeless street kid, the tycoon passed his umbrella back to Julius who quickly raised it above his boss' head letting only a few rain drops land on the tycoon's shoulder.

"May I ask your name boss?" I asked following my new employer out of the alleyway and back towards the entrance to the restaurant, "Of course, if we're going to work together you're going to have to call me by name aren't you?" the tycoon spoke "My name is Samuel, Samuel Blake" the tycoon replied leading me into the restaurant. The maître D' examined me for a moment before noticing Blake's expression and nodded his head holding the curtain to one side, that curtain symbolised more than just what would later be the best and only steak I had ever eaten but also the gateway to my new life under the employment of Samuel Blake.

## Chapter 24
## My past is questioned

"Any questions?" I asked looking at the stunned expressions of all my friends who were struggling to decide on what exactly to say next after I had told them the story of my change from the life of a homeless kid to the early life of an employee on two hundred dollars a week. "Blake … you said Samuel Blake, right?" Will questioned his jaw almost hitting the floor "Who is Samuel Blake exactly?" Katie asked one eyebrow raised high in confusion and looking over at Will.

"Samuel Blake, the C.E.O. of Blake industries?" Will replied staring at Jen and Katie who both had absolutely no idea who Blake was, "Blake industries is a weapons development company, they provide tech and weapons for half the world and the military, the guy is practically richer than God!" Will added waving his arms in the air. "Damn, that is rich" Katie joked looking over at me, "Although he is a bit of a recluse, he only makes appearances at the occasional conference or if he's captured by the paparazzi walking into a restaurant that you would need at least four figures to your name just to eat for two" Will spoke rubbing his chin with his thumb and forefinger.
"Yeah there's a very valid reason for that" I replied scoffing at my statement, "Why?" Jen asked me leaning forwards in her seat and clasping her hands together, I paused and studied my friends feeling my heart thunder in my chest "Because Samuel Blake is an arch-demon" I replied.

Honestly, I swear to you in that moment, on a speeding train flying through the countryside, in a booth with four teenage Protectors, the child of an Angel, Demon, Hunter and Half Angel, Half Hunter …. You could have heard a pin drop against the carpet. "Blake is an arch-demon? Are you sure?" Jen asked me trying to formulate words, "When your employer who you trust decides to show his true form to you one night believe me, I'm sure" I replied rolling my eyes.

"That was my first encounter with a demon and why I asked you when we first met if demons were the bad guys" I added looking over at Jen. "What did sort of work did Blake have you do exactly?" Will asked me, I paused trying to decide what to tell them next, they already knew that I was working for an arch-demon in my past and the last thing I wanted them to know was the full truth of the work I used to do for Blake. "At first it was simple stuff, take this envelope to this location bring what they give you back, sit in the car with Julius and count people coming in and out of a building, clean the apartment when Blake was out and then the work became … less than legal" I spoke deciding to leave it at that simple statement.

"Less than legal? I always figured Blake for a shady character but a crime boss? Really?" Will asked as the conductor announced that we would shortly be pulling into Wichita central station, "He is an arch-demon after all and they aren't exactly known as being honest individuals" Katie replied pulling her backpack over her either arm. "True, but hurtful, I am the child of a demon after all, my dad may have only been a minor demon but still" Will spoke slinging his backpack on and tugging at the collar of his now ripped leather jacket after the battle with Isaiah.

We disembarked in Wichita and used the last of our mortal dollars to buy four tickets direct to Dallas on the Amtrak train taking our seat in our own private booth, "How you feeling?" Jen asked me resting a hand on my shoulder. "For the trip to see my ex-employer, arch-demon, owner of the faceplate of Dante's compass and the impending doom of the opening of the gates of hell in 4 days? Just fine" I joked running my hands through my hair and letting out a nervous laugh, "Nothing like laying out all our troubles in one statement" Will replied passing the conductor our tickets before slumping back in his chair.

"Sorry guys ... it's just, I don't know how I'm going to do this" I spoke intertwining my fingers repeatedly, "I know how" Katie replied smiling at me and clenching her hand around mine stopping the constant shaking and intertwining of my hands, "Together, we've got your back with this Jason" Katie added. Jen reached over and placed her hands on top of Katie's and smiled at me "To the bitter end" Jen spoke looking over at Will "To Hell and back" Will added materialising a cigar in his hand resting it between his teeth and propping his feet up on the small side table.

Jen, Katie and myself all stared at Will with full sarcastic expressions written across our faces "Are you mad about the Hell and back statement or the cigar?" Will asked moving the cigar from the right side of his cheek to the left side using his teeth. "Both and don't put your feet up on the table" Katie replied removing the cigar from his teeth and slapping his feet at the ankles knocking them off the small side table "Sorry mom" Will joked rolling his eyes at her and flashing his same wicked cheesy grin.

Throughout this entire journey and what would happen next in the future I knew in that moment that these three Protectors in this cabin with me, my friends and family would have my back to the ends of the earth and beyond but knowing what we were about to face when we arrived in Dallas tomorrow at 7pm ... I feared for how Blake would react when we came face to face. After two years since the day I ran away from him and all the work that we had done together, whether or not he would kill us on the spot or more terrifyingly ... welcome us all with open arms, no matter what ...

I would never allow myself to become the man Blake had forged me into all those years ago.

## Chapter 25
## Dallas, Home to Cowboys and Arch-Demons

A full 8 hours later we disembarked our Amtrak train and stepped off into Union station and exited onto the streets of downtown Dallas. My nerves felt like they were on fire as we walked down the city streets passing the local mortals who had no idea about the dangers they faced in their city and the madman that ran it in secret, I could almost feel his presence in the air as I gazed up at the surrounding skyscrapers and listened to the loud horns of the city traffic, since becoming a Protector it seemed like my already heightened senses had doubled and I could see through the haze with ease.

Everywhere I looked I could see the occasional passing demon or minor league monster on their way to the office or home depending on what demons did in their spare time, "So, how do we find him?" Will asked me as we continued our walk through the city ... and then I sensed him "We don't need to, he's found us" I replied stopping at the entrance to an alleyway on my right.

At the end of the dark and foul-smelling alleyway ahead of us I spotted one of Blakes most useful messengers, he used them for day-to-day access to contact his thugs whenever he had no desire to leave the building or use his phone lest someone listen in on his call and use the information against him. "Is that?" Will questioned but I ignored him completely and approached the messenger ... a pure white wolf with blue eyes (Not what you were expecting right).

The wolf examined me curiously with its beyond bright blue eyes and sniffed the air as though trying to determine whether or not I was a threat or a friend, his fur ruffled as the cool Dallas air passed through it and he let out a slight howl/whimper at my approach. I knelt down in front of him and stared deep into those stunning canine eyes so full of wisdom and loyalty, "Tell the boss I want to talk, just give me a time and a place" I whispered to the wolf who promptly bowed his head with a low howl and ran off down another alley.

"Did you just talk to that wolf?" Will asked me slowly approaching from behind, "He's a messenger for the boss, best way to reach him without ..." I replied a sudden low howl piercing the air grabbing my attention, my wolf friend had returned bowing his head and looking at me with puppy dog eyes (I know it's a wolf but you know the look I'm talking about).

I approached the wolf who currently had a white envelope held between his teeth "Good boy" I mumbled removing the envelope from the wolfs mouth and patting him on his head scratching him behind his ears, the wolf barked and turned running out of the alley blending into downtown traffic.

The envelope was stamped on the back with Blake's coat of arms in wax, two wolf heads on a shield with a flame in between them, "Good thing the haze can hide the wolf as a dog or people would ask some serious questions" Will joked trying to break the thick tension that it was in the air, the envelope may as well have been a two-ton weight the way my hands shook while breaking the seal and opening it. "Where are we going?" Jen asked as I unfolded the letter "Corner of Ross and Olive, our ride will meet us there" I replied crumpling the note and casting it into the air, the moment it left my hands the letter burst into flames and crumpled into ash.

The walk over to the corner of Ross and Olive was intense for me yet again, the air felt impossibly thick when I spotted the black town car parked waiting for us, I knew before the car door opened that it was the one waiting for us, God knows that I'd seen every single car that Blake owned enough to know one that belonged to him and him alone. The car door opened and my soul temporarily jumped out of my body before re-entering it in a panic at the man exiting the car "Hey Julius" I mumbled spotting the hulking beast of a minor demon climbing out of the car.

It had been two years since I had last seen Julius but he hadn't changed at all, his bald head still shone under the Dallas sun and his muscles rippled underneath his suit as he stood with both hands clasped in front of him secret service style. "Parker, been a long time" Julius growled glancing over my shoulder at Katie, Jen and Will who were all primed and ready to jump into battle at a moment's notice, "Who are they?" Julius added shrugging his head in the general direction behind me.

"My friends, they're going to be coming with us" I replied my eyes never leaving Julius' gaze, "Boss only sent me for you, I'm not taking them as well" Julius spoke folding his arms applying pressure to his already ridiculously muscled torso. I could feel something primeval bubbling in my soul at Julius' outright command and statement against me, emotions bubbled to the surface that I hadn't felt in a long time ever since I had started to work for Blake all those years ago.

"Fine, then you go back and tell Blake that his most valued employee refused to return because you wouldn't allow three extra people in the car" I replied my gaze locking with Julius feeling the fire and fury flooding my soul. Julius stared at me intensely trying to break my gaze but the one thing I knew about Julius was that despite all his muscle, despite all his power as a demon and his reputation in Blake's organisation … he was far more scared of me than I was of him. "Fine … watch where you sit I just had the leather treated" Julius mumbled stepping aside and opening the car for us to enter, I climbed in first followed quickly by Katie, Jen and Will who were now all staring at me utterly confused and wondering who I was at this moment.

I stared at the floor as Julius shut the door behind us and returned to the driver's side climbing into the front seat and starting the engine before pulling out into traffic which seemed to part like the red sea for Moses. "Boss has been searching for you a long time, why did you come back?" Julius asked me "I need his help" I replied bluntly keeping my gaze on the fine Egyptian wool carpet at my feet "His help? After all these years? You must be desperate" Julius laughed, "I don't feel like talking Julius put the visor up" I replied running my hand softly through my hair.

"I don't take orders from you anymore kid" Julius replied locking his gaze on the rear-view mirror and on me, that same primeval anger flooded through my system yet again as I fixed my gaze on Julius' cold black eyes, "Either put the visor up Julius or I will ... and your head will find itself placed in the gap" I growled. Julius paused for a moment and then pressed a button on the dashboard raising the black visor until he disappeared from sight sealing us in the now soundproof, bulletproof, bombproof, magic resistant limo "Dude?" Will spoke utterly shocked at my courage against Julius "Please, don't ask anything until this is over" I replied turning my attention to the window watching Dallas pass by me while my friends watched wondering who they were really sat with in the back of this limo.

The ride to Blake's apartment building was more awkward than any situation you can imagine in your entire life, more awkward than your first kiss or first dance, any situation you may have faced in high school or any awkward situation in life that you can impossibly imagine until we finally pulled up outside the apartment block.
 Blake told me when he first brought me here that he refused to buy the entire apartment building for himself unless it had a hundred floors exactly no more, no less and even now it was as impressive as the first day I had seen it.

The building stretched high up into the sky and had a silver frame with black windows that on the outside barely gave a reflection but on the inside could be seen out of as clear as though the window wasn't even there. Blake had told me that it was because he wanted to stand out from the surrounding buildings but once I found out he was an arch-demon I realised that for him it was all about power and statement. "You okay?" Jen asked placing her hand on my shoulder "Let's just get this over with" I replied trying to shut off all emotion while entering the building I had called home for over a year through the sliding automatic doors.

The interior of the building looked exactly like any other apartment block lobby you might see aside from the two security demons with horns and hooves who were sat behind the desk reading a newspaper and watching football. "I'm here to see the boss" I spoke, the demon holding the newspaper looked at us and nodded before pressing a button on his console opening the elevator behind him, Jen took position first in the elevator followed by Will and Katie so that in the end I was in front and staring at the open lobby waiting for the doors to close.

Julius approached after me trying to squeeze his massive frame into the already cramped elevator, "What do you think you're doing?" I asked him pushing him away, "Riding up with you guys, What? Do you think I'm going to let you go up without me?" Julius scoffed. "There's no room, don't worry about the boss you know we're of no threat" I replied, "Not happening kid" Julius spoke trying to force his way into the elevator yet again "Julius" I spoke the power raising in my chest. "If you take one step into this elevator, I will break every bone in your body until you beg for mercy" I added grinding my teeth together (Scary, right?) Julius stared down at me before nodding his head and stepping back allowing me enough time to press the button for the Penthouse and watch the doors slowly shut on his face.

The elevator groaned and shouted as it began its ascent while I stood shaking and clenching my fists repeatedly feeling the cool sweat pouring down my back, "It's not too late you know, we could open the door, run as fast as we could out of Dallas and find the gateway without him" I mumbled anxiously ready to press the stop button. From behind me I suddenly felt Jen grasp my hand having approached me from the side taking Will's place who was now stood at the back of the elevator smiling at me, "Don't worry, we can do this, together" Jen replied softly trying to calm down my nerves, Jen reached down and intertwined her hand with mine which did actually make me feel better but my body still tingled with anticipation as the elevator finally arrived at the 100th floor.

I ignored the open expanse of the living room where several guards were currently sat laughing and shouting at the same football game that the security guard downstairs had been watching completely oblivious to our entrance. The walk down the hall to his office echoed against the hardwood floor with every footstep like those moments in horror movies where each footstep sounds a hundred times louder than it actually is, his doors seemed to get further away the more I approached until finally my hand rested just slightly away from the door.

I took a deep sigh and knocked twice and three times "Come in" Blake called out from the other side of the door, I seriously considered running quickly to my right and leaping out of the window plunging a hundred stories down to the concrete street below rather than opening this door in front of me but I knew that if our assignment would ever be complete then I had to open the door. I slowly lowered the handle and stepped into the office followed closely and cautiously by Katie, Will and Jen.
Blake had his back turned to me staring out the window at his empire below, his office was the epidemy of power when he had first had it designed, weapons hung from the wall from various era's, a tommy gun that had once belonged to Al Capone sat in a glass cabinet to my right on his precious bookshelf and his solid mahogany desk stretched 4 feet across the room in the dead centre of the room precisely (Blake has serious O.C.D. by the way).

"Welcome back Jason, it's been far too long" Blake mumbled slowly turning to face me with his cold black eyes that provided comfort to me and fear to his enemies, his sleek black hair shone under the artificial light of his office and his freshly tailored suit that showed no sign of a crease of stain hung on his athletic build frame. I'd admired the man for most of my young life and would have done anything for him, when I left I was terrified of what would happen if he ever caught me and brought me back but now stood in front of him not as a helpless street child but as a Protector, the child of an Angel and a Hunter ... I'd never felt more powerless. I fixed my gaze with his and breathed a deep heavy sigh to calm my nerves "Hi dad" I replied his blank expression slowly turning to his wicked grin.

## Chapter 26
## Meeting with the boss

Well, if I hadn't shocked you before with every secret that was suddenly revealed to me and the demons hidden in plain sight then I'm guessing that last sentence made you very confused. "Dad?" Katie asked utterly stunned staring directly at me, my head hung in shame as I fixed my gaze between my friends and Blake who was currently stood flashing his wicked grin at me. "Glad to see your manners haven't changed son" Blake responded walking over to a nearby cart with a crystal decanter filled with a fine scotch and pouring himself a drink with two ice cubes clearly cut and even on all sides, two fingers exactly, no more no less (Like I said, O.C.D.).

"I try to keep them in check still" I replied my gaze fixed on Blake trying to hide the fear in my eyes at Blake's intense stare, "Good boy, you always were my favourite" Blake spoke taking a drink of his scotch with a heavy and intense sigh at the strong, cool liquid pouring down his throat. "We need your help" I spoke breaking the slowly building tension in the room "I presumed so Jason after all, it's been … what is it? Two years now" Blake replied placing his glass on the table and taking a seat in the plush leather sofa in the middle of the room.

"Yes, two years exactly almost in fact" I replied shifting awkwardly from foot to foot "Such a shame to be parted for so long Jason, please have a seat" Blake responded pointing to the couch across from him, Katie, Will and Jen all looked at me as if wondering why one of us hadn't just driven a sword through Blake's smug face the moment we had arrived. "While we're young Jason" Blake added gesturing to the seat once again his facial expression shifting to one that screamed "*Do it now or else*", with no other option I sat down central on the sofa with Katie on my right and Will and Jen on my left all staring at the arch-demon.

"I must say, having the child of a Hunter and an Angel in my office is certainly an experience" Blake mumbled his gaze fixing onto Katie and Jen "Wish we could say it's our pleasure" Jen responded without a second thought. "Feisty this one Jason, I admire that" Blake laughed his gaze fixed on Jen trying to decide how serious of a threat she truly was, "I'm glad to see you finally discovered your heritage too, I never got the chance to tell you after all" Blake added turning his gaze to me.

"YOU KNEW I WAS A PROTECTOR AND YOU DIDN'T TELL ME?!" I screamed raising from my seated position and clenching my fists in anger, "Sit down Jason and watch your tone" Blake replied his gaze never leaving his glass of scotch slowly turning the crystal clear glass in his hand. "You didn't have the right to keep that from me" I spoke holding back the mixture of emotions bubbling up in my soul "Jason … sit" Blake whispered his gaze locking into me, those cold eyes … God how I hated those eyes, the black eyes that could radiate the difference between great anger, joy and disappointment.

 I sighed and sat back down onto the couch like the loyal puppy dog I was. "Good, now if you'll allow me to explain, I knew shortly after we met what you truly were, I could sense the power emanating from you but if I had told you then you would have run away searching for answers and found yourself at the academy and I could not allow that, you were too valuable and precious to me" Blake spoke softly (The guy has a nasty way of seeming kind and evil). "I still deserved answers" I replied "I know Jason and I'm glad you finally found them, but I suppose we should discuss business after all that's why you're here isn't it?" Blake asked reclining back onto the sofa stretching his arms across the back.

"We need the Faceplate of Dante's compass and we know you have it" I spoke clasping my hands together, "I see Isaiah let that little piece of information slip out, didn't he?" Blake asked "Call it last words" I replied, Blake smiled at me and clapped his hands "Something's never change, do they?" Blake spoke the same smug and wicked grin growing across his face.
 "The Faceplate Blake … please, we need to stop the gates of hell opening" I begged "Of course Jason, believe me, I want the gates of hell to remain sealed too" Blake spoke placing his hand against his chest.
"But you're a demon, wouldn't you want the gates opened?" Will questioned,
"My boy, most of my business comes from mortals buying my products, if all the mortals are either in heaven, dead or being chased by demons then business isn't going to go well for me is it?" Blake placed his glass onto the table licking the remaining scotch from his lips.

 "So, can we have the Faceplate?" I asked, Blake studied me for a moment and then smiled "Of course son, I'd be happy to" Blake replied climbing up from the sofa leaving his scotch on a placemat on his desk approaching the safe that he kept hidden bookshelf that opened by tugging on Treasure Island by Robert Louis Stevenson (I swear that's honestly the book he chose).

After a brief glance over his shoulder to make sure that we couldn't see the combination to the safe Blake punched in the four digit code and then scanned his thumb print using an iris scan to open the heavy steel safe. Blake removed a small black box from the safe and held it in his hand as he approached us "Here it is" Blake spoke opening the box.

True to his word the Faceplate of Dante's compass was staring back at us, it looked no different to a regular compass faceplate that you might find in any campers kit with a N, S, E, W in four directions, except for the demons perfectly carved into the Faceplate at South with the gates of hell painted just underneath the North. I reached for the Faceplate and retreated my hand as Blake suddenly slammed the case shut, "Now Jason, you know well enough that nothing in this world comes for free" Blake spoke smiling at me, "Damn it" I muttered under my breath and retreated my hand,. "Shame … and I thought we would be able to do this the easy way" Jen mumbled moving quick as a flash removing her hair pin and extending it into her ivory bow, an arrow knocked in it before I could even blink "JEN … NO!" I shouted too late as Jen let the arrow fly directly at Blake's heart.

The arrow flew through the air with perfect speed and accuracy, the ultimate weapon in demon killing, it was forged from Hunter steel and designed specifically to kill all supernatural beings, as the arrow flew through the air towards Blake's chest he smiled and laughed … the arrow passed harmlessly through his chest like he was a ghost and lodged into the wall behind him.
"What?" Jen spoke barely above a whisper "You're lucky that Jason is such a friend to you or I may take offence at that" Blake spoke flashing his wicked grin, "That's impossible … you should be dead" Katie mumbled trying to form some semblance of an answer.
"That is true young angel, that arrow should have turned me to a smouldering pile of dust … if weren't for this that is" Blake replied reaching into his shirt and raising the necklace that he always wore "No" Jen mumbled turning to see my head hung in shame, Blake held his shining silver pendant wrapped around his index finger dangling in clear view for us to see encrusted with black onyx jewels and a small crystal ball containing two droplets of blood "A blood bond" Katie added turning her gaze to me.

## Chapter 27
## Blood is thicker than water

"The most sacred and loyal gift anyone can give to a person" Blake spoke placing the necklace back underneath his shirt. For those of you unfamiliar with a blood bond it is the most loyal gift two people can share, in return for a droplet of blood and a small amount of magic two people can form a bond bound to every fabric of the universe that makes a member of the party of choice essentially immortal. No weapon can break the skin of that person and as such that person can only be killed by the person who shares the blood bond, a gift that is the very semblance of loyalty.

I couldn't meet my friends shocked expressions at the shame I was feeling, I'd made the pact with Blake shortly after he'd taken me in and I'd started working for him, I trusted him and he trusted me, it was the perfect symbol that I would never hurt him and part of the reason why I was so high in his organisation compared to the demons around me. "Jason was such a loyal worker to me, when I asked him to perform the blood bond he happily agreed, when he left it hurt but I knew that he would never harm me after all … I'm basically a father to him, aren't I Jason?" Blake spoke looking over at me but I still hadn't taken my gaze away from the carpet.

I couldn't form any sense of words at the shame I was feeling, I had made that blood pact with Blake shortly after he had welcomed me into his home with open arms and into his business along with showing me his true identity, back then I would have done anything to get any semblance of approval from him … now, with what I knew about myself and my heritage … I wish I could take it all back. "What do you want for the Faceplate?" I questioned my gaze remaining on my shoes, "Nothing yet Jason, it is late and I'm sure you all need rest" Blake replied placing his empty glass next to the decanter licking his lips once more removing any leftover residue of scotch, "We need the Faceplate, we only have four days before the gates of hell open and the world comes to an end, we don't have time to rest!" I shouted standing my ground against Blake meeting his steely gaze.

These were the moments when I showed my influence and power with Blake compared to the rest of his loyal lap dogs and how I had earned his trust over the years, I didn't back down in an argument like the rest of his men when he scolded them, I challenged him and he challenged me back, two stubborn men ready to tear each other apart at a moment's notice.

"Jason, you are exhausted, you haven't slept well in days I'm guessing and likely haven't eaten a true meal since you started your little assignment" Blake mumbled a sliver of his black hair slipping down across his forehead before he quickly pushed it back into place precisely where it needed to be. "You have two choices, you can stay and receive the Faceplate after the payment I desire tomorrow or you can leave now and the Faceplate shall never be yours" Blake continued.

I clenched my fists together and felt my knuckles tense in frustration as I desperately wanted to punch him in his smug face but I knew how that would end, I'd done it before (A week alone in my room in case you were wondering). "It's okay Jason, we'll stay" Jen spoke from behind me resting her palm on my shoulder, the tense pulling sensation that both pulled me and Blake towards each other and pushed each other away broke as I realised that we were going nowhere yet.

"Okay, fine Blake, we'll stay but as soon as I do your job tomorrow, I want the Faceplate and we are leaving" I grunted gesturing towards Blake "Very well Jason if that is what you desire then so be it, your demon friend William can stay in your room it's still as you left it" Blake replied catching me off guard slightly, I hadn't been in that room for over 2 years and he hadn't changed a thing? "Did he know I'd be coming back one day?" I thought to myself. "As for your Angel and Hunter friend, well I'm sure Cassandra wouldn't mind sharing her room with them" Blake added as I felt my heart literally skip a beat, "Cassie .... Cassie's still here?" I asked utterly stunned "She never left, she's in the study currently, dinner is at seven" Blake replied flashing his smug grin and turning his attention to the hole in his wall where the arrow had struck.

Sensing the tension, we left as Blake shouted for Julius to call the contractor to fix the damage immediately (The guy took less than ten minutes to get there and fixed it in twenty, bet you wish you could get contractors like that huh?) but my soul focus was on Blake's last statement as I walked down the hall towards the study past my room and Cassie's, the soft melody sang in the halls emanating from the study, "*If I die young*" by '*The Band Perry*', it was Cassie's song.

It sound's strange since the song was slow and kind of depressing but she loved the song, it was her favourite and she would listen to it insistently and even now as we approached the study I could hear her singing from inside, "Who's Cassie?" I heard Katie whisper to Jen who simply shrugged her shoulders back at Katie.

I slowly pushed the door open and spotted her from behind dusting the tall bookcases that stretched across the back wall of the study singing along to her song. Her scarlet hair danced down her back as she danced from side to side, she was wearing blue jeans and a dark green tank top that fitted her form flawlessly, the small birthmark on her right shoulder that looked like a flower could just be made out on her tanned Columbian skin.

I approached cautiously from behind while Will, Jen and Katie remained at the door watching me intently, if I spoke her name now I knew she'd jump out of her skin in fright and likely start beating me in anger so I decided to do an old trick that I had done years ago. I snuck over to her wireless speaker as the song continued to play and pressed pause cutting the music off mid-sentence "Hey! Who turned off ..." Cassie spoke spinning around to face me.

Her dazzling sea blue eyes with green flecks spotted me immediately and danced in shock and excitement, her pink lips moved from shock to joy and tears could be seen in the corners of her eyes "Hey Cass" I mumbled barely able to form words at her beauty. "An old friend?" I vaguely heard Will whisper but my gaze was still fixed on Cassie, "Jason?" Cassie questioned in shock.
Wasting no time I rushed over to her and embraced her tight in my arms weeping into her shoulder and running my hand through her hair as she cried onto my shoulder in joy, "You're here ... you're actually here" Cassie stammered a single tear rolling down her cheek "I told you I'd come back" I replied as Cassie made the first move and kissed me, my heart lit aflame at her touch, one that I hadn't felt in two years and had longed for since then, we broke apart and rested our foreheads against each other smiling "Or maybe not" I heard Katie mumble as I held Cassie tight.

## Chapter 28
## The love of my life

I'm sure that may have come as a bit of a surprise to you, well I'll explain, shortly after Blake took me in and gave me my job I was introduced to Cassandra Adam's, the most beautiful and amazing girl I had ever met. She was the same age as me at the time when Blake had took me in and I knew from day one that I was crazy about her (I know, it's sappy but it's the truth), Cassandra had started to work for Blake when she was eight years old although not in the sense that I did ... Cassandra was a slave for Blake.

You see, Cassandra's father Anthony was a no good, gambling drunk and he owed a lot of money to Blake and when I say a lot, I don't mean break your bank account type of debt, I mean the kind of debt where you would break the bank and punch a hole in the economy, Blake had sent goon's to break her father's thumbs, smash his car, wreck his home, all threats to get him to pay but Anthony was a drunk who could barely hold up a job.

Eventually the debt became too great and Blake dragged him into his office by Julius who had already broken one of Anthony's kneecap's leaving it a bloody mess, Blake warned that if Anthony didn't pay up his debt then he would suffer consequences beyond imagination and since Blake was an arch-demon (Although Anthony didn't know that) then he could truly make Anthony suffer. In return for his debt, Anthony offered up his only daughter as a servant to Blake to complete any household chores he may have until he could pay up the debt (I know, he was a Jerk right?).

Blake sensing an opportunity accepted the offer and took Cassandra away from her father as his own personal slave/servant, Cassie's mom had died during childbirth so she wasn't an issue that Anthony would then have to face once handing Cassie over. Shortly after Cassie's 9th birthday and yearlong servitude to Blake, Anthony wandered home from the casino drunk as a skunk once again and fell in front of the oncoming subway train, Blake could have given Cassie up on the spot but decided she was still useful and kept her as his slave.

When I was hired by Blake and I first met Cassie, I knew that I had met the most amazing girl and that I would be happy for the foreseeable future, I would always be there for her. The first time she really recognised me was when one of Blake's goons went to lay a hand on her and I used a letter opener (Which I later found out was a relic made out of Demonic obsidian) to remove the goon's hand from his wrist, after that day, the friendship I had formed already with Cassie blossomed into attraction and then from attraction into dating and finally dating into Love.

When I ran away from Blake, I tried to take Cassie with me but in the process of escaping we found ourselves trapped at a steel door, only one of us could make it and get away, before I had the chance to offer myself up as the sacrificial lamb, Cassie pushed me through the door and locked it behind me from the other side.

I was stuck like a fish in a tank watching as the guards dragged Cassie away and tried to break down the door that I was currently trapped behind, I knew that if I didn't run then that I would never escape from Blake and so I ran, as fast and as far as I could. Until this moment I had no idea what had happened to Cassie after that day but now, stood holding her in my arms I was thankful that after all these years I had been forced to return to Blake.

"I can't believe you're here!" Cassie spoke pressing her hands and feeling the new found muscles in my arms, "You've changed so much … what happened to your hair?" Cassie asked running her hands through my scraggly street hair "I haven't had a haircut in two years" I replied placing my palm against her cheek. "But you haven't changed a day, you're still the same beautiful girl I fell in love with" I replied, lost her in stare I heard a fake coughing noise come from Will behind me and returned my focus back to my friends.

"Right sorry, Cassie these are my friend's Jen, Will and Katie" I spoke turning Cassie to them and gesturing to each of them in return "Guy's this is Cassie" I added pointing at Cassie who gave a cute little awkward wave and smiled. "It's a pleasure to meet you but since when do you have friends? And what happened to you?" Cassie asked turning to face me again and squeezing the muscles in my arms. I looked over at Will who was smiling his smug grin and nodding his head up and down, Katie and Jen who looked utterly and equally stunned at this sudden interaction and then turned my focus back to Cassie "We have a lot to catch up on" I replied simply.

For the next hour I told Cassie all about what had happened over the past two years from my time on the streets to being rescued by Jen, to discovering my family heritage and discovering that I was a Protector, the Academy, the assignment and I showed her my wings (Don't be rude!). "And that's everything up until now" I spoke folding my wings back into my body from our seated position on the couch, Cassie stared at me trying to form some semblance of words and looked over at Will, Jen and Katie who had also shown their family heritage just to add to my tale "I always knew that you were more special than I already knew what you were" Cassie spoke placing her hand on my forearm.

"I can't believe I'm back here with you again" I replied smiling at the love of my young life, "Me neither but you shouldn't have come back, Blake has been searching for you for years and now that he has you back …" Cassie stopped holding her tongue and looking around the room (Blake has eyes and ears everywhere in his Penthouse).
 "I know, but don't worry, once I pay what I owe and get the Faceplate I'm leaving … and I'm taking you with me" I replied clasping Cassie's hands tight.
 "How?" Cassie asked,
 "Once Blake gives me the task tomorrow, I'll demand your freedom as well in return, Blake is loyal to a fault with me and if I ask he'll give it to me or he'll suffer the consequences" I replied
"Consequences?" Jen inquired, I turned my focus to Jen and nodded before turning back to Cassie.

"If Blake refuses to let you go … then I'll make sure that he can't hold you hostage anymore" I replied pondering over whether or not I would actually be able to do what I had just promised.
"Could you do that? Really?" Cassie asked me,
 "I honestly don't know … but I guess we'll find out tomorrow" I replied shaking my head from left to right,
 "Then for the time being we need to get your friends to my room and get you a haircut because frankly you need once" Cassie spoke standing up running her hand through my messy mopped hair "That I do" I replied laughing and smiling at her touch.

After escorting Katie and Jen to Cassandra's room who quickly deposited their items and crashed on the spare cots that Blake's butlers had dropped in Cassandra's room for them, I showed Will to my room while Cassandra finished up her jobs for Blake, "Here we are" I spoke opening the door wide to the room I had lived in all those years ago.

True to Blake's words my room hadn't changed at all, the four poster mahogany bed stood pressed against the wall with its fitted Egyptian cotton sheets and thick duvet. Across from the bed was a large plasma screen TV and gaming console and at the back of the room was an en-suite bathroom and walk in wardrobe fully stocked with fresh clothes in my size (Blake has personal shoppers on hand at a moment's notice).
T

he thing I was ashamed to admit was that my old room looked exactly the same as my one at the academy aside from the magical roof of the four poster bed "Nice place" Will spoke flinging his bag onto the couch in the room at the foot of the bed. "You mean aside from the homicidal arch-demon running the building then yeah it's perfect, here give me a hand with this" I replied removing the cushions from the couch and pulling out the futon with Will, "Looks comfy" Will mumbled pressed his hand against the hard springs.

"Yeah, I never used to have many guests" I spoke running my hand against the base of my neck,

"Cassie was never in this room?" Will asked with a single eyebrow raised,

"Dude I was 13! What the hell is wrong with you?"

"Sorry man, she seems amazing though"

"She is" I replied laying on my bed resting my head against the cushion.

"I'm going to get some shut eye before dinner" I mumbled feeling my tired body descend into the comfy mattress, "First good idea you've had all day" Will replied landing with a heavy squeak and thud onto the futon. "Ow" Will mumbled laughing and rubbing the back of his head, I burst out laughing with Will until my eyes started to water from the laughter and I drifted off into slumber.

## Chapter 29
## And you think your family dinners are bad

For the first time in a long time, I slept soundly for the next 3 hours without a dream or horrifying vision taking place which now meant that I had to attend a dinner with my old boss and father figure (I hate my life). "You okay man?" Will asked me borrowing one of my brown leather jackets and black t-shirt from my wardrobe, "I'm about to attend a dinner with both an arch-demon and the guy who took me in when I was 13 years old" I replied straightening the collar of my smart blue shirt and double checking for any creases in the material "I'm doing great" I added sarcastically leaving the top two buttons of my shirt undone.

We met Katie and Jen in the hall who had both changed borrowing some of Cassie's clothes from their torn gear that they had been wearing since the battle with Isaiah and headed down the hall towards the dining room. Blake was already there waiting for us in a black shirt and red tie immaculately pressed without a single crease or stain, the white tablecloth was set up precise and flattened on the table again without a crease in the cloth (Like I said, Blake is very OCD).

Each plate, knife and fork for all of us was immaculately organised and lined up to the perfect angle each utensil exactly an inch apart no more, no less, a centrepiece of black roses sat in the dead centre of the long table that seemed to suck all life and joy out of the room and into their dark petals.

Julius and Marcus another one of Blake's gorilla sized demon bodyguards stood stoic behind Blake with their hands folded together watching every step that I made into the dining room and Cassie stood against the wall smiling at me avoiding Blake's gaze.

"Jason my son, glad you could finally join me, I trust you rested well?" Blake asked fixing his intense stare onto me, "Yes, I did thank you dad" I replied cringing slightly at calling him dad now that I knew my true history. "Excellent, well then without further ado, please sit, join me" Blake spoke pointing to the four chairs each facing each other on either side of the table in direct line of eyesight, I sat closest to Blake with Will at my side and Jen and Katie across from us.

"Now, let's eat shall we, I'm starving" Blake announced a large grin spreading across his face, from behind Marcus clapped his hands twice and waiters and waitresses descended from the kitchen placing down a starter course of Tomato Prosciutto on golden toasted bread and filled our glasses with the finest mineralised and purified water money could buy. Within an instant every plate had food on it and each glass was filled to exactly halfway up the glass "To my son's return" Blake spoke raising his glass into the air, I raised my glass and nodded slightly at Will, Katie and Jen who were all sat unsure before following my lead and raising their glasses in return.

Carefully and precisely we dined with Blake, I had rehearsed a hundred times to know that I followed each forkful at the exact same time as Blake to keep in touch with his OCD aside from my friends who were eating casually unsure of whether to touch the food or not. "So, tell me Jason" Blake mumbled wiping the corners of his mouth with his napkin and placing it on the now empty plate right before a waiter descended removing the plate and speeding out of the room before anyone could even blink, "How are they treating you at the academy?" Blake asked fixing his cold dark eyes on me.

"I only spent a few days at the academy before I was sent on the assignment but it feels like home" I spoke looking over at my friends and smiling, "And what is this place for you exactly?" Blake asked offended looking at each of my friends in turn and stretching out his hands gesturing to the room around him.
"This was always a refuge Blake but you and I both know that it was never a home for me" I replied watching a waitress take my empty plate away and three more waiters and waitresses' descended removing Will, Katie and Jen's plates before disappearing back into the kitchen.

"Jason, please, mind your words or I may find offence at them and you and I both know how well I take offence" Blake growled his calm voice shifting slightly from its usual steady baritone, "I'm sorry" I replied with a heavy sigh and looking over at Cassie who hadn't removed her gaze from the floor. "I accept your apology son" Blake replied tapping the rim of his now empty glass, Cassie grabbed Blake's crystal decanter and ice bucket placing exactly three perfectly squared ice cubs into the glass and filled the glass up to the halfway point with scotch, the inside of my soul wanted to punch Blake in his smug face as he watched Cassie serve him but my better half knew to keep my anger level's to myself.

"Can we talk about the job tomorrow?" I asked as the servants brought us rack of lamb each with mint sauce and a side salad, "Now Jason, you know we don't discuss business at the dinner table" Blake replied tucking the napkin into his shirt checking the freshly brought to him utensils for any blemishes or scratches.

"I understand Blake, but time is of the essence as you know, if I knew what the job was then I could better prepare for tomorrow" I replied arguing my case, Blake chewed a chunk of the lamb in his mouth and swallowed before breathing in a heavy sigh "Let's just say it involves work you're already well familiar with" Blake replied his intense stare never leaving mine.

A small part of me knew that whatever Blake had planned for me tomorrow couldn't be good but I also knew that if we were ever going to get the Faceplate then I needed to do whatever Blake asked. "What time?" I asked my reduced appetite denying the lamb currently sat on my plate, "First thing tomorrow morning, 8 am sharp, Cassandra will come to collect you" Blake replied digging into his meal.

Blake finished his rack of lamb leaving behind his knife and fork on the plate, quick as a flash like always a servant who I knew was a lower class demon descended from nearby removing the plate and ducking away, unfortunately, in the process he dropped the knife from the plate.

Time seemed to slow down as the knife plunged towards the table cloth a thin sheen of juice from the lamb coating the blade, I watched helpless as the knife spun and landed on the table leaving behind a faint crease and a brown stain on the pristine white cloth.

The servant froze, I froze, my friends stared in confusion and Cassie looked away knowing what was coming next, "I'm so sorry sir! It was an accident, I ..." the servant stammered stopping when Blake held up his hand, "Relax Maximillian" Blake replied barely above a whisper his voice flat and monotonous as always.

"Accidents happen" Blake added slowly picking up the silver knife from the table taking the plate from Max placing it on the table,

"Really sir?"

"Yes" Blake groaned his gaze fixed solely on the blemish on his perfect table cloth, "And mistakes ... can always be corrected" Blake added.

I should have reacted faster, jumped in to help the Max's plea and accidental fumble but I knew it was too late, the damage was done, Blakes perfect organised world had been damaged. I watched helpless as Blake slowly stood up placing his hand softly on Max's shoulder ... and drove the silver knife into Maximillian's heart.

Max took one last breath in shock before bursting into a pile of ash, "It truly is hard to find good help these days" Blake groaned returning the knife back to the plate angling it precisely next to the fork in a straight line. "Shall we continue onto dessert?" Blake asked a wicked grin tugging at the corner of his lips. Jen, Will and Katie all sat open mouthed waiting for me to react but I knew better "Just let it go" I whispered smiling up at the heartless demon before me.

The rest of the night passed by surprisingly easy despite the constant tension between Blake, me and all my friends who had sat itching to cut down everyone in sight and somehow steal the Faceplate from Blake's private safe until the servants took away all utensils and plates from the tables clearing it completely down to the perfectly pressed white sheet.

 "Until tomorrow Jason" Blake spoke standing up brushing down the creases in his suit "Until tomorrow … dad" I replied watching as Blake walked down the hall to his bedroom followed by Julius and Marcus, his loyal lap dogs who followed him into his room and closed the door behind them to discuss business with Blake.

Katie and Jen followed Cassie back into her room after dinner, I kissed Cassie goodnight promising that I would discuss her freedom with Blake first thing tomorrow and Will and I walked back into my room closing the door behind us. "What do you think he's going to ask you to do dude?" Will asked changing out of my leather jacket and hanging it onto a coat hanger in the closet "I don't know, maybe it'll be just a drop or a delivery but … I have a feeling it may be something else" I replied placing my dress shirt back into the wardrobe and changing into an old shirt and jogging bottoms before slumping down into my bed and staring up at the ceiling.

Tomorrow would be a new day and whatever Blake had planned … I had no doubt it would be bad.

# Chapter 30
## Sleep eludes me

Well, after a full four hours of staring at both the back of my eyelids and the ceiling above me I decided that my chances at sleep tonight were very unlikely. At 2 am I snuck past the very loudly snoring Will who was currently laid on the futon drooling onto his pool drawing in the shadows around him cloaking himself in a comfortable cocoon of darkness and tip toed out into the hallway shuffling across the bare carpet feeling the comfort of the texture underneath my bare feet wandering through the silent penthouse.

At this time of night, the penthouse was completely silent aside from the almost silent honking and hustle and bustle of the city outside, another one of Blake's issues with his apartment is in order to sleep or conduct any business he needed absolute silence. The windows were two feet thick and ingrained with demonic symbols to keep divine beings out, the walls were six feet thick with soundproof padding and the carpet underneath was heated to provide both the comfort of hell for Blake and his demons and to keep out the winter chill.

Blake sent home all the servants and workers every day when night descended to make sure that not a single noise disturbed him (Not out of the kindness of his cold black heart as you may think). I shuffled out towards the balcony and opened the door carefully and silently before closing it tight behind me listening to the roar of the city and the wind blowing against my cheeks.
Above me the few stars that managed to peek through the light pollution shone in the dark night sky, the smell of the warm Texan air tickled at my nostrils, despite all Blake had done … he was right when he said I felt at home. "Penny for your thoughts?" Jen spoke from behind me snapping me out of my trance and appearing onto the balcony dressed in a white tank top with flowered pyjama bottoms, she was barefoot like me, a small purple drawl covered her bare shoulders and her hair was pulled up into a tight bun the three coloured stands hidden in the tangle.

"Hey, sorry, couldn't sleep" I replied resting my elbows on the cool metal handrail, "Thinking about the job Blake is having you do tomorrow?" Jen asked leaning her waist against the handrail and staring directly at me "Is mind reading one of our Hunter abilities?" I asked jokingly never taking my gaze away from the city landscape.

"Call it more woman's intuition" Jen replied,

"All those years ago when Blake first found me, I had nothing, I was living on the streets and barely surviving" I muttered the memories of my past running through my head while Jen remained totally silent listening to my story.

"At first working for Blake wasn't a problem, I picked packages up and dropped them off, I attended meetings and stood in the backdrop and then I did things that ..." I added staring down at the city streets below. "What kind of things?" Jen asked me folding her arms across her stomach showing her Hunter tattoo on her forearm, the Proud 'H' stood in front of the flower that symbolised her master of Nature Magic seeming to come to life in the city lights and the twin arrows pierced through the flower that symbolised her mastery over Archery.

"Things that I'd rather not discuss" I replied shutting down the conversation,

"Okay, so do you think Blake is going to ask you to do ... those things again?" Jen asked me. The thought had crossed my mind the moment Blake had told me I had to do a job for him but the idea also made me want to vomit over the edge of the balcony.

"I think so ... I just don't know what to do" I replied hanging my head so that I was staring down at the city streets below us.

"May I offer you some advice?" Jen edged slightly closer to me

"Please, God knows I need it" I replied feeling Jen place her hand on my shoulder

"Don't corrupt yourself for Blake's benefit, if what he asks you to do tomorrow is too bad for you to handle then say no and we'll find some other way to get the Faceplate, if that means fighting our way through every demon on this floor and breaking open the safe in Blake's office then so be it" Jen replied rubbing her hand across my shoulder blade

"No matter what, we've got your back" Jen added smiling up at me.

"Thank you" I replied smiling up at Jen and hugging her in appreciation feeling her hands on my back and mine on hers, this was not a romantic hug in the way that I held Cassie but rather a hug between friends, the kind of hug one would receive from a mentor or a parent after a job well done. "When did you get to be so wise?" I asked leaning back on the railing with Jen stood next to me resting her elbows on the cool metal surface as well

"When I first came to the academy, you learn a lot in ten years" Jen replied catching me off guard.

"Wait … you came to the academy when you were six?", Jen stared outwards at the city her eyes reflecting the buildings glow.

"Can I trust you?"

"With anything, I give you my word" I replied studying her expression,

"I'm an oddity in the academy compared to the other students … both of my parents are mortal" Jen replied dropping this information on me like an atom bomb.

"But I thought that all Protectors came from a parental supernatural being?" I asked stunned,

"Usually they are, sometimes it skips a generation, my grandma was a Hunter who married my grandfather who was mortal, she had my mother and she thought that one day she would have to send her to the academy to have her identification ceremony. But when she turned thirteen, no latent abilities appeared, she tried sneaking her a small drop of the sacred liquid into her drink but when my mom drank it nothing happened" Jen explained filling my mind with more information that I thought I could handle.

"So, life went on, my mom grew up and met my dad and then had me, when I was six years old, we were in a car crash, a drunk driver" she spoke her voice wavering and a tear starting to form in the corner of her eye. "Did they?" I asked unsure if I should break the silence "They were fine, still are, they live in Seattle" Jen replied smiling at the memory in her mind.

"After the crash I woke up first but my parents were still unconscious, I can't explain what happened but my body seemed to go into overdrive and I somehow got free of the wreckage and ripped off the hinges of the car door on my dad's side and dragged him out to safety and then did the same with my mom's side" Jen added. "Your Hunter abilities … they activated when you crashed" I spoke as Jen simply nodded her head in agreement.

"After that my grandma realised what had happened and explained our family heritage to me, she took me to the academy and I went through the identification ceremony and sure enough, I was a Hunter like her" Jen spoke a smile in the corners of her mouth.

"What about your parents? Do they know about the academy?"

"No, they think I'm in a high school for the advanced, before that I was in middle school for the gifted, the haze does work wonders" Jen replied smiling and laughing at the comment,

"Do you miss them?" I asked remembering the pain of not even having my own parents to talk to let alone have both my parents be mortal and have no connection to the supernatural world.

"All the time, I see them during the holidays, occasionally visit in the summer but it's best that I stay away as often as possible, you know as well as I do that we don't exactly live without any kind of danger" Jen replied glancing over at me and rolling her eyes.
 "What about your grandma?" I asked
"She passed shortly after I went to the academy" Jen replied a hint of sadness in her eyes, "I'm sorry"
"Thanks" Jen spoke bumping against me slightly.

Jen looked over at me and studied my expression "You miss your grandma too don't you?" Jen asked me,
"Truthfully, I don't remember much about her, I was only six when she died but she was the only connection I had to my parents, now that I know what they were and what I am ... I wish I had had more time with her" I replied feeling a tear rolling down my cheek.
"Well, I think whoever your parents were ... they would be immensely proud of you" Jen replied resting her head on my shoulder
"Thank you" I replied resting my head on top of hers.

"So, Cassie huh?" Jen spoke standing back from me and smiling "Oh shut up" I replied pushing her away playfully, "What? She only told us some fun stories before bed" Jen spoke turning and walking back towards the apartment. "Wait ... what stories?" I asked following her back inside, "Nothing important ... although New Orleans sounded fun" Jen replied winking at me and continuing down the corridor "Damn you Cassie" I mumbled smiling.

# Chapter 31
## The Job

Surprisingly, after my late-night chat with Jen I actually managed to sleep until 7 am when I woke up, showered, shaved and dressed ready for whatever job I would be doing for Blake today. "You nervous?" Will questioned staring at his reflection and combing gel into his black hair backwards like a 1960's greaser
"If I told you no would you believe me?"
"Relax dude, you've got this" Will replied dipping his comb into a cup of water and turning to face me, "I've got your back from here to the end" Will added placing his hand on my shoulder and smiling with the same wicked grin he always had, "Thanks man" I replied tapping his hand with my own.

A sudden knock on the door snapped me and Will out of our tender brotherly moment as Cassie slowly opened the door, "Are you all decent?" Cassie asked holding the palm of her hand over her eyes. "If I said no would you take down that hand?" Will asked smiling at Cassie "Well, I obviously now know that Will is decent" Cassie replied placing her hand on her hip removing her other hand from her face scoffing at Will.

"Ignore him, is Blake ready?" I questioned rolling my eyes at Will,
"Yes, he asked me to bring you to him",
"Awesome let's go" Will added clapping his hands starting to walk towards the door before Cassie held up her hand for him to stop.
"Actually, he only wants Jason" Cassie mumbled looking over Will's shoulder at me.
"Alone? No way man!" Will shouted turning to face me.

A small part of me knew that Will was right and that I should demand that my friends be allowed to join us but I also knew enough about Blake knew that if he wanted to see me alone, then no one else would be allowed with ten foot of that room. "Don't worry Will, it's okay, let's go" I spoke tapping Will on the shoulder on my way out following Cassie out into the hallway.
"So, I hear you've been talking with Katie and Jen? About New Orleans?" I asked raising an eyebrow at her
"Wow, you would think you Protectors could keep a secret from each other" Cassie replied blushing and tucking a strand of her scarlet hair back into alignment.
"Yeah, my friends don't exactly understand the meaning of boundaries" I replied laughing.

These moments like this were the moments I missed most of all after I left her, walking down the corridor with Cassie laughing about the stupidest little things, I couldn't wait until I bought her freedom and we could go and travel. "So, I'm going to ask Blake for your freedom today at the job, after that when we've got the Faceplate I'll find you somewhere safe and when this is all over, you and I are going to go travel, say maybe ... Paris?" I asked raising an eyebrow stopping Cassie dead in her tracks "Paris? Seriously?" Cassie asked utterly stunned and staring straight up at me smiling.

I reached up and brushed a strand of hair behind her ear resting my palm on her cheek, "Really" I replied "You always wanted to see the Eiffel Tower and I'm going to make sure that happens" I added smiling at her. Cassie blinked away a few tears and then kissed me, the feeling of her lips against mine were hypnotic even if it was for a brief moment.

"Isn't that touching?" Blake spoke breaking my concentration on Cassie, the whole time we'd been stood in front of the door to the room Blake was waiting in, he was smiling that same smug grin he always had, the one where I wanted to punch him in his perfect teeth. "Shall we?" Blake asked stepping into the room, I reluctantly followed him in with Cassie keeping my focus locked on the dark room in front of us.

"Alright Blake what's the ..." I asked before looking to my right feeling my soul drop to the earth underneath my feet. In the next room behind a thick plane of double sided glass was one of Blake's guards that I had spotted yesterday, he was tied to a chair in the middle of the room.
I could see that three of his ten fingers were broken and horribly mangled, blood was dribbling from his mouth as he hung his head staring directly at the floor, "Meet Oliver, one of my finest employees for a while, he joined shortly after you left Jason" Blake whispered, Cassie was staring at me horrified, clearly she had no idea that Blake had planned this little encounter.

"Why is he here?" I mumbled barely forming words
"Oliver in there stole from me, five hundred thousand dollars to be precise" Blake replied, "Wow, stealing from you, your employees are far less loyal now aren't they?"
"Regardless" Blake spoke his calm tone shifting slightly to annoyance.
"He stole that money but we caught him before he could spend it which means that somewhere in Dallas is my money and I want you to find out where it is" Blake added (If my soul didn't already feel heavy, it certainly did now).

"You can't be serious" I asked utterly stunned,
"You were my best interrogator Jason, break him and the Faceplate is yours, refuse ... and you will never get what you need to stop the gates from opening" Blake replied. I had had a horrid feeling in my gut that Blake might have asked me to do something of this calibre for him once again but I had hoped my thoughts would be wrong.
"Blake please, anything but this" I begged,
"Sorry Jason but these are my terms" Blake replied folding his arms,
"Then I want something else as well as the Faceplate" I replied knowing this was my best chance "Two things for one task? I hardly see how that is fair Jason"
"I want Cassie's freedom from your control" I demanded squaring up to Blake.

Blakes cold eyes bore into mine as we stood staring off at each other like two gunslingers in the old west, "You know as well as I do that you'll never break him without me" I added. Blake blew air out of his nostrils in frustration and glanced over at Cassie, "Very well, you have a deal" Blake replied crossing his arms.

I saw Cassie's face shift slightly to joy at her freedom but also concern at what this would cost in exchange for her freedom, "The room still work how it used to?" I asked centring my mind and soul, "They never changed it from your original design" Blake replied. I breathed in and out slowly focusing my mind on the simple task ahead of me, the job I had done countless times for Blake in the past, I channelled my very soul into the man that I used to be, preparing myself for what I had to do next, "Here we go" I mumbled slowly opening my gaze as the lights went out in the next room and I stepped into the wall.

## Chapter 32
## If you're squeamish go to the next chapter

Okay so I'm sure that last section may have confused you so I'll explain, years ago shortly after I started to work for Blake, I discovered a hidden talent for interrogating prisoners and getting them to confess to the information we needed by any means necessary, we built The Vault, an interrogation room equipped with everything I needed including a magical wall that you could walk through so that the prisoner would never know where the exit is. I hated this side of me with a passion but Blake wanted me to break Oliver in exchange for the Faceplate and Cassie's freedom and if that meant I had to break someone to get that … Well then, I guess the ends justified the means.

"Well, well, well, who do I have here?" I whispered slowly walking around the room in the darkness occasionally tapping Oliver on his shoulder so that he couldn't track where exactly in the room I was, "Who is that?" Oliver questioned,
"Your conscience asking you to tell the truth, where is the money you stole Oliver?" I asked again leaning against the space where the double sided window was.
 "Nice try but I'm not telling you or anyone anything" Oliver spat a clod of blood to his right.

"Fine, I guess we're going to have to do this the hard way" I replied centring my mind once again,
"Tell me, you've been in here a while, I'm sure they've done everything to try and break you, broken fingers, regular beatings, turning the lights on and off occasionally or as it is otherwise known Sensory Deprivation, I bet you couldn't even tell me what day it was let alone whether it was day or night am I correct?" I asked, Oliver stayed completely silent the sound of the wheezing from his broken nose filling the room.
"I'll take your silence as a yes" I continued "Well … all these things you've been exposed to aren't exactly demon methods of torture, so the thing you have to ask yourself is" I added pressing the hidden button under the window ledge that made the darkened room suddenly fill with light reflecting the white surfaces all around us, it became blinding to anyone who had been in darkness for a long period of time "Who do you think taught them?" I asked locking eyes with Oliver.

You could literally smell the fear in the room as the recognition clicked in the back of Oliver's mind, "You're Jason … the boss' kid" Oliver stammered trying to back the bolted to the floor chair away from me.

"He's not biologically related but he did take me in so I can understand the confusion" I replied pressing a panel on the side wall revealing a short dagger than had been left in a brazier of boiling hot coals for so long that the blade of the dagger glowed a bright orange from the immense heat.

"Now, I'm going to ask you kindly once more and then this is going to get far worse than you can imagine" I spoke twirling the dagger in my hand making sure that the razor sharp and steaming blade never touched my skin.

"I'm not telling you anything" Oliver whimpered,

"Very well, you know there's an old scripture in the Bible that mortals love so much, Exodus 21 verse 24, the scripture speaks of punishment for one's actions" I spoke subtly taking a deep inhale through my nostrils "Now how does that go again …" I asked pressing my index finger against my teeth pausing for a moment, "That's right!" I announced clicking my fingers "An eye for an eye" I replied (You were warned!).

I pressed the heated flat blade of the dagger over Oliver's right eyelid burning the flesh, Oliver let out a blood curdling cry as his skin burnt and scabbed until I pulled the blade away and placed it back into the brazier. Oliver ground his teeth and growled in agony at the pain, he would never see out of his right eye ever again I knew that much, his iris was now completely white and scabbed frantically darting from left to right when the pain wasn't too intense trying to get a lock on anything in the room.

"Now that's just one eye, I can easily take the other one" I mumbled feeling my insides boiling with disgust, "You see when I break prisoners, I like to take it one step at a time, the body regardless whether it be supernatural or not can live with only one of almost everything, I can take a kidney" I spoke pressing my fingertip into his lower back "A lung … half of your liver … I could even take half of your brain, a mortal actually survived that once isn't that amazing?!" I asked clapping my hands.

"The only question you have to ask yourself is how much do I have to remove before you tell me what I want to know … Where is the money Oliver?!" I shouted grabbing and squeezing his already broken fingers "I'll never tell you" Oliver replied through staggered breaths (You have to admire his resilience).

"Fine, what's next? Oh yeah!" I exclaimed grabbing some pliers from the nearby table, "A tooth for a tooth" I jammed the pliers into his mouth and grabbed one of his molars, Oliver screamed and thrashed as I twisted his tooth from left to right loosening it before ripping it clean from his gums throwing it to the other side of the room, the tooth turned to ash before it hit the ground leaving only the clattering of the pliers against the wall. If Oliver's mouth hadn't been bleeding enough from his beating before it certainly was now "And the best part is you have 31 of those left which means I get to continue for longer!" I shouted returning for the now once again burning blade.

"Where's the money Oliver?! Don't make me ask again" I spoke as I felt the primeval fury enter my body that I experienced every time I tortured a prisoner for Blake, it was like adrenaline poured through my body as the prisoner begged for mercy before breaking (I know, gross, but bear in mind Oliver is a demon and Blake is an arch-demon with a heavily corrupting influence) "No" Oliver mumbled through a gargled mouth full of black blood.

"Okay, well I've done eye and tooth, I'm missing something … that's right!" I exclaimed snapping my fingers, "An ear for an ear" I added slicing the blade upwards in an arc removing the flesh part of Oliver's outer ear cauterising the wound as the blade passed through it with another deafening cry of anguish from Oliver.

"TELL ME WHERE THE MONEY IS OLIVER!!!" I screamed throwing the dagger downwards lodging it in the chair inches away from the most valuable part of his anatomy, "Oops, I missed" I added removing the blade from the wood (Yeah, I didn't miss). "The next one I assure you will meet its mark, this is your last chance Oliver, I don't want to hurt you but I will" I spoke pointing the tip of the blade at Oliver. "Please" Oliver mumbled, I raised the blade high into the air and prepared myself for separating the next limb from his body, "STOP!!!" Oliver shouted seconds before the blade was due to leave my hand. "It's down in the warehouse district, warehouse 13" Oliver mumbled hanging his head "Where in the warehouse Oliver?"
"Box 2213, along the right wall" Oliver mumbled his one seeing eye never leaving the floor "If you're lying" I growled holding the blade higher, "I'm not I swear!" Oliver replied gasping for air.

"Did you get that boss?" I asked approaching the intercom in the corner pressing the red call button, "Julius and Marcus are on their way to the warehouse now, we'll have an answer in thirty minutes" Blake replied, "Then for now it's just us Oliver" I said leaning back against the window and folding my arms feeling the ice cold beating of my heart that I sensed whenever I interrogated a prisoner.

Time passes differently in The Vault with a prisoner, I didn't know whether it had been thirty minutes, an hour or two minutes so I was left with a bleeding and gasping prisoner wincing in pain every time his ruined eye tried to blink. "We've got it Jason, the money was where he said it was" Blake announced suddenly though the intercom, I looked down at Oliver and felt pity for him knowing that as soon as I left this room he would be left at Blake's mercy would suffer a punishment him far worse than I ever would.

"Did you know Oliver that I'm a Protector?" I asked pacing back and forth like an animal in a cage, Oliver looked up at me and squinted with his working eye "A Protector?" he asked stunned. "Yeah, turns out Dad was an Angel and Mom was a Hunter and they had me, do you know what a Protector's most important job is?" I asked staring at the white washed wall with small flecks of black blood stained onto it, Oliver stared up at me with a quizzical expression on his face trying to gauge my reaction ...

"We keep the balance" I added bringing Divine Fury to life in my hand before driving it through Oliver's chest, Oliver looked up at me before bursting into ash in his chair.
I could feel the smile on my face knowing that I had successfully broken another prisoner, a smile that I didn't want to show but grew across my face like it was muscle memory, I turned on the spot and my smile disappeared ... as I stared at the image of my three friends all staring at me horrified whilst Blake stood next to them clapping his hands.

## Chapter 33
## Welcome back

(Okay, for those of you who skipped the last chapter let me give you the run down, I tortured the prisoner, he confessed to everything, I killed him to prevent him from the harm Blake would do to him and I smiled before turning to see the horrified faces of my friends in the next room, all caught up? Good let's continue).

I couldn't look my friends in the eye as I left The Vault and stood in front of Blake and my friends who were still staring at me utterly horrified, "Bravo my son, Bravo" Blake spoke clapping his hands approaching me slowly before patting me on the back. "See? What did I tell you? This kid is a pro at breaking even the toughest of prisoners" Blake added as I continued to stare at the floor in total and utter shame.
"The Faceplate Blake?" I mumbled daring to look at my friends faces who now were also avoiding eye contact with me, "Of course, a deal is a deal, tell Cassandra that she is officially free from under my employment, as for the Faceplate …" Blake replied slowly heading towards the door. "You will receive it after a celebratory dinner tonight in your honour" Blake added twisting the golden doorknob, "I'm proud of you Jason" Blake finished opening the door walking out leaving me alone with my three closest friends.

"How much did you see?" I asked keeping my gaze locked on the now closed door after Blake had left, "Blake sent Cassie for us, we came in shortly before eye for an eye" Will replied a gruffness to his voice, "I'm sorry you had to see that" I replied rubbing my eyelids with my index finger and thumb feeling the tears form in the corners of my eyes.
 "Dude, the torture I could get, Blake made you do it but … you smiled" Will spoke, I finally gathered the courage to turn and face my friends feeling the tugging guilt in my heart.

I looked over to Katie who was looking at me with a mixture of "What happened to you? And who are you?" and looked over to Jen who refused to make eye contact with me, "The first time I tortured a prisoner was by accident" I explained sitting in the one metal chair in the viewing room that Blake always sat in. "The guy had some information for Blake and he wouldn't give it up, Julius was beating this guy senseless but he wouldn't talk and I remembered something from a movie about sensory deprivation" I added running my hands through my hair, "So we put the guy into a room for six hours and constantly turned the lights on and off, by hour four the guy couldn't even tell us whether it was day or night outside, he broke on hour six and from then on …" I mumbled "Blake had you become his personal breaker" Will interrupted.

I nodded my head and looked over at Jen who had finally made eye contact with me, "I hate this side of me, I hate it with a passion, it's something he does, he brings the worst out in me and then I act without thinking, the smile you saw … it was muscle memory, when I saw the look on your face's I was horrified" I spoke feeling the tears begin to run down my cheeks.

"It's Blake" Jen finally spoke slowly approaching me, "Huh?" I asked,

"Blake is an arch-demon, you should be totally under his power but because of your bull-headed stubbornness" Jen tapped my forehead with her knuckle, "He manipulates your emotions into what he desires, that's why you feel like you're not in total control around him, it's not your fault" Jen finished resting her hand on my shoulder.

I was utterly stunned, I had expected a good beating or being screamed at or even having my friends storm out in anger but they all looked at me with such … pity,

"But I did those things not Blake" I spoke as Will and Katie approached me now as well, "No, Blake forged your emotions into doing those things, you may have acted but Blake is the puppeteer, the boy I know would never willingly hurt someone just for pleasure and I know another reason why you are not what Blake thinks you are" Jen continued staring at me letting her hair hang down her side, "Because you killed that demon so that Blake wouldn't get his hands on him, that is mercy and that is something that Blake has nothing of" Jen spoke rubbing her hand on my back.

(Are you crying? Well, I certainly was) After a brief (Okay, long) weeping session I hugged my friends and thanked them for their support, "Thank you" I mumbled pulling Jen in tight to me, "You're welcome, now go tell Cassie the good news" Jen replied pushing me away.
I smiled at them all and ran out of the room and down the hall to Cassie's room bursting through the door causing Cassie to jump in shock and surprise.

"Jason! Jesus, you scared the …" Cassie huffed before I grabbed her and planted a longing kiss dipping her down slightly before raising her back up, "Well, hello to you too" Cassie joked brushing a strand of hair away from her field of vision. "Sorry, couldn't help myself … you're free Cass" I spoke as her face changed from joy to joyous shock (You know the emotion I mean) "Free?" Cassie asked utterly stunned "Free as a bird, Blake told me himself" I replied.
Cassie's eyes began to fill with tears as she pulled me in for another hug and wept into my shoulder, "Thank you" Cassie mumbled,

"Tonight we get the Faceplate, then we stop the gates and then we start our life together, we'll see the world, I'll even try and find us a home on the Academy grounds, you may not be a Protector but if they don't let you in then I'll leave" I spoke holding her at arm's length smiling at her.

"But ... your job as a Protector, it's your heritage, your future",
"No Cass, you are my future, always have been, always will" I spoke as Cassie ran her hand through my hair.
"My hero" she mumbled resting her palm against my cheek.
"I love you Cass"
"I love you too, but we need to do something about this hair first" Cassie joked straightening my scruffy street hair, "Deal" I replied noticing the sudden and not so subtle cough from behind me.
"Make sure to get the sides and the top, he definitely needs it" Jen joked winking at us before continuing down the corridor laughing with Katie and Will the whole way. "You're going to have to get use to them too I'm afraid" I spoke rolling my eyes "Worth it" Cassie replied reaching up and kissing me again softly on the lips.

I sat down on the metal chair in Cassie's room as she tied a towel around my neck and started to cut my hair back to a more acceptable level cutting off long scraggly lock after lock, "And done!" Cassie spoke a few minutes later as she pulled the towel away with a flair and spun me to face the mirror.
 "Damn, I look different" I mumbled, Cassie had shaved the sides of my hair around my ears to buzz cut level and had trimmed the top of my hair neatly and precisely so that I resembled a sort of warrior, punk rocker look "Much better" Cassie spoke running her hands through my shortened hair checking for any spots that she might have missed.

 "Am I more handsome?" I asked with a swagger and a wink. Cassie slowly raised her hand and rested it on my chest, "Handsome? Questionable, goofy idiot? Always" Cassie joked eliciting a laugh from me as I pulled her in tight and kissed her on the top of her head. I loved her beyond words can express, even after two years separated it felt like no time had passed and a few days from now once the threat was over, I would be travelling the world with her ... all I had to do is get through one more evening with Blake.

After another awkward dinner we met Blake on the roof of the Penthouse at 7pm as per his request given to us by a very angry and frustrated Julius who had now been assigned the job of messenger after Cassie had been granted her freedom, Julius stormed down the hallway huffing and moaning like a stubborn mountain goat.
 Blake was already waiting for us at the edge of his rooftop balcony staring out over the city landscape holding the Faceplate in one hand and a scotch with three ice cubes, halfway filled precisely in his other hand.

The rooftop was a place Blake rarely visited but was one of his proudest accomplishments in the entirety of the Penthouse, a rooftop infinity pool stretched in a perfect 10x10 square at the corner of the rooftop glowing under the dimming light of the Dallas skyline. To the left of the rooftop was an open bar and seating area around a glowing firepit for entertaining business clients who if Blake was annoyed with, could easily have them thrown off the roof by one of his guards, the gravel crunched under our feet as Myself, my friends and Cassie all stood waiting to say goodbye to Blake forever.

# Chapter 34
## The Exchange

"Impeccable timing as always Jason, one my most favourite qualities about you" Blake spoke never even turning to face or acknowledge us, "Alright Blake, I tortured the prisoner, I stayed for dinner, now give me the Faceplate and we can be on our way" I spoke edging ahead of my friends breaking the hold Cassie had on my hand and approaching Blake from behind. "Of course Jason, I am a man, well … a demon of my word, this belongs to you" Blake spoke turning to face me and throwing the Faceplate towards me.
I could feel the power coursing through my veins once I caught the Faceplate and held it in my hands, the whole device seemed to emanate evil almost as if the shadows around me were being drawn into the Faceplate like a blackhole removing any and all light from the world, I turned to face Jen and passed it to her, Jen took the precious item and slipped it into her pocket ready to equip it to the rest of the compass after we left.

"Thank you Blake, now if you'll excuse us, we only have a few days left till the gates open and every demon in hell comes pouring onto the earth" I spoke slowly edging towards the door to the roof, "Ah yes, about that" Blake spoke swallowing the last of his scotch before placing his glass onto a nearby table, before I had a chance to react Julius placed his heavy frame in front of the door blocking our only escape route off the roof.

"Blake? What are you doing?" I asked hoping that this was all some kind of stupid joke, "I must say Jason when I saw the commander had placed a bounty on you I was worried" Blake mumbled giving us the mysterious name yet again. "But this is what I have to do Jason, you are far too valuable to me both as a worker and a son to let go" Blake replied edging across the roof placing each foot precisely on each stone slab without missing the centre. "Blake … you gave me your word" I spoke noticing Jen who was stood ready for combat, "Well actually Jason, if you'll remember correctly, I promised you the faceplate which I have delivered and I promised you Cassandra's freedom which I have granted, first lesson of business … always read the fine print" Blake spoke clasping his hands together.

I went to clasp my fist together ready to bring Divine Fury to life and end this mayhem once and for all before I found myself suddenly grabbed by Marcus from behind prying my hands open and holding me tight so that Divine Fury stayed in it's useless ring form. I looked over my shoulder to see three other guards grab Jen, Will and Katie before any of them had the chance to jump into combat ready to do battle and slay Blake where he stood along with the 10 other demons on the roof including Julius who was now stood laughing at our predicament. Blake edged ever closer to me and smiled tapping the palm of his hand on my new haircut like one would a puppy dog, "Oh, Jason, my dear boy" Blake spoke maniacally his cold black eyes boring into my soul flashing his wicked grin at me "You always were so naïve" Blake added as I struggled against the demons grasp on me.

# Chapter 35
## The Choice

"I can't believe I thought you would actually help up us" I screamed at Blake struggling to break free from Marcus who was gripping his fingers tight into the crook of my elbow, "But I am Jason can't you see that? I'm making you into a better man not what these Protectors are trying to make you" Blake replied in disgust staring at Katie, Will and Jen. "I chose to be a Protector, no one forced me into it, you are the only person who ever forced me to do something I didn't want to do!" I yelled in anger watching my friends who were trying their best to break free from the demon's hold.

"Jason, my boy, I never forced you to do anything you did not want to do, despite all the good that is in you, deep down inside in your very soul" Blake spoke staring directly at me with his deep black eyes "You are exactly like me" Blake added his eyes glowing with the same intensity that they always did when he began his speeches.

"You will work for me once more Jason I guarantee that" Blake mumbled gesturing with his index finger wagging up and down at me, "I will never work for you again ever!" I yelled back struggling in vain to break free from the Marcus' grasp,
"Jason … I wish you would have done this the easy way but sadly we'll have to do this differently, you see my associate Marlin over here" Black spoke as a sorcerer dressed in black robes his face hidden under the darkness of the hood leaving only two glowing red eyes emerged from the shadows behind Blake. "Is an expert at memory erase spells, he's going to reset you back to the days when you worked for me, with some improvements of course" Blake added with a wicked grin.

"That will never work! Jason has free will you can't just manipulate him like that it's not how it works" Katie shouted "Don't you think I know that!" Blake screamed back the shadows bending around him, "Which is why I'm going to crush his free will before the spell is cast" Blake added smoothing back his black hair and lowering his voice back to its usual calming tone. "How?" I asked utterly confused "Jason … you are amazing at everything you do but the one thing you could never do is function when your emotions weren't in check, which is why I'm going to crush your soul so it can be remade … by removing a loved one from the conversation" Blake replied pulling a gun from the waistband of his pants.

"So, who will it be Jason? The best friend?" Blake questioned pointing the weapon at Will "The one you love as a sister?" Blake added moving the gun over to Katie, "Or the mentor and trusted ally?" Blake asked pointing the gun directly at Jen and tilting it from left to right tapping the trigger just light enough for it not to go off. "Please Blake don't do this, I'm begging you" I pleaded looking at my friends who were shaking with determination and fear.
I couldn't lose any of them, I loved them all and I needed them in my life, if Blake took them away from me now … I knew that my spirit would be crushed and I would be totally under his power. "Well, there's only one fair way to decide then if you won't" Blake spoke aiming back at Will, "Eenie, meanie, miny …" Blake mocked moving the gun from Will to Katie to Jen with each mocking word. "Moe" Blake mumbled "NOOO!!" I screamed right as Blake pulled the trigger.

# Chapter 36
## Goodbye

Time seemed to stop as the bullet flew through the air, I looked at the bullets trajectory expecting it to be heading straight towards Jen …. And then Cassie stumbled back a few inches a slow trail of blood cascading down her white shirt from her chest, "CASSIE! NOOO!" I screamed bringing my head back breaking Marcus' nose behind me running over to Cassie catching her right before she hit the ground and holding her in my arms.

Katie let out her heavenly glow in shock and fried the demon behind her turning him to dust before materialising her two Shui daggers and dispensing of the guards holding Jen and Will, Katie rushed to my side while Will and Jen stood guard with their weapons drawn forming a barrier between me and the approaching demons. "Cassie … Cassie baby talk to me" I mumbled running my hand through her scarlet hair, "You look worried" Cassie mumbled smiling up at me, Katie stretched her hands over Cassie *"Sana"* Katie whispered her healing incantation and slowly began to glow at her fingertips as she tried to heal Cassie's wounds.
"Me? Worried? Of course I'm not, you're going to be just fine isn't she Katie?" I asked turning to face Katie who stared into my eyes with utter sorrow but nodded her head anyway, "Liar" Cassie laughed choking up a clot of blood "Sshh, Cassie stay calm, I'm going to get you out of here, we still have so much to see, the open plains of Utah, London, Paris and the Eiffel Tower, we can see all of that if you just hang on" I whispered tears slowly rolling their way down my cheek.

"That would have been amazing, but you and I both know that it's too late for me … you can stop now" Cassie spoke looking over at Katie who nodded her head and stopped her healing magic collapsing onto her butt gasping for air, clearly the magic had taken its toll giving Cassie a few more precious seconds at life. "Cassie … don't do this to me, please I need you in my life, I love you more than anything else in this whole world, you're all I have and need, please don't leave me" I mumbled propping her against the top of my leg and pulling her up slightly off the ground.
Will and Jen looked over their shoulders at me with tears on their cheeks and utter sorrow in their eyes, Katie watched with tears pouring down her cheeks as Cassie slowly began her final breaths "I Love you too, never change who you are, because me and your friends are the only ones who know how truly amazing you are and I'll never leave you, not really anyway, after all …" Cassie mumbled her breath becoming staggered "We'll always have San Francisco" Cassie whispered, she took one long breath releasing it slowly, the light of life disappeared from her eyes and she breathed no more.

"Cassie ... Cass ..." I muttered but I knew that she was gone, the girl I had loved since I was 13 had been taken from my life by someone I thought I could trust from all those years ago, "Pity ... she was such a good servant" Blake mumbled but I could barely hear him over the beating of my heart. It felt like it had been broken in two, I could feel my body burning with rage, I pulled Cassie in close and kissed her forehead before lowering her gently to the ground running my non-blood covered hand over her face closing her eyes.

"Rest in peace finally my love" I whispered as the rage continued to build but this was not the rage of anger but more of a constricting feeling, the kind of feeling you can only experience if you've lost someone you love ... grief and pain. My body felt like it was on fire as my fists shook and I clenched my teeth grinding them together and growling letting out tiny spots of spit flow through the gaps in my teeth. "What's happening?" I heard Blake whisper although it could have been a shout for all I knew my ears seemed to have stopped functioning, "Oh god, WILL, JEN, COVER YOUR EYES!" Katie screamed, Will and Katie nodded and shielded their faces before ducking to the ground.

The pain was intense and was building up inside me more and more like a dam being pressured by a flood, the power in me had built too high as I felt tears pour down my face in grief and pain, my felt fists clenched together so tight that if I had been holding coals they would have turned to diamonds, I screamed at the top of my lungs so loud that the whole city seemed to echo my roar ... and then I blew up.

## Chapter 37
## I blow a hole in the Penthouse roof

Surprise yet again, I'm still alive but the demons who had been surrounding me and the few who had been in front of Will and Jen were long gone with only flecks of ashes remaining in the air, I looked to the floor under my feet where a crater had formed almost making the roof collapse from under me. My hands were glowing impossibly bright before slowly beginning to dim to a slight glow like you might see from a light bulb or an early sunrise, I'd released the full force of my Heavenly glow, the ability that Angel Protector children possess (I know, awesome right?) and destroyed any demon within five feet of me and blinded a few others who were now stumbling around the rooftop crashing into random objects screaming "I can't see".

The sorcerer wandered too far back desperately trying to find his way blind before he fell off the roof when he got too close to the railing, "Jason" Katie mumbled staring at me but my gaze had shifted to Blake who had managed to shield his eyes but was groaning in pain at his severely burned right arm.
"Kill them all, leave no survivors, but not Blake … he's mine" I growled unfurling my wings bringing Divine Fury to life in my hand, "He's all yours" Jen replied rushing to face the demons on her right with Will by her side cutting down any in their path, Katie lunged to the left and began slicing her way through any demon in front of her.

 I pointed my sword directly at Blakes chest and stared deep into his eyes that once had been filled with confidence but were now filled with utter fear. "Uh oh" Blake mumbled before I screamed and lunged at him aiming directly for his head, Blake materialised his sword at the last second dropping his gun and blocking my strike, "Jason let's talk about this" Blake muttered as our blades locked over and over again in a full force battle, each of my strikes were aiming for his torso or neck to strike a killing blow but he blocked every strike.

"YOU KILLED HER!!! I'M GOING TO END YOUR MISERABLE EXISTENCE!!" I screamed spinning on the spot using my wings to sweep Blake's legs from under him, my wings collided with his ankles and he did a full backflip before landing on his knees with a heavy crunch, Blake screamed in pain as I my sword came down towards him. Blake raised his sword to block what he thought was a killing blow but right before my blade collided with his I twisted Divine Fury and removed Blake's left hand from his wrist.
 Blake screamed in pain and dropped his sword as it and his hand turned to ash, I used my free hand to grab Blakes left arm and burned it with my divine light turning it almost to charcoal and much worse than his right arm, I raised my blade high up into the air and above his head ready to bring it down on top of him … only I couldn't do it.

Despite all he'd done … when I looked at his pitiful and fearful eyes all I could see was the man who had taken me in all those years ago, a lonely kid living on the street who he'd given a home, a warm bed and three meals a day and a life with some semblance of a purpose. "You can't do it can you?" Blake laughed as my sword wielding hand shook trying to bring it down and drive its way through his thick arrogant skull, "You know why?" Blake asked "Because I am who I made you to be, I forged you into the man you are today" Blake ranted, "As much as you try to deny it, I created you … I moulded you … I'm the only one who knows who you truly are!" Blake shouted laughing that same arrogant and cocky laugh.

I looked over at Will and Jen who were locked in battle with demons, my best friend and the woman who had brought me to the Academy, I looked at Katie who was currently using a combination of her wings, divine light and her Shui to cut down any demons in her path and I looked over at Cassie's body lying on the ground a shimmer of light seeming to descend from the night sky and shine down on her.
 I had loved her from day one, the only one I had ever trusted with every fibre of my being like none I had before ever since my grandma had died, I imagined the future we could have shared before Blake had taken that away and a truth I'd never thought of before came to life in my mind.

I looked down at Blake and locked eyes with him as the look of arrogance in his smile turned once more back to fear, I pulled Blake closer to me with his burned left arm his face inches away from my own. "I don't need you or anyone to tell me who I am" I muttered bringing Divine fury straight down from its raised position running it through Blakes chest … Blake looked at me in shock and burst into ash the blood bond smashing against the ground into stardust.

I stared at the pitiful pile of ash that had once been the closest thing I'd had to a father and my former boss and scoffed before kicking the ashes away, "Let go of me!" Jen shouted catching my attention as my wings folded back into my body the adrenaline that forced them out in the first place now slowly leaving my system. I looked over as Jen grappled with Julius and backed slowly towards the edge of the building "JEN LOOK OUT!" I screamed all too late as Jen slipped backwards with Julius and fell over the railing of the roof.

"NOOO!!" I screamed running to the edge of the railing and swan diving off the building. "JASON!" I heard Will and Katie shout simultaneously but my gaze was fixed on Jen who was still falling to the ground, Julius disappeared in a puff of ash as Jen kicked him into a nearby flagpole skewering him like a kebab and tried to slow down her descent. I stretched out my hand trying to reach hers, our fingertips just briefly touched …  and we missed grabbing each other's hand (I missed, she missed it doesn't matter just don't ask Jen) and she fell faster spiralling like a top.

"No, not again" I growled unfurling my wings once more and using them to launch me forwards like a jet engine, I was inches away from Jen now who was still spinning (Thank god Blake had to have a 100 storey building) and pointed my body forwards like a pencil pulling my wings closer to my body ... and grabbed Jen pulling her in tight against my body.

"Got you" I spoke over the rushing air around us, "Nice catch" Jen replied with a sigh of relief looking down to the street and then back up at me. "Right ... falling still, don't worry, I've got this" I replied unfurling my wings fully outstretched and flapping them repeatedly, "Yes! I'm flying!" I mumbled before I realised, I was more slowing our descent than actually flying.
 "Uh oh" I mumbled as my wings decided that now would be the perfect time to stop their attempt at flying the same way a chicken might hover and hang their uselessly. "What do we do?" Jen asked noticing the fast-approaching ground, "The only thing I can" I mumbled folding my wings around Jen encasing her in a protective bubble "What are you doing?" Jen shouted trying to loosen the grip I had put on her to prevent her from leaving my grasp "Saving you, I won't lose another person I care about ... make sure Cassie gets the goodbye she deserves" I mumbled looking over my shoulder at the final five storeys "Jason ... no!" Jen screamed as I turned so my back was facing the ground and landed directly on top of Blake's Mercedes and then everything went black.

## Chapter 38
## What does it take to kill me?

"How's he doing?" I heard Will mumble from somewhere nearby as I tried to regain consciousness, the world was spinning every time I tried to open my eyes and my ears rang with a high-pitched whistle, "In and out of consciousness I think, Jason can you hear me?" I heard Katie mumble briefly seeing her blue eyes through my foggy vision, we were in a car, I was pretty sure from the sound of the roaring engine and the beeping of traffic "Cassie?" I mumbled.

My whole body felt like it was on fire from the pain and agony as I shuffled around on the seat of the car, I was pretty sure a few bones were broken and I definitely had some bruising on my body, there was also a blinding stinging pain in my back around my shoulders and a warm wet sensation running from my shoulders, "Blood? Yeah, probably blood" I thought to myself trying to sit upright to the screaming and throbbing of my head before I collapsed back down and faded into darkness.

"That was a bad fall he took, he's lucky to be alive" Jen muttered as consciousness started to return to me, we weren't moving now which meant that we were no longer in the car and I could feel the comfort of a mattress underneath me the rough springs pressing into my back. I'd started to heal now (Thank you advanced healing powers), some of my bones had started to mend together and my vision was all but completely cleared as I stared up at the ceiling fan above me spinning around and around like a record. "You know it's rude to talk about someone while they're asleep" I mumbled slowly pushing myself upright to the groaning and shouting of my aching muscles, "Woah, easy there buddy" Will spoke approaching me from behind aiding me up into an upright seated position, "Thanks man, where are we?" I asked looking around the room.

The whole motel room that we were in screamed *"old school"* and *"never been used in years"* (Think Bate's motel and you've got it). The brown flowery wallpaper was peeling off the wall in the corner revealing a horrid sick green coloured paint on the wall behind it and a few flecks of what I hoped was red paint although I had the feeling it may be something with a little more iron in it. The green carpet underneath my feet did nothing to compliment the gloominess of the room and the TV across from me that I could only guess was from the early 1970's judging from the suitcase sized case on the back of it made the motel room less than the ideal place to wake up in.

"How are you feeling?" Katie asked me passing me a glass of water which I promptly gulped down like a fish out of water, "Like I fell a hundred stories and landed on a Mercedes" I replied looking over at Jen who had a few cuts and scrapes on her cheeks revealing her blue blood like mine. "How are you feeling?" I asked Jen who was staring at me with a mixture of thanks and disappointment on her face, "Better than you I'm sure" Jen replied leaning against the dresser that the TV was placed upon.

"How long have I been out?" I asked rubbing my forehead trying in vain to ignore the throbbing sensation, "About 12 hours" Katie replied, "12 HOURS!" I shouted in utter shock "You broke your leg, both of your wings and three ribs not to mention the shard of glass that was stuck in your shoulder and then there was the detonation of your heavenly light that drained you" Jen scolded me like an angry mother scolds her son.

"That would explain the throbbing sensation in my back" I joked tensing in pain every time my shoulder moved in its socket. "That was a stupid move jumping off the roof" Jen said her expression remaining the same, "I'm sorry but when exactly did you grow wings?" I asked raising a quizzical eyebrow "And you can't fly even with them" Jen replied shrugging off my comment, "I'm sorry, what I should be saying is thank you" Jen added sitting down next to me on the bed and placing her hand on my shoulder, "Anytime" I replied putting my arm around her giving her a warm hug.

A horrid tugging sensation reappeared in my heart as memories of the day before began to return and I remembered what had happened on the roof, "Cassie" I mumbled remembering every detail from the roof, the moment when Blake pulled the trigger, Cassie falling to the ground when the bullet hit her and her final breaths leaving her lungs before she left me forever "I'm sorry man" Will spoke sympathetically trying to gauge a reaction from me.

"Her body?" I asked (I know last thing I should be thinking of),
"The police have her, news has been going crazy since we ran away after the crash, they found Cassie on the roof and matched the bullet to Blake's gun, he's wanted for suspicion of her murder … shame they'll never find him" Katie replied.
I remembered the moment when I had taken Blake's life after he had taken Cassie's, I hesitated even after all he'd done, even though I had killed him eventually I still couldn't believe that I'd hesitated before killing him, he was an Arch-Demon and I was a Protector, it was my job to kill him and I'd hesitated.

"I should have killed him sooner" I spoke thinking back to all the times I'd had the opportunity and now because I'd hesitated Cassie was … no, the pain was too intense to think about, "We need to find the last piece of Dante's compass and finish this" I added standing up on shaky legs like Bambi on ice.

"Easy there" Jen spoke standing up and straightening me "You're still healing, we gave you a bit of Holy Water and Robur Elixir but you still need time" Jen added, "I'll be fine, we still have to find the needle first, do we have any idea where it is?" I asked shrugging off Jen's offer of help shutting down the pain and grief that bubbled to the surface every few seconds.

"No, we tried figuring it out while you were resting but the needle hasn't been seen for over a hundred years, it could be anywhere" Katie replied, I looked over to the other bed in the room where multiple books from an apparent local library were scattered around including a few newspapers highlighted with any suspicious circumstances.

"Great, so we've got three days to figure out where the needle is, retrieve it, add it to the rest of the compass and find the Gates of Hell before they open and all before Sunday when the world will come to an end if we fail" I grumbled pacing the room in frustration trying to ignore that constant pain in my heart.

"Actually" Jen replied "We've only got two days, it's Friday" Jen added, I looked out the window for the first time since waking up spotting the slowly setting sun on the horizon lighting up the sky in an array of orange, blue and purple.

As if the news couldn't get any worse since my recovery we now had less than two days to find the needle to Dante's compass before the world came to an end, time was running out and because of my decision to refuse to kill Blake from the beginning we were now stuck with absolutely no idea where to go and had lost precious time in our busy schedule. "It's not your fault … Blake tricked us" Katie spoke consolingly "If I'd have killed him myself when we first arrived then we wouldn't be in this mess!" I shouted slamming my fist against the wall in frustration.

"Easy, you don't need any more broken bones" Jen argued, she was right of course (Don't tell Jen that) my fist was throbbing from the impact against the stone wall "Dude, Blake was like a father to you, my old man was never around but even I know that if I ran into him and he was a major threat I wouldn't be able to kill him" Will said, "I wish I'd done it sooner maybe if I had Cassie would still be …" I replied ignoring that pain again.

"Jason …" Jen mumbled staring at me with kind eyes, "Let's just find the needle and we'll figure the rest out later" I replied grabbing the nearest book on the American revolution and scanning the pages for any hint about the needle. Someone had marked in the book a section about George Washington crossing the Delaware River and Paul Revere finding his way through the dark whilst warning that the "*British were coming*", "They used the needle to find their way?" I asked running ideas through my mind ranging from checking the museum to digging up George Washingtons corpse.

"Best guess, I'd say so, but the needle disappears sometime around the end of World War one" Jen replied, "Well, that's helpful, anyone happen to know anyone who's been around for a hundred and four years?" I asked.

"Actually, I think I can help with that" a deep voice suddenly boomed, every single one of us jumped a foot into the air and brought our weapons to life in our hands ready for combat "Easy kids, try not to destroy the message, they're awfully difficult to send" the voice continued, a voice we all knew all too well as we stared at the shimmering image of Coach Jones in the middle of our motel room.

## Chapter 39
### Coach Jones calling, do you accept the charges?

"Coach Jones?" I asked curiously staring at the hazy image in front of me, somehow, Coach Jones was stood in the middle of our hotel room like a hologram in star trek, he was encased around his feet in a veil of what looked like fire slowly licking at the cuffs of his black suit trousers. He was dressed different to his usual sports attire opting instead for a three-piece black suit with a white shirt and red tie like a supernatural Mad Men character.

"The one and only Jason" Coach Jones replied stretching his arms outwards and spinning in a circle, "How are you here?" I asked curiously turning Divine Fury back into its ring form, "Pyros message my boy, the best and safest way for Protectors to contact each other, all you need is a fireplace and a silver coin, modern quarters will do the job fine but you won't have long" Coach Jones replied glancing behind him before returning his attention to us.

"I'm here to see how your assignment is coming along" Coach Jones asked looking behind him again, "Is something wrong Coach?" I asked trying to see what he was looking at but apparently Pyros message only applied to the person and not their surroundings "Sorry, we're preparing for Sunday, the academy is in mayhem at the minute as we try to maintain our weapons and make the appropriate preparations for the coming battle" Coach Jones replied.
 I'd never even considered for a moment that while we were trying to stop the gates from actually opening the rest of the academy would have to focus on the usual supernatural threats that attacked the world every Sunday anyway, "The assignment is going okay but we've hit a snag, we don't know where the needle is" Jen spoke up approaching me from behind having returned her bow back to its hairpin position, Coach Jones stared at the floor and then rested his thumb and index finger on his chin lost deep in thought.

"The needle has been lost for over a hundred years but there have been rumours of its location" Coach Jones asked remaining fixed to the spot as the flames started to flicker slower at his feet, "Do you know where it is?" I asked hopeful,
"The needle of the compass has the gift to show the wielder to their hearts most desire wherever that may be, the last time it was wielded by someone in History was by J. R. R. Tolkien" Coach Jones replied (I know, bombshell right?).

"As in writer of the Lord of the Rings J. R. R. Tolkien?" I asked utterly stunned and a little star struck,
"How do you think he got the idea for Lord of the Rings? A Journey across the land to deliver a ring to be destroyed, getting lost and finding your way with the help of elves and dwarves? He met several supernatural beings while he was fighting overseas in World War one" Jen replied. "Please tell me we don't have to go all the way to England and dig up Tolkien to the needle" Will said laying flat on his back on the bed letting out a heavy sigh, "No, William, I assure you the needle is definitely in the United States" Coach Jones replied glancing behind him once again.

"The needle was stolen from Tolkien shortly after the war by an American which is precisely why he never liked the Americans in his letters" Coach Jones spoke, "I heard a rumour that the needle was being held by an adventurer his name was … Axel, Axel Collins" Coach Jones added snapping his fingers at the sudden realisation of Axel's name.
 Will suddenly jumped up from his position on the bed and ran over to us knocking Jen across the room and into the nearby wall in the process "AXEL COLLINS?! I love that guy!" Will shouted like a crazed teenage girl at a Jonas' brother's concert.

 "You know who he is?" I asked confused "Yeah, Axel Collins is an explorer and born adventurer, the Brits have one like him I think they call him Bison or Bull or some kind of animal" Will mumbled. "Anyway, the guy is awesome, he's a hunter and survivor who's been travelling the world for years with his hit TV show team" Wil added clearing up many details that I really did not need to know with the vast multitude of information that was already getting pumped into my brain (I was starting to get a headache).

"Okay, fine, so where is Axel Collin's now?" I asked "He's in Yellowstone National Park" Katie suddenly spoke up from behind, "How did you know that?" I asked spinning to face Katie who had turned on the TV during this conversation.

"*Hello their guy's I'm Axel Collins and this is Born to adventure*" a voice with a rough New York accent came through the TV, on the screen was a middle aged man dressed in a black jumper with green camouflage trousers and a large backpack sitting heavily on his back, he had salt and peppered black hair with flecks of grey and was classically handsome with what appeared to be years of stress etched across his brow and freckles from being out in the sun for a long period of time.

"*I'm coming to you from Yellowstone National Park where I will be spending the next week living solely off the land and surviving only with the tools in my pack, I will teach you all the tools of the trade for how to survive in the open wild yourself, I'm Axel Collin's and welcome … to Born to Adventure*" Axel spoke as the TV let out a tune of several drums being beaten and lit up with the title of the show, "Okay, looks like we're going to Yellowstone" I spoke looking back over to Coach Jones.

"Good luck kids, we're counting on you" Coach Jones spoke with a kind smile, "*Sir, we have a problem the recruits are …*" a voice spoke from behind Coach Jones interrupting the connection before being dismissed by a frantic dismissal waving from Coach Jones. "Who was that?" Jen asked "Just a student addressing some concerns, I've got to go, safe travels" Coach Jones replied with a smile stepping backwards, the flames around him disappeared and the connection broke leaving me and my friends alone in the Motel room staring at a blank wall.

"Let's go" I spoke searching for my backpack before realising it was back in Blake's apartment letting out a groan of frustration, "And how are we supposed to get to Yellowstone National Park exactly?" Jen asked. She was right of course, we were still stuck in Dallas with no money, no I. D's and no resources. "I know a way" Katie spoke up, "How?" I asked curiously, Katie stared at me looking me up and down and smiled biting her lower lip "We fly" Katie replied "Again, I just sort of learned how to use heavenly light, I can't fly, I think the dent in Blake's Mercedes is testament to that" I argued, "Which is exactly where I come in" Katie spoke approaching me and placing her hand on my shoulder

"Jason … I'm going to teach you how to fly" Katie said winking at me and smiling.

## Chapter 40
## Flying lessons with Katie

The next morning I met Katie, Will and Jen on the top roof of the motel as the sun slowly began to rise on the horizon filling the day with a sense of dread and panic knowing that in two days the gates of hell would open and the world would come to an end … and I was having flying lessons (I really hate my life).

"Alright Jason, this is the best spot for teaching you how to fly" Katie spoke gesturing around the empty grey tarred roof, "Two storeys up so if you fall you won't immediately die and high enough that the winds can give you maximum lift rather than taking off from the ground" Katie added pacing from left to right like a teacher in a classroom.

"First things first, show me your wings" Katie spoke folding her arms across her chest, "And you didn't even buy me dinner first" I laughed relaxing my posture focusing on that internal fight or flight instinct I carried with me and stretched the muscles on my back releasing my wings from my body, Katie smiled at me and clapped "Excellent, now flap them" Katie said.

I focused on the wings on my back and tried to move them in an upwards and downwards motion like you would see for the flaps on an airplane but instead they just hung their uselessly feathers blowing in the wind, "This is stupid and we're wasting time it's not going to work" I moaned in frustration. "Because you're thinking too much, your Hunter abilities are connected to the fight or flight instinct in your mind during battle but your angelic abilities are connected to your emotions, that's why you never used your heavenly light ability until …" Katie paused spotting the grief stricken expression across my face "Until Cassie died" I mumbled slumping and sitting down on an air duct tube for the ventilation system.

The traffic seemed to become louder filling the empty silence that had overtaken the roof during my moment of distress, it had been less than a day since Cassie had died and I hadn't even found the time to grieve truly for it yet but there was still too much to do, I had to stop the gates of hell from opening and then after that I could grieve but every time I closed my eyes all I could see was her smiling every time I said her name or the time when we'd watched TV late into the night and fell asleep together on the couch in each other's arms. The memory of her breathing her last breath as her soul left this world flashed through mu mind, "We'll always have San Francisco" her last words echoed in my mind over and over again like a broken record,

A stray tear rolled its way down my cheek before I wiped it away and stood up regaining my composure, "Let's try again" I spoke relaxing the muscles in my body ignoring the pain and grief in my heart,

"Jason, if you want to take a break then we can …"

"No … I need this, I need the distraction" I interrupted Katie before she could finish ignoring the pitiful expression written across her face.

"Let me try and help you fly" Will stepped forwards unfurling the dark scaled wings from his back and hovering a few feet off the ground before landing once again, "Easy as that, emotions work the same in demons too, I think about my suave and debonair style and it lifts me up" Will added winking at Katie and Jen with a smile on his face who both rolled their eyes at him in disgust and frustration.

"Will's right, I think of Christmas dinner with my dad and sisters, the happiness and love I felt and it lifts me into the air" Katie said with a smile flapping her wings and hovering a few feet off the ground landing softly and gracefully back onto the roof.

I tried to focus on my memories with Cassie to fill myself with joy like Katie had advised me to but every time I tried I had the same image replay through my mind of Cassie's death and Blake's mocking tone, "It won't work, let's find another way to get to Yellowstone" I grumbled walking away from my friends. "Alright let's try Plan B or as I like to call it, trial by fire" Will spoke from behind charging towards me, before I had a chance to blink Will kicked me in the chest and sent me flying backwards off the roof.

My wings fluttered frantically as I stared up at my friends on the roof before landing with a heavy 'THUD' into the dumpster behind the motel, "Just like old times" I thought to myself groaning at the pounding pain in my wings, Will landed down next to the dumpster and looked at me as Katie landed next to him holding Jen "You were supposed to fly!" Will shouted "Maybe next time a little warning?" I replied removing a stray banana peel that had found its way down my shirt.

"We're running out of time, we need to find another way to Yellowstone, you can figure out how to fly later" Jen broke the tension giving me a hand as I scrambled out of the foul stenching dumpster brushing the dirt and trash off my clothes.

"Maybe we can still fly to Yellowstone" I mumbled a crazy idea forming in the back of my mind "How?" Jen questioned scrunching her eyebrows together in a quizzical look.

"We steal a plane" I replied clapping my hands together,

"Steal a plane? How and where are we going to find a plane let alone fly it?",

"I did see a small airfield on the way here, if we can borrow one" Will spoke using quotation marks with his fingers on his borrow idea "We may be able to fly there" Will added materialising a cigar into his hand.

"But we don't know how to fly a plane" Katie replied turning to argue with Will, "You may not but I do" Will spoke placing the cigar between his teeth "How do you know how to fly a plane?" Jen asked staring at Will surprised that he had the knowledge to fly a plane. "Mom dated a crop duster for a while when I was twelve, he used to take me up and let me fly the plane with him, bet I could do it again if we can find the right aircraft" Will spoke moving the cigar from left to right with his tongue.

"Okay, so we steal a plane, fly to Yellowstone, find Axel Collin's, ask him for the needle and find our way to the gates of hell … sounds easy enough" I said with a small aura of confidence ignoring the extremely difficult and dangerous path ahead of us, Jen groaned in annoyance and pinched the bridge of her nose.
"Remind me why we keep planning ideas that could get us killed" Jen spoke breathing through clenched teeth "Because we're Protectors, when do our plans never involve us likely getting killed?" I joked putting my arm around her shoulder, "I really hate you" Jen mumbled turning to face me "And that's what makes us great" I replied winking at Jen and smiling, "Alright then, let's go steal a plane" Jen said shaking her head from left to right.

# Chapter 41
## Come fly with me

We hitchhiked a ride from a friendly farmer who was more than happy to help four sixteen year old kids who were just trying to get to the airfield nearby to find their way home (Mortals will believe anything) and arrived at the airfield an hour later. We waited near the fence and watched as the few security guards that patrolled the grounds waddled from hangar to hangar checking for any intruders, the airfield itself was miniscule by any sense compared to larger airports that people regularly used but this airfield was solely for small planes that were privately owned or needed to land in order to refuel before continuing on their journey.

 "Over there" Will spoke passing me the binoculars that he had "borrowed" from the farmer who had given us a ride, I stared through the binoculars at where Will was pointing spotting a small yellow aircraft fit for four passengers maximum. The paint was peeling off on the side of the plane revealing the slowly rusting metal underneath it and the propellor looked as though it was about to fall of any moment.

"That plane? Seriously? It looks like the plane from Indiana Jones" I joked passing the binoculars to Katie who looked at me confused along with Jen who was sharing the same look, "Indiana Jones? Harrison Ford? One of the greatest movie series of all time?" I asked remembering the moments on the streets when I had caught glimpses of Indiana Jones through the window of the TV store in the bitter cold to try and distract me from the hunger in my stomach.
 Jen and Katie continued to look at me with blank and puzzled expressions "I need new friends" I added jokingly squinting across the landscape at the hangar.

"Okay, so I say we start a small fire to distract the guards, run across the airfield, jump in the plane and take off, are you sure you can fly it Will?" I asked Will who simply nodded his head and winked.
 "That sounds like a bad idea" Jen spoke wrapping the binocular strap over her shoulder, "Well, you know what they say … All the best plans start with a bad idea" , Jen looked at me in confusion and concern
 "Who said that?"
"I did just now" I replied.

"That's a terrible saying! Why would you say that? Bad idea's get you killed" Jen replied "Well, excuse me for being the only one with a plan" I remarked in frustration, "As ridiculous it is … it is a good plan" Jen replied.  "Okay then, I'll start the fire on those boxes over there and distract the guards while you, Will and Katie get the plane up and running and I'll meet you on the runway" Jen ordered before standing up and running in the direction of the pile of wooden boxes "Let's do this" I mumbled running with Katie and Will towards the airplane hangar and our temple of doom yellow plane.

True to her word a few moments after we had started our panicked run across the runway and towards the hangar the boxes Jen had chosen burst into flames catching the attention of the guards who dropped their routine to battle the blazing inferno. "All aboard" Will ordered climbing into the pilot's side of the plane with Katie in the co-pilot's seat leaving me to scramble into the small backseat of the aircraft.

I had to admit I was impressed with Will's confidence and reaction speed as he flicked several switches on the plane dashboard that made the Star Trek enterprise look easy to fly and the airplane buzzed to life the propeller spinning wildly threatening to fall off and shred anything unfortunate to find itself in its path.
"Here we go" Will spoke pushing the throttle forwards slowly guiding the plane out of the hangar and towards the runway, Jen immediately started running towards us after causing several vines to burst out of the ground around the guards' feet pinning them in place.

"Come on Jen!" I shouted over the roar of the engine pushing open the door opposite to me and leaning out stretching my arm for her. Using her natural Hunter speed and Agility Jen quickly caught up and grabbed my hand and I pulled her in moments before Will pushed the throttle to maximum speed and pulled back on the wheel to the groaning of the engine taking us up into the air and away from the airfield, "Next time … we take the train" Jen spoke through staggered breaths.

An hour into our flight towards Yellowstone we passed over the open plains of Colorado enjoying the sights of the wide-open grasslands, natural lakes and mountains stretching high up into the sky, the world below looked peaceful and the mortals below were enjoying their weekend looking forward to their lazy Sunday blissfully unaware that if we failed on our assignment there would be no more Sunday's and no more peaceful Colorado.

"You, okay?" Jen asked snapping me out of my trance of the peaceful landscape and bringing my attention back to our current predicament "Yeah, just thinking that's all" I replied staring at my hands and clasping them together repeatedly trying to get rid of the image of them being stained with Cassie's blood when she had died. "Is it about Cassie?" Jen asked seemingly reading my mind yet again "In a way, she would have loved this, flying through the air, not a care in the world, just the silence and peace of the landscape" I replied picturing Cassie sat next to me smiling at her new adventure.

"She was amazing and she loved you deeply, I only wished we would have had more time to get to know her" Jen replied clasping my shaking hand with hers, "The funny thing is … even after all that time I spent with her, I feel like we still knew so little about each other" I thought my gaze drifting back out the window.
"I can still smell the lavender shampoo she used and remember the way she used to smile whenever I told a bad joke, I wanted to spend the rest of my life with her even after I found out that I was a Protector and that I had responsibilities, I wanted to spend every day with her, a half breed and a mortal … we would have made quite the pair huh?" I joked feeling tears start to cling to my eyelashes. I knew that I should be focused on the mission and ignoring all other emotions but everything I saw reminded me of Cassie, the way she smiled, the way she laughed, the scenery that she should have seen but never got the chance to and now never would.

"What happens to us when we die? As Protectors I mean?" I questioned shifting the conversation,

"Well …" Jen replied "When a Protector dies, they go to the Realm of Protectors, a sort of rewarding afterlife for us" Jen added with a smile.

"What is it like?"

"The stories say that the Realm is the ultimate reward for a Protector, it's supposed to be paradise" Katie added to the story "Fields of rare and beautiful flowers as far as the eye can see that dance up to your knees in the breeze" Katie continued as the image started to form in my mind.

"Rivers of crystal blue water refreshing beyond imagination, a sky so blue that you would think the ocean was reflected above you, open planes of grass with wildlife where Protector's would rest under the glorious sunshine" Katie continued "Mighty cities home to legends and small villages for those who wish for a simple afterlife, a night sky filled with millions of stars and galaxies spread out before you with a moon so big that you feel like you could reach up and touch it" Jen added, "Food so sweet they make your tastebuds dance and a coliseum to do battle in should you feel the urge, you don't die, you are simply reborn the next day to continue your afterlife again" Will spoke his attention never leaving the sky.

"It sounds like heaven" I replied imagining myself in the fields, relaxing under the blue sky, reunited with my parents and grandmother, my family in my arms all the questions I ever desired answered for me and a certain girl with Scarlett hair dancing through the plains with me. "Do you think Cassie will be there?" I asked Katie who was the only one in the plane with the closest connection to any sense of heaven, "Cassie although mortal was a Protector at heart … There's no doubt in my mind" Katie replied turning to face me and smiling, I could see tears in the Katie's eyes and in Jen's bringing me comfort that at least I wasn't the only one who missed Cassie deeply.

"Alright here we are, Yellowstone National Park" Will shouted over the roar of the engine after another hour and a half of flying, I glanced out of the window at the open valleys of Yellowstone national park. The whole park was filled with more trees of various kinds than the brain could possibly comprehend filling the valleys with a multitude of colours and patterns, cars slowly buzzed through the winding roads with mortals heading out for camping adventures or a day out exploring for the weekend.

Mountains stretched high into the sky around the park and old faithful the geyser that attracted so many tourists shot a plume of steaming hot water into the sky, it was the picture of perfection, a small part of me wondered if this was what the Realm of Protectors looked like.

The sound of loud beeping coming from the cockpit dashboard attracted my attention as Will frantically stared around at the various buttons and dials around the dashboard "That's not good" Will mumbled pressing buttons (Not what you want to hear or say when someone's flying a plane) "What's going on?" Jen asked leaning forwards "I think we may be out of fuel" Will replied calmly as the plane began to slowly descend.

The engine sputtered and the propeller tried to stay alive as we dropped closer to the landscape below, "FIND US A PLACE TO LAND QUICK!" Katie shouted in a panic, Will glanced over at Katie and then back at me and Jen with an uncomfortable expression written across his face, "Slight problem with that … I don't know how to land" Will replied calmly creasing the corner of his mouth.

"You don't know how to land? How is that possible?" Katie questioned as the plane began to descend faster towards the forest,

 "Well the guy never taught me how to land just how to fly and take off isn't exactly rocket science but landing is the problem" Will replied trying in vain to keep the plane from falling out of the sky.

 The forest canopy below grew ever closer as the front of the plane around the propeller began to let out a thick plume of black smoke and the propeller came to a complete stop in mid-flight "The Lake! Aim for the lake!" I shouted pointing over at the crystal-clear blue water of Yellowstone Lake. "Hold on tight" Will spoke pointing the front of the plane towards the lake diving at incredible speed as the plane spun in a circle in free-fall, the lake was coming up fast "Here it comes!" Will shouted pulling back on the wheel levelling the plane out slightly right before we slammed into the cold lake surface.

## Chapter 42
## If you go down into the woods today

"The train … definitely the train next time" I mumbled coughing up clods of water from my lungs spitting it onto the shore clearing my lungs before lying flat on my back my wet clothes clinging to my skin. We'd hit the lake and pushed our way out of the broken doors and windows from the impact before swimming our way to shore soaked to the bone and struggling for breath.

Katie was sat down next to me wringing out her long blonde hair sending a cascade of water onto the earth providing refreshment to the plants growing underneath our presence, Will was stood nearby leaning against a tree and peeling his now completely ruined leather jacket off his frame throwing it away and into the forest in frustration and Jen was stood at the shore staring over at the slowly sinking plane.

"Nice landing Will" Katie mumbled flicking her hair and around smacking me across the cheek with it in the process, "Sorry" Katie added as a red mark slowly grew across my now stinging cheek. "It's not my fault we didn't have enough fuel, just be happy we didn't hit the tree's" Will groaned wringing out the hem of his shirt "She means good job, now how do we find Axel?" I asked looking around at the space around us.

We were completely surrounded by woodland with no visible markers or hiking marker routes in sight, birds sang overhead in the trees in the morning sunlight and fish bobbed to the surface of the lake swallowing the occasional bug that landed on the surface of the water. "I think I can help with that" Jen spoke wringing the lake water from her denim jacket.

"How?" I questioned curiously

"With a little bit of help from my Nature magic" Jen replied kneeling down onto her right knee and placing her hand against the earth closing her eyes.

Jen reopened her eyes to reveal that they were now glowing a bright green like the tree canopy above us, the sunlight reflected in her iris making it seem like she had the forest in her eyes, the earth underneath her hand glowed and cracked with veins of light disappearing into the forest in various directions and spreading off into the distance "Wow" I muttered unable to form any other words in the English language.

The veins that had once been glowing in the earth retreated back to Jen's hand and up her forearm before Jen's eyes turned back to their usual blue, the green light disappearing from them.

"Found him" Jen mumbled collapsing backwards onto her knee gasping for breath. "Are you okay?" I asked kneeling down and helping her up onto her feet, "Yeah … just took a lot out of me that's all" Jen gasped breathing heavily "Axel is doing a speech at the moment for the camera's, he's about two mile in that direction, if we go now we should catch him before he moves on" Jen added pointing to what I guessed was North in the forest "Into the woods we go" I spoke walking with my friends into the thick expanse of the forest.

Every few dozen? Fifty? Hundred? Feet I honestly had no idea how far we'd travelled from the lake, Jen would touch the earth once more spreading out the tendrils of life in her nature magic and pointing in the direction we needed to go before continuing on our trek through the woods making me feel like little red riding hood heading to grandma's house the further we went.
 "How much further?" Will asked curiously
"We're nearly there he should be just over …",
*"Hello folks, I'm Axel Collins and welcome to born to adventure"* the voice cut through the forest nearby cutting Jen off mid-instruction.

We climbed the last few feet up the steep hill we had just spent the last thirty minutes climbing up and came face to face with Axel and his camera crew who needless to say were surprised to see four teenage kids slowly drying after a dip in the lake and gasping for breath after a steep climb. "Hi" I spoke waving right before two security guards appeared from a nearby tent blocking our path to the TV star, "This is a closed set, no visitors allowed" the hulking ogre of a guard on the right growled with his arms folded across his muscular chest.

"I know and I'm sorry but we just need to speak to Axel about something important and we'll be on our way" I spoke hoping for luck to shine down on us, "Turn around kids, the trail back to the campgrounds is twenty feet that way" the guard on the left spoke pointing to the east "Well that makes the show I've loved for so many years a lot less spectacular" Will grumbled from behind me.
 "It's okay guys let them through" Axel spoke from behind, his guards stepped aside allowing us to step past them watching every step we made and I honestly thought the guard on the right actually growled like a dog.

Axel looked exactly as he did on the TV show, salt and peppered black hair and dressed in a black jumper with green camouflage trousers and black army boots with a kind but curious smile spread across his face. "What are you kids doing out here?" Axel asked us concern in his tone, "Looking for you actually sir, my names Will and I'm a big fan" Will pushed forwards nearly knocking me down to the ground in the process like a crazed fan girl at a boy band concert grabbing Axel's hand and shaking it up and down repeatedly.

"Well, it's always nice to meet a fan" Axel replied breaking the death grip Will had on his hand, "You said you needed to talk to me about something?" Axel asked scratching the stubble on his chin.

"Yes, we're sorry but we're looking for something of ours that we lost a while back and we think you may have it, it's the needle of a compass, should be red and look a little like …" Jen spoke right before Axel tugged the chain he had around his neck revealing two military dog tags and a red compass needle with demonic sand script etched into the metal "Like that" Jen added pointing to the compass needle on his chain.

"You came all the way here for this?" Axel asked holding the needle in his hand, "It's a family heirloom, it fell out of the compass my grandpa gave me and we've been looking for it for a while, I saw it on your show a few weeks ago and recognised it immediately and we just had to find you" Will said edging closer to Axel slightly. "I suppose you have proof that this belongs to you?" Axel asked watching each of us intently "Yes right here" I spoke holding out my hand for Jen to pass me the compass which she did hesitantly, I showed Dante's compass to Axel pointing to the clear fact that it did not have a needle.

Axel tucked the necklace back into his jumper and started to laugh "The commander was right, for Protectors, you are all terrible liars" Axel spoke that same name echoing again making me wonder if we should be looking for this 'Commander' as well. Axel cracked his neck and watched us with hungry eyes (I think you know where this is going), "I'm sorry what's a Protector?" I asked dumbly watching the camera crew slowly put down their equipment.

The two hulking guards who had blocked our path earlier cracked their knuckles in the palm of the opposite hand with a deafening pop, "Like I said … terrible liars" Axel growled and when I say growled, I mean literally growled like a hound.

"Axel, we don't need to do this" I spoke looking out of the corner of my eye at Jen who was already reaching for her hairpin, "Actually I do, you honestly thought you could sneak up on me? I smelled you coming from a mile away" Axel replied stretching every muscle in his body. "Do you want to know why I'm always out in the wild?" Axel added his breathing becoming heavier and the growling becoming louder "Enlighten me" I mumbled ready to bring Divine Fury to life in an instant when the time came.

"Because a pack always sticks together and always feels most at home in the forest" Axel growled before barking like a dog and then letting out a loud deafening howl. His eyes were the first thing to change turning from a deep brown to a dark yellow and a large black pupil, his teeth elongated into large fangs, his nose begun to shift into a long snout the teeth fitting into place, his salt and peppered fur began to sprout across his face and down his neck.

Axel's guards had also started to transform like Axel in the same way, their eyes changing colour, fangs sprouting in their mouth and fur growing around their ears "Well, damn it" I muttered right as Axel shifted into his full form ... a large 8 foot Wolf standing on four legs with salt and peppered fur growling and dribbling pools of saliva onto the floor. "For once why can't we do things the easy way" Will groaned pressing the fob on his watch bringing Tenebris to life in his hand, Jen brought her ivory bow to life and drew an arrow, Katie flicked both her wrists and brought both of her daggers to life in her hand and I spawned Divine Fury into my hand "Because then it would be boring" I joked rushing towards the angry and growling wolf that had once been Axel Collins.

## Chapter 43
## The Big Bad Wolf

If any of you reading this have seen the twilight movies then I hate to disappoint you but Werewolves are not kind, gentle, handsome creatures, they are vicious, brutal and have breath that could knock a giant unconscious. We were each locked in battle fighting the pack and preventing ourselves from winding up as a chew toy for the wolves, "Bad dog" Will joked slashing Tenebris down separating the head from one of the wolves who had launched through the air at him leaving behind a yelp and then a pile of dust on the ground.

Katie was stood near the centre of the camp with her wings outstretched sliding on her knees across the ground whenever a wolf dived at her moving with the grace of a ballerina almost like she was dancing with the wolves in the battle. Both wolves launched themselves at Katie from either side teeth bared and growling in hunger but Katie had clearly planned this, with a quick beat of her wings Katie launched herself up into the air sending the two wolves crashing into each other before dropping back down driving her daggers into each wolf just around the scruff turning them both to dust adding more soot to the already dead campfire.

I dodged an attack from Axel slamming him with the flat of my blade as he surged past and watched as Jen fired two arrows simultaneously at the two wolves who had once been the security guards striking them both in the chest as they lunged through the air, Jen smiled and spun her bow pointing the tip towards the ground as both wolves burst into ash and scattered into the wind. Each of my friends fought with utter grace and balance in the fight having grown up in or around the academy, I could only rely on my natural Hunter instincts and the few training sessions I had spent with Blake and Sir Galahad so my fighting style resembled clumsy monkey rather than fierce warrior.

Sweat was pouring down my back as I continued to dodge Axel's attacks waiting for my opening to strike, with a low growl and howl Axel lunged through the air teeth bared with chunks of meat spread between the gaps of what I hoped were rabbit or deer, "Now" I thought to myself side-stepping the launch and slicing Divine Fury in a downwards arc leaving a large gash against Axel's side who let out a loud howl and dropped to the ground black blood leaking from the wound.
Axel collapsed near to his tent slowly shifting back to his human form clenching his hand against the wound, "YOU KILLED MY PACK!" Axel shouted grinding his teeth in agony trying desperately to crawl away from us, as I approached him something caught my eye to the left of me in a tent, there were backpacks stuffed into the corner but not the kind that a camera crew would carry … and that's when my worst fears and thoughts were confirmed.

The first thing I spotted was the large yellow camping backpack with the Osprey logo etched onto it and a pink water bottle attached to it. Red marks that I knew to be blood covered the top of the backpack around the shoulders, around the large camping backpack were several others of various sizes including a large duffel bag and … a small pink one with a white daisy that could only have once belonged to a child.

Rage filled my body and soul as I turned my gaze back to Axel letting in and out loud breaths of air that made Axel shiver in fear, "How many have you killed?" I commanded clasping Divine Fury so tight that my knuckles turned white, Axel frantically looked between me, my friends and the backpacks in the tent.
 "You wanted the needle right?" Axel asked tearing the piece of Dante's compass from the neck chain, "Here take it just please have mercy" Axel added throwing the needle so that it landed in front of my trainers but my blood continued to boil in rage at the thought of the countless hikers and campers who had been killed by Axel and his pack.

"Mercy? You want me to show you mercy?" I questioned turning Divine Fury back to its ring form choosing instead to grab Axel by the front of his shirt with my left hand clenching it tight so he couldn't escape. "Did you show them mercy?" I asked bringing back my right arm and driving my fist into Axel's face, a deafening crunch sounded as his nose broke from the impact and black blood poured from his nostrils across his lips and dropping off his chin.

"HOW MANY OF THEM BEGGED FOR MERCY?" I shouted the rage filling my body as I drove my fist again into Axel's nose,
"HOW MANY PLEADED TO BE SPARED?! TO HAVE THEIR LIVES SAVED! TO LEAVE THEIR CHILDREN ALONE!" I shouted driving punch after punch into Axel's face. Black blood gushed from his busted lip and the corner of his eyes as bone broke under each punch, cartilage snapping with each direct hit, "Jason!" Jen shouted from behind trying to break me out of my raging state but my stare was fixed solely on Axel.
 "HOW MANY DID YOU KILL AXEL?! HOW MANY?!" I screamed grabbing Axel with both my hands before throwing him across the campsite in rage, Axel slammed into a nearby pine tree with a deafening crunch several bones breaking on impact "JASON STOP!" Katie shouted now trying to bring me out of my blind rage to no avail.

"THIS IS FOR EACH LIFE YOU TOOK!" I shouted grabbing the near unconscious Axel by his throat driving my fist into his ribs with every ounce of Hunter strength in my body,
"FOR EVERY PERSON WHO DESERVED TO LIVE! …
FOR EVERY SOUL YOU SENT TO THE AFTERLIFE! …
FOR EVERY PARENT WHO SCREAMED AS YOU MURDERED THEIR CHILDREN!" I screamed driving a punch into his ribs with each scream, tears clung to my eyelashes as the rage and pain continued to flood my system.

"STOP IT JASON!" Will shouted running up behind me and grabbing my right arm "GET OFF ME!" I shouted bringing my elbow back into Will's nose with a loud crunch sending him backwards a few feet.
"FOR EVERY PERSON WHOSE LOVED ONE YOU TOOK!
DID THEY DESERVE TO DIE!
DID ANY OF THEM?! …
DID CASSIE?!!" I screamed driving a final blow into Axel's sternum.

A deafening crunch sounded once more and Axel went limp in my arms, "Jason … stop" Jen mumbled slowly appearing at my side placing a consoling hand on my shoulder.

I let go of Axel and stared at my hands for the first time since I had started my raging beating on Axel's body. The skin on my knuckles was broken and torn almost down to the bone, my blue blood ran down my hands and clung to my sleeves around my wrist, I was at least eighty percent sure that I had broken several bones in my hand and they refused to stop their shaking, my body deprived of the adrenaline it had been flooded with during the beating.

The last words echoed in my mind like a broken record "Did Cassie?", I'd taken all my anger and grief that I had been feeling since Dallas and poured it onto the beating I had given Axel who was now nothing more than a pile of ash after the last of his breath had left his lungs. "I'm sorry" I mumbled collapsing to my knees grabbing fistfuls of dirt, the tears that had clung to my eyelashes were now pouring down my cheeks tracing their way through the black blood that had splashed onto me during the beating, "I'm so sorry" I cried weeping in utter and complete indescribable grief, I felt Jen pull me in close to her body in a loving hug and two other bodies against my back and opposite side that I guessed were Will and Katie "It's okay" Jen whispered like a mother would to a child as I continued to cry and scream in pain.

## Chapter 44
## With Friends like these

The popping of the burning wood did little to comfort the pain in my heart as the campfire burned late into the night filling the air with smoke and the gentle embers from the flames, we'd decided after the fight and after my grief filled rage beating on Axel to settle in for the night and we hadn't spoken a word to each other since. Three hours of deafening silence once the tears had finally stopped and I was left to my own thoughts, "Here, drink this" Jen spoke passing me a cup of warm tea that had been boiling over the campfire, Jen and Katie had raided the backpacks of the camera crew of Axel's victims after I'd collapsed staring into space from the grief and had found several energy granola bars, bottles of water, herbal tea bags and sleeping bags.

"Thank you" I mumbled feeling the warm metal cup pressed against my fingertips warming my entire body, overhead countless stars shined across the night sky each one like a beacon shining down on us, the sounds of the animals who thrived in the night howled throughout the forest ranging from owls to coyotes each one making their presence known to us. "How are your hands?" Katie asked, "All healed now, sorry about your nose Will" I replied looking down at my knuckles that had now completely healed and over at Will who was smiling back at me "It's okay man, it's been a while since I've had a good punch to the face" Will joked his nose now completely healed.

Will and Katie were both roasting marshmallows over the campfire gasping in agony when they placed steaming hot treat on their tongues. "How are you feeling?" Jen asked me trying to make eye contact with me, "I honestly can't describe it in words" I mumbled placing the warm cup onto the soft earth and intertwining my fingers repeatedly trying to keep my hands busy.

"Maybe I can help with that" Katie said approaching me and sitting down next to me crossing her legs,
"How?"
"I can sense emotions and visualise them with a touch" Katie replied her eyes fixated on mine, "Katie you're an empath?" Jen asked stunned "What can I say it's a gift" Katie replied shrugging her shoulders. "An Empath?" I asked feeling like the odd man out on the story, "Empath's are incredibly rare in the children of Angels, they can sense emotions in another person and in some cases replay memories that have strong emotions attached to them" Jen answered.

"So … may I?" Katie asked again slowly reaching her hand up to my chest, I struggled to form any words so instead just simply nodded in agreement, Katie placed her hand softly against my chest and I felt the magic of her empath ability tug at the corners of my mind and the beating of my heart. Katie's eyes began to glow slightly and a blue glow emanated from her fingertips, "Wow" Jen mumbled in wonder but Katie's expression was entirely different.

 I knew she was staring into my very soul and feeling the same grief that I was feeling, "Oh, Jason" Katie whispered taking her hand away tears pouring down her cheeks, her eyes slowly turning bloodshot "Welcome to me" I replied wiping away a tear from the corner of my eye.
Katie looked like she might collapse from the emotions she had felt from within me, I had spent years pushing down any sense of pain or grief from my parents' death, my grandmothers passing, the foster homes that had been destroyed after attacks, the years living on the streets barely surviving and my time with Blake and Cassie which had now all been pushed straight into Katie's mind who was still shedding tears wiping them away with the back of her hand.

Both Will and Jen were staring with compassion in their eyes at me, they didn't have the ability to read emotions like Katie did but they could tell from her reaction how much pain I was truly carrying in my heart, "I'm sorry Katie, are you okay?" I asked clasping her hands, "How do you do it?" Katie replied meeting my gaze,
"How do I do what?"
 "Cope … go day to day … fight and function with so much grief and pain?" Katie questioned "Simple, I survive" I replied with the most basic answer I could give to her.

In truth, I had spent years trying to focus my mind on the task at hand and forget about any pain I may be feeling so that I could be the strong one, the person anyone could rely on, but since Cassie's death … that emotional barrier keeping the pain away seemed to collapse at all the wrong moments.
"It's all Cassie, isn't it? That's why you took all your anger out on Axel" Jen asked me pulling her knees up to her chest, "She was my anchor, the thing that gave me hope and kept me grounded and now …" I replied the tugging at my heart strings screaming at me in agony again causing me to clutch my chest, "We miss her too" Katie spoke placing her hand on my shoulder.

"She was so much fun and awesome, like the sister I never got" Jen said poking the ashes of the campfire with a small twig, "She told us so many stories about you, New Orleans, the time you made her laugh so hard that milk shot out of her nose but there was one story she never told us ..." Jen spoke catching my gaze "San Francisco" Jen added the words stabbing into my heart at the thought of her final words to me.

"It was a precious moment between the two of us, the most important day in both of our lives" I replied struggling to stop myself from bursting into anguished cries once again, "It was the first time we said I love you to each other" I added the memory starting to tug at the corners of my mind "I can still see it now" I whispered with a small smile.

"Can I see it too?" Katie asked me wanting to use her empath ability to replay memories as well

"Yes" I replied simply.

"Can we come along too do you think?" Jen asked stepping forwards with Will, I nodded at my friends in agreement and waited as Jen grabbed Katie's left hand and used her right to grab Will's, Will used his free hand and clasped mind and I turned to face Katie holding up my left hand "Here we go" Katie whispered wrapping her right hand delicately around mine letting out a wave of energy as the scenery around us fell away.

# Chapter 45
## San Francisco

"Where are we?" Will asked looking around at the space around us "The Golden Gate bridge" I mumbled looking out over San Francisco Bay under the night sky. The fog slowly rolling in from the hills covering the bridge and surface of the ocean in a thin layer of mist, I didn't need the vision to remember this moment, I had thought about it incessantly since Cassie had died and used the memory as her final words.

*"Come on Jason"* I heard a voice giggle through the fog, a voice I knew all too well, a voice that belonged to the only person I had ever loved.

Two figures slowly emerged from the fog running along the footpath on the Golden gate bridge laughing with utter and complete innocent joy. *"Slow down, I swear you have the patience of a Jack Rabbit"* my voice echoed through the fog croaky and on the verge of breaking in my teenage years, a moment later Cassie emerged through the fog 13 years old but still as beautiful the day she had left me.

"Cassie!" I spoke reaching out my hand to grasp hers as she ran past but my hand passed through hers like she was a ghost, "I'm sorry Jason, this is just a memory ... no touch" Katie whispered placing her hand on my shoulder, I came into view 13 years old and laughing chasing after Cassie until we were both stood about halfway across the bridge next to one of the large towers that spread across the bridge.

My past self-caught up with Cassie and pulled her in a tight hug placing my arms around her waist, her back pressed into my chest laughing in glee as I lifted her up and spun around on the spot with her before lowering her back to the ground.

*"You caught me"* Cassie spoke spinning on her heels and turning to face me, her Scarlett hair danced in the lights of the San Francisco bridge, the San Francisco Bay to our back the honking of car horns and barking of Sea lions the only sounds disturbing the moment. *"I'll always catch you, no matter what"* past me whispered kissing Cassie softly on the lips and brushing her hair behind her ear.

"When is this?" Jen asked me, "Six months after Blake took me in, we came to San Francisco on a short business trip but we were told to never cross the bridge fully, something about threatening other cultures that lived outside San Francisco I don't know" I replied (I never did understand why Blake never let us cross the bridge on car or foot). "Same with New York, Protectors are banned from visiting anywhere in the entire state" Jen spoke watching the scene unfold before us, I did wonder about the reason behind New York being under eternal ban but right now I was too obsessed with watching the memory continue.

*"When did I become the lucky one to win you over?"* Cassie whispered pressing her head against past Me's chest, *"I think I'm the lucky one, I never had anything growing up and I always felt empty ... and then I met you"* past me spoke softly cupping his hand against Cassie's cheek making a small part of me want to smack him and tell him to get his hands off "My girl".

"*I love you*" Cassie blurted out suddenly locking her eyes on his "*Damn*" past me spoke with a big grin across his face, "*I'm sorry, I just blurted it out and …*" Cassie stammered backing away from past me slightly "*No, it's not what you think*" past me spoke grabbing her and pulling her back towards him. "*I only said it because I was annoyed … that I didn't get to say it first*" Past Jason spoke "*I Love you too*" Past Jason added.

That single moment filled my pain and grief with a flush of joy, something about seeing the scene actually play out rather than just imagining it in my mind. I watched as Cassie reached up and pressed her lips against past Jason and the scene unfolded wrapped in a haze of fog until we found ourselves once again sat in the forest canopy under the night sky.

"Jason? Are you okay?" Katie asked me, I hadn't even noticed the tear rolling down my cheek until my friends were staring at me with concern. "I've never been better … thank you" I replied hugging Katie like the little sister she was to me, "That was beautiful, she really was amazing, wasn't she?" Jen asked.

I paused staring up at the night sky and smiled imagining Cassie up there somewhere in the Realm of Protectors staring down at me smiling at the work and effort I was putting into keeping the world safe from threats and the day ahead of us, "She was" I replied feeling the grief and pain in my heart feel slightly easier to carry. "So, tomorrow is Sunday which means we've got till Sunset to find the gates and make sure that they stay shut, shall we?" I asked taking Dante's Compass case from my pocket, "Let's do it" Jen replied passing me the needle that had once belonged to Axel Collin's.

I placed the needle slowly towards the compass Faceplate. Suddenly, the Needle attracted to the Faceplate like a magnet and locked in place spinning around frantically in a circle trying to decide on a destination, the wind rippled in the air around us and dirt flew into the air pushed away from the compass' power, even we struggled to stand our ground against the buffeting of the winds until the winds stopped and the needle stopped spinning.

"Is something supposed to …" Will mumbled once the winds stopped before a bright window of flame hovered in front of me like a gateway to another world, "Wow" I whispered unable to form any other words in the English language as the image shifted to show the Gates of Hell that I had seen in my dreams. The black looming gates pulsated ready and prepared to burst open the moment the sun set on Sunday releasing all demons and supernatural beings that waited for us on the other side.

"So, how do we find the location? Do I blink and bob my head? Or wiggle my nose?" I joked "Open Sesame?" Will joined in trying to break the tension. "Maybe we just ask?" Jen spoke taking Dante's compass from my hand, "Show us how to get to the Gates" Jen added, the compass remained silent showing only the same image of the gates, "I don't think it ..." I muttered before stopping as the image zoomed out away from the gates through a dark tunnel with bats, Stalactites and cracks in the ground before opening up to the location to the Gates of Hell.

 "Of course, I should have guessed" Jen spoke throwing her arms up in the air in frustration, "If we leave now and take one of Axel's old trucks I bet we can make it there by noon tomorrow" I spoke looking over at one of the Range Rover 4x4 vehicles parked a short distance away "Then we better get a move on" Jen replied stamping out the flames on the campfire and grabbing her backpack.

I closed the compass and stored it in my pocket to use later when we would find ourselves near the gates, "I'm driving" Jen shouted snagging the keys from the visor over the driver's seat, "Why do you get to drive?" Will moaned throwing his backpack into the trunk of the car. "Because the last time you drove us somewhere we crashed into a Lake" Katie replied climbing into the backseat "I'm never going to live that down am I?" Will groaned climbing into the backseat with Katie, "Sorry buddy, but definitely not" I replied jumping into the passenger side in the front seat.

Jen turned the key in the ignition bringing the roaring engine to life and the radio burst into life causing us all to burst into laughter instantly, "Honestly, I swear before you guys these coincidences never happened" I joked, "What can we say ... it must be fate" Jen replied backing down the hill as the radio blasted out *Viva Las Vegas* by "Elvis Presley" both a great song and our destination, the City of Sin and the Gateway to Hell.

## Chapter 46
## Viva Las Vegas

The sun was slowly peeking its way above the horizon of the Nevada desert as the Las Vegas strip skyline came into view and our 4x4 continued to power its way down Route 66 the windows down blowing the hot desert air into the already scorching car. It was Sunday morning which meant that we had until sunset to find the Gates of Hell and find a way for them to stay shut to prevent the rapture (I know, easy right?).

"Hey pull over there, me and Jason need to collect some resources" Katie shouted from the backseat pulling her feet from the car window frame she'd leaned them on, Jen veered off into the car park of one of the classic Las Vegas mini churches.

"We'll be right back" Katie spoke jumping out of the car and I jumped out with her following her to the church. The white wooden paintwork did little to disguise the fact that this quaint little church had seen more marriages in its short time on this earth than every other church on the planet, a small sign glowed in neon outside reading "*Marriages now only 30 dollars, Divorces also available for 50*" bringing an even greater gloom to the church.

We pushed our way through double doors into the altar room and ignoring the shouting of the receptionist who tried to chase after us towards (I swear to God this next part is true), Elvis Presley stood front and centre of the podium. Of course this wasn't the real Elvis considering his black wig kept sliding off revealing a bald head with white hair on the side, his large aviator glasses hid his age from us reasonably well but his frame under the jumpsuit made me fear that he might wither away and turn to dust at a slight breeze.

"Hey kids, I'm all for free love but if you kids are looking for a marriage license I'm going to need to see some I.D" The impersonator spoke in his Californian accent dropping the Elvis persona instantly. "Me and him?" Katie replied letting out a loud scoff and rolling her eyes at me smiling, "While I'll try not to be immediately insulted by that" I said looking over at Katie "We're actually here for some Holy Water" I added pointing to the small basin in the corner.
"Why do you want Holy Water?" Elvis asked curiously, "Vampires" Katie joked winking at the impersonator "Fine don't tell me, who knows what you kids are up to these days, take as much as you need" the impersonator replied dismissing us with a wave of his hand. Katie and I filled both of our canteens that we had stolen from Axel's camp and filled them with the clear liquid before heading out of the church "Thank you, Thank you very much" I mumbled to the impersonator in my best Elvis impersonation shaking my hips "Come on you" Katie spoke grabbing my ear by its tip and dragging me back outside.

"So, how are the newlyweds?" Will joked leaning out of the window of the car laughing at us the creases of his mouth almost touching the brim of his aviator sunglasses, "Apparently the idea of marriage to me is ridiculous so not very well" I replied rolling my eyes and jumping back into the passenger's seat next to Jen, "You do remember I'm gay right?" Katie asked sliding into the seat next to Will stealing the sunglasses off his face and placing them on her own.

 "Yeah, but still, I mean am I that bad?" I replied lurching slightly when Jen slammed down the accelerator and pulled us back out onto the open road, "No, if I was straight then I would maybe ..." Katie replied looking me up and down "Oh come on!" I shouted to the enjoyment of everyone in the car who burst out laughing with joy.

 In such a short time I'd gone from homeless with no friends and surviving day to day however I could, to surrounded by three friends who I considered more as family and given not only a home back at the academy but a purpose. I was a Protector, born to defend the world and I would fight till my dying breath to do it, for all those who lost their lives who I held so close, for my parents, for my grandmother, for ... Cassie, the pain of thinking of her was still beyond intense, the vision I'd been granted had helped but any mention of her name made my heart physically ache from the grief.

"This can't be good" I mumbled when we finally parked up on the Las Vegas strip, (I don't know if any of you reading this has ever been to Vegas but I'm sure you know that what I'm about to tell you next isn't normal).
 Vegas was empty ... and I mean empty, the only sound in the entire city was the desert wind blowing through the streets and the gentle lapping of the water where the fountains should be dancing but instead had apparently disappeared with every soul in the city ... Vegas was a Ghost town.

"It's the Haze, look" Jen said pointing to an electric warning sign reading "*Gas leak, all residents must remain indoors until further notice*". Apparently, the Haze, the thing that kept mortals from coming too close to danger from the supernatural world had told every mortal in the city to run and hide lest a stray cigarette blow the Las Vegas strip to smithereens, because of course the alternative of the Gates of Hell opening and hundreds of demons pouring onto the earth was so much better (Yes, that was sarcasm).

"Let's find the Gates before anyone asks why we're out here" Jen mumbled, I took the compass from my pocket and opened the case revealing the spinning needle constantly turning in a fast speed circle like a centrifuge. Suddenly, the compass stopped spinning and pointed due North "I guess we just follow this?" I questioned following the compass instruction, "Here's hoping it's in the city" Will replied walking alongside me, the compass leading our path.

After another hour of walking in circles following the compass directions we found our way into Caesars palace, apparently the message of the gas leak hadn't spread to the mortals in this casino who were betting every last dime of their hard earned wages on slot machines, blackjack, poker and every other game that you can possibly imagine.

"The entrance must be somewhere in here" I shouted over the roar of the casino machines "Let's try and remain indiscreet so we don't attract the guards attention, that means you Will" Jen ordered turning on the spot to face Will who had vanished into thin air "Will? … Will?" I asked spinning in a circle searching frantically for my best friend and brother,

"Of course" I added rolling my eyes when I finally found him.

Will, the ever charming 16 year old that he is, was currently stood leaning against a post flirting with an attractive cocktail waitress ten years older than him dressed in a white toga that clung to her hourglass physique stopping just before her knees with golden bracelets on her wrists, she was wearing the classic roman soldier sandals and had her blonde hair braided in a plat that ran down the back of her neck down to her cleavage and the rest of her hair pulled into a bun, she was smiling at Will and laughing at his awful jokes and pick-up lines.

"I've got this" Jen spoke slowly walking over to Will faking anger turning her cheeks blood red storming over to Will like a bull, "WILLIAM! HOW COULD YOU?!" Jen shouted pulling Will to face her and slapping him incredibly hard across the cheek.

"Jen what the …?"

"Who are you?" the waitress asked,

"I'm his girlfriend!" Jen shouted, I tried my best not to burst into laughter as the incredibly embarrassed waitress ran away from the scene.

Will and Jen walked back over to us, Will rubbing his cheek and Jen laughing like a hyena at Will's predicament. "What was that for?" Will questioned pulling his hand away from his red cheek that had a Jen shaped handprint left on it, "Next time don't wander off on mission or I'll put you on a leash" Jen replied "Kinky, I like it" Will joked back resulting in a smack to the back of his head from Katie "OW!" Will shouted chuckling and rubbing the sore spot from the smack.

We wandered through the casino dodging any security guards who happened to glance our way whenever the haze dropped slightly revealing our true age to the guards, "The compass is going crazy" I mumbled looking at the needle which was now spinning around incredibly fast unable to decide on a direction. "The entrance must be somewhere around here" Jen added glancing at the space around us, the only thing nearby were slot machines that were "OUT OF ORDER" and yellow tape cutting off the section "You don't think" I spoke spotting a lone slot machine stood in the corner all by itself.

The machine look different to every slot machine we had seen in the casino so far, it seemed ... older, the entire machine was covered in a thick layer of dust and was labelled as "*The Devil's dealer*" in bright neon letters but the thing that truly caught my eye was a square slot positioned in the middle of the sign, a space of an ideal fit for the compass. I looked over at Will, Jen and Katie who all nodded at me in confirmation to go for it and I slowly and cautiously placed the compass into slot.
For a short while nothing happened and then suddenly the machine burst to life, the lights glowed bright for the first time in what seemed to be decades, the machine let out a low sound of evil laughter and continued to glow "Maybe" I thought pulling the slot level downwards, the dials began to spin stopping one by one on a small picture of a cartoon devil face and a loud hiss sounded from the back of the machine.

I walked around the side of the machine and grabbed the small slot that had appeared at the back of the machine pulling with every ounce of my strength, Will and Jen also grabbed the large slot machine as well and helped me pull back the machine revealing a tunnel leading down into darkness, the low howl of screams sounded from the tunnel and a cold chill passed through our very bones, I looked over at my friends and then turned back to the tunnel of doom "Only one way to go" I replied grabbing Dante's compass from the slot space, taking the lead to be the first one to begin the descent down the staircase.

## Chapter 47
## Welcome to the Pearly gates (Wait … wrong direction, sorry)

"Seriously, how far down does this thing go?" Will asked through the darkness his voice echoing off the walls and down the infinite path. It feels like we've been walking for hours or has it been days? months? I honestly don't know any more as we continue our descent. The darkness is excruciating as though the very air from your lungs is being ripped out of your body, our only source of light is the occasional candle placed upon the top of a skull, there's only enough room for us to go single file one behind the other reducing our chance of fighting as a group.
 The halls seem to shift and move with each step at some point I'm walking with my back flat against one side of the wall and my stomach pressed tight against the other barely squeezing through, Katie has panic attacks every time we slip through a small gap that she's going to get stuck halfway through (Katie is severely claustrophobic) only for us to find ourselves in another winding, never ending tunnel.

"Check the compass again" Jen asked me, I removed Dante's compass from my pocket and flipped open the case but nothing happened, the needle sits motionless pointing north when I turn like a normal compass would. "Show me the Gates" I command but the compass just sits there in my hand staring back at me, we push through another small gap and stop to gauge our next path … except there isn't one.

The room we're in is completely sealed off, there are seven walls all facing each other the only way out is the gap we've just come through. "This can't be right" I mumble slapping Dante's compass against the flat of my palm, "Where are the Gates?" Will asks placing his hands on the wall searching for secret buttons or compartments but nothing happens "This can't be it" Katie moans checking for any paintings or signs that we may have missed.

"Maybe we missed a turn, let's head back and try again" Jen spoke, we reluctantly agreed since there was no other option only to find ourselves with another problem … the gap was gone … we're completely sealed in … no way in, no way out. "Where did the entrance go?" Jen added pressing her hands up against the wall like Will had been doing but nothing, happens the gap is gone and we're stuck.

I was starting to panic now as well and Katie was stood in a corner of the room hyperventilating and clutching her body trying to ease her shaking nerves, "Did I do something wrong? What have I done? Now all my friends and myself are going to die in this room because I couldn't follow a damn compass!" I thought to myself clenching the compass so tight in my hand that I fear it may crack. "Okay Parker, think, you've been in stickier situations before" I mumbled slowing down every breath that left my lungs tuning out all other sounds around me, the only sound I can hear is the beating of my heart and the air leaving my lungs, my friends are still searching the seven-sided room for … "Wait … Seven sides" I whisper as my brain begins to connect the dots.

I remember one of the first things that was taught to me when I arrived at the academy, Seven is a Sacred number amongst all the known universe. There are Seven deadly sins, Seven angels in the book of Revelation for the apocalypse, the world was created in Seven days and we're stuck in a seven-sided room, "This can't be a coincidence" I spoke out loud finally standing in the centre of the room and staring at each wall.

"What are you thinking?" Jen questioned joining me at my side, "A seven-sided room that's supposed to be on the way to the Gates of Hell, surely there must be something we're not seeing, did we check every wall for any slot openings or anything?" I asked watching Will and Katie who had also turned to face me now, "Nothing, they're just walls" Will replied slamming his hand against one of the tough stone walls.

I stood deep in thought trying to get my brain to put the pieces together "Jason … the floor" I heard a voice whisper in my head, "Great now I'm hearing voices" I thought to myself shaking my head from left to right, "The floor, Jason … looks underneath you" the voice whispered again into my ear and when I looked down I realise maybe I'm not going crazy after all.

There are four slots in a circular shape in the dead centre of the room each the precise shape for a piece of Dante's compass, a small tall diamond shaped hole matches the shape of the needle, a large circular shape matches the Faceplate, a small square shape matches the magnet from the compass and a larger space matches the shape for the compass case.

"Well, I'll be damned" I mumble tearing the compass apart piece by piece "Jason what are you …?" Jen mumbled before I placed the needle into the slot on the floor. The space where the needle slotted began to glow on contact and locked tight on the needle securing it in place and I knew that I couldn't move it now even if I tried, "Please let this work" I whispered placing the Faceplate into the appropriate slot like a two-year-olds wooden game (You know the one I mean).

Each slot piece glowed and locked with each piece that I placed into it, "One more" I spoke placing the compass case into the last slot and closing the lid. A large clunk sounded when the compass case secured itself in the hole and the whole room began to shake, "Oh that can't be good" Will spoke grabbing onto my shoulder trying to steady himself.

The whole room started shaking violently like an earthquake and we held onto each other hoping that the roof wasn't going to collapse down on top of us, the pieces of Dante's compass slowly began to descend into the floor underneath the stone and then a large orange flame symbol burned itself into the ground in the middle of the septagon shape of flames.

A final rumble sounded as the floor cracked, each corner connected to the other with a line spread across the expanse and the room finally stopped shaking, "Is that it?" I asked and then the shaking continued slower this time, the floor underneath us began to separate at the cracks in the floor peeling apart slowly.
 "It's opening! This must be the way!" I shouted ready to see a staircase that would lead us down, the only issue with the plan … that there isn't a staircase, the pieces are slowly separated revealing a large hole that descended into total darkness. We perched on our toes pressed tight against each other on the last bit of stone left to stand on as the floor slowly retracted itself back into the wall "I really wish I'd stayed in the casino" Will mumbled as the remaining foot space for us disappeared and we plunged into the hole.

After a lot of girlish screaming some from Katie and Jen but mostly Will (Okay yes, and me too) we land with a heavy 'Thud' into the earth, I looked back up to see how far we'd fell but all I could see is the rocky roof with multiple stalactites pointing down at us. I clenched my hand and felt the earth beneath us slowly running through my fingers, "Is this?" I mumbled picking up a loose handful of sand.
The sand was blood red and covered the entire area around us like a vast desert, dunes raised high up above us and black rocks protruded from the earth around us like teeth, "Where are we?" Jen mumbled slowly standing up and rubbing the back of her head at the base of the skull, "I think … it's safe to say that we're in the right place" Katie replied pointing behind us and my jaw almost hit the floor.

About two mile ahead of us were the two gigantic black gates from my nightmares. The gates connected to a large rock wall on one side and then to the rock wall on the other, an impenetrable barrier that no being could escape from, razor sharp spikes sat on the top of the Gates like arrows preventing anyone or anything from climbing over, in front of the Gates were the seven braziers from my dreams six of them glowing with bright green flames and the sound of screaming and screeching could be heard coming from the opposite side "We're here" I spoke slowly pushing myself to a standing position.

## Chapter 49
## How to close a Gate

The Gates of Hell were a truly terrifying and awe-inspiring place, I'd been introduced to the meaning of being a Protector pretty quickly leaving little time to fully accumulate to the environment and the change from living on the streets spending every day fighting for my life, to living on the Academy ground's and fighting every day for my life and everyone around me (Yeah, my life doesn't change much).
"Alright, how do we do this? Do we just wait for the Gates to start to open and then lock them shut or put some rope around the handles?" I asked walking with my friends across the sandy dunes towards the Gates.

The desert seemed to be never ending as though each step we took brought us no closer to the gates themselves. Each push of my body weight onto my foot with each step caused my muscles to tighten and scream in protest to the vicious climb over the sand dune, at one point I nearly slipped and slid all the way back down to the bottom but luckily Jen caught me and pulled me back upright before I could drop, "Thanks" I mumbled leaning on Jen for support "Any time" Jen replied leading the way towards the gates.

"The Gates of Hell haven't been approached for over 700 years at least by anyone who found them and made it back alive anyway" Jen replied wiping the sweat from her brow. "The rumour was that Dante Alighieri upon finding the Gates of Hell, travelled throughout the nine circles with the help of the compass he'd crafted, when he found his way back out he sealed the Gates with a binding spell from the outside so that no armies of demons could follow him out, but in order for it to work then the Gates need to be open" Jen added pausing with the rest of us to catch our breath.

The Gates were only a mile away at least, a large and imposing Sand dune in front of us raising up into the air hid the base of Gates from us which made me feel like we were staring at Mount Everest. "But if the Gates are open won't all the demons just pour out?" I asked stretching the muscles in my shoulder blades, "The Gates will open slowly, only a few demons will manage to squeeze through and attack, if you guys can distract them long enough then I can use the binding spell to seal the Gates again" Jen replied taking the lead in climbing the colossal sand dune in front of us.

"Simple enough, kill any demons that come through the gap, shut the Gates, return home and dance the night away" I joked trying to break the tension between us, truthfully, I had a strong feeling in my gut of horror and fear, I'd already lost Cassie to this damned mission and now my battle senses were telling me that someone wouldn't be coming back to the academy with us but I wouldn't lose anyone else, if the time came for someone to sacrifice themselves … then I would be the one to do it.

As we neared the top, Jen and Will who were taking the lead suddenly paused in shock before spinning back around tackling me and Katie slamming us into the ground, "What the hell?" I asked Jen who was lying prone of top of me before slapping her palm across my lips. "Don't say anything … we're not alone" Jen replied pointing behind her subtly, my senses were in overdrive when we crawled on our bellies up the sand dune to the crest peering over the edge "Damn it" I whispered at the sight in front of us.

There were easily a Hundred demons and beasts waiting outside of the Gates engaging in idle chatter, roasting some sort of creature over a spit tearing the meat from its bones as it spun, a few were practising sparring with their demonic blades ready for the upcoming battle. "This is bad" Jen mumbled her iris turning yellow and pupils expanding and shrinking like an owl as she scanned the field ahead of us, "No kidding" I replied feeling the power flow through my vision enhancing it like Jen, I stared ahead of us at the Gates waiting patiently to open.
I knew that there was no way we would be able to reach the Gates and stand ready to close them without the army of demons spotting us which meant we had only one option, fight and pray that the odds were in our favour despite being outnumbered massively, "I've got an idea" Jen whispered pointing to a large black rock about 20 feet away from her, "I'll stand up there and fire down at the demons to cause a distraction" Jen spoke reaching for her hairpin.

"Okay and we'll go down and fight them on the battlefield, if we can cut enough of them down then maybe we can keep the rest of them distracted while you close the Gate" I replied fixing my far seeing gaze on the demon army searching for the weak link in the chain. "There" I pointed to six demons sat in a circle, three of them had their backs to us reclining by a fire, the demons were massive and easily the largest of the army which meant one thing.
 "If we take down the big ones first then the rest will be so stunned we can sweep through them like a wave" I whispered looking at Katie and Will for confirmation, "We've got your back brother" Will replied "To the Gates of Hell and back" Katie added placing her hand on my shoulder "Let's do this" I replied nodding to Jen who slowly and stealthily snuck her way over to her perch.

Katie, Will and myself rolled ourselves over the crest and slid down to the bottom of the dune until we were down on the flat surface leading to the gates, the sandy landscape had turned to solid cracked ground like the open plains of Death Valley near Vegas. "Move slowly" I whispered walking forwards slowly placing the heel of my foot onto the ground rolling the flat of my foot until my toes touched the floor and repeating the process with the other making each step almost silent.

Katie and Will were on either side of a demon now ready to bring their weapons to life and I was stood behind the third, its hairy back hiding me from the others and the horrendous stench emanating from him that burned my nostrils made me want to vomit right then and there.

I looked up at the Jen's perch to see her stood proud and strong in an archer's stance three arrows on the drawstring aiming for the three demons opposite me, Jen was the greatest shot in the entire academy and there was no doubt in my mind that her arrows would strike true and precise. I raised my left hand with three fingers so my friends could see and counted down lowering a finger at a time, on one I brought Divine Fury to life and drove it through the demons back.

The demon let out a howl of rage the blade protruding out of its chest before it burst into ash leaving me facing the three other demons who were staring at me in shock, Will and Katie brought their weapons to life and killed their demons, "Protectors!" one of the three demons shouted with a loud roar to the rest of the army.

"Smile and wait for the flash" I joked, the demons looked at me in confusion right before an arrow each lodged into their foreheads and they burst into ash the shocked expressions never leaving their face.

Jen was stood on the rocky outcrop smiling down at us with pride drawing another arrow into her bow, the rest of the demon army had stopped their activities now and were stood facing us with rage and fear in their eyes at our sudden appearance. "Okay ... who's next?" I asked spinning Divine Fury in my hand charging at the first demon who moved with Will and Katie at my side.

# Chapter 49
## The Battle

The battle erupted so fast that I barely had time to blink as we cut our way through the army, Jen stood on her perch firing arrow after arrow down at the army striking each demon with precision sending them back into the pits of hell before moving onto the next target. Katie danced through her attack's sliding on one knee stabbing demons in the thigh before driving the other dagger into the base of its skull or slashing the dagger across it's throat sending black blood spraying across the battlefield and rushing through the ash to fight her next target.

Will had made his own kill circle spinning with the grace of a ballerina (Feel free to tell Will that I said that) slicing any demon that was unfortunate enough to reach him, each demonic blade swing that came too close found itself either blocked by Tenebris or hitting empty air when Will dodged under the strike.

My Hunter instincts were the only thing keeping me alive as the demons began to encircle me fully, I'd lost count how many we'd cut down so far "Twenty? Ten? Thirty?" I thought right before bringing my wings to life from my back and using them to sweep the feet from an approaching demon tripping him over before driving my blade through his heart and moving onto the next one.

"Jason!" I heard Katie shout to my left, she was completely surrounded on all ends letting out the odd burst of heavenly light to keep the demons at bay, "WILL! THIS WAY!" I shouted cutting my way through the crowd towards Katie, Will enveloped himself into the shadows and appeared at Katie's side standing back-to-back with Katie forming the perfect kill circle, I jumped into the fray each of us circling the demons that surrounded us.

Jen was still perched on the rock but the demons had drawn closer to her now too causing her to constantly switch from using her bow as a weapon to fire arrows and using it as a staff to bat away any approaching demons.

We were completely surrounded and beyond screwed, there was easily at least another fifty demons left and we were spent, every ounce of our energy had been used in the battle leaving us gasping for breath with sweat pouring down our brows and backs. Black blood ran down my face and body from each demon I had killed and my adrenaline fuelled body struggled to allow my brain to function once again.

"Game over, Protectors" A large demon growled slamming his large demonic obsidian club against the palm of his hand, I looked over at Jen who had pressed her palm against the rock surface shifting the earth underneath her to form a tall column elevating her another twenty feet above the demons but with little space to freely move around. The demons below her had begun to scramble up the column their nails digging into the stone leaving large scratch marks behind with each scramble.

"Any ideas?" I asked Katie looking at her out of the corner of my eye, "I'm stumped, Will?" Katie replied glancing over at Will "Nope sorry" Will spoke jabbing at a demon who was too eager to finish his kill finding himself instead turned to a smouldering pile of ash, in that moment I knew what I had to do to end this and keep my friends safe.

"Katie, Will, when I give the instruction use your wings and take flight away from here, grab Jen and find another place to stand your ground" I whispered grasping Divine Fury even tighter turning my knuckles white as a ghost.

"But you can't fly, how are you going to escape?" Katie asked me but one look from the corner of my eye told her all she needed to know, "That's not happening! We're not leaving you behind" Katie argued slightly above a whisper the sound of the demon's growl drowning her out, "I know you won't ... which is why I'm not giving you a choice" I replied drawing in the last of my strength and remembering a spell I had seen in my first magic lesson in what seemed like years ago *"LEVARE"* I shouted slamming my palm into the dirt between Katie and Will.

A loud blast of air and the shifting of the earth sent Will and Katie launching away from me towards Jen like a rocket screaming my name and spreading their wings to stop them from crashing back down to the earth leaving them hovering a few feet off the ground. "That was a dumb move Half breed, now you're going to die all alone" the Demon with the club growled edging towards me "Yeah" I replied my left arm hidden behind my back ... "But I'm taking as many of you sons of bitches with me as I can" I added. I drew onto my last remaining bit of power deep in my soul, *"IGNIS"* I commanded bringing a ball of fire into my hand shifting it until it formed a second blade leaving my skin charred slightly but the adrenaline in my veins kept the pain hidden from me.

I ducked to the right as the demon brought his club down towards me missing the heavy instrument by inches before driving my flaming sword into the demons' leg and using the strength in my legs to propel me upwards before separating the demons head from his shoulders, the giant demon detonated into ash leaving his followers looking at me in confusion before attacking.

The rest of the battle seemed to go by in a flash as I slashed and stabbed aiming to take as many down with me as I could, but using so much magic was starting to get to me. I could feel the adrenaline leaving my body until I felt like I might pass out, my vision started to blur and my ears rang while I tried to remain conscious on the battlefield.
A blow to my left from a demon's shoulder barge sent me sprawling across the terrain leaving me lying flat on my back staring up at the dark ceiling.

I knew that this was it, after all I'd been through this would be how I died, flat on my back at the Gates of Hell surrounded by demons, my friends about fifty feet away from me shouting my name begging me to "GET UP!" but my strength was gone. I couldn't force myself back up even if I tried, the demons stood over me now fighting over which one would get to kill me first, "You fought well Half Breed but now … I'm sending you onto the next life" a demon growled raising an axe over his head.

The afterlife, my final rest, I would be in the Realm of Protectors for all eternity surrounded by my fellow warriors from ages past, maybe my grandmother was up there waiting for me to welcome me with open arms, my parents beaming with pride, Cassie might be there too she'd died a free woman and by my side so why shouldn't she.
I could see her Scarlett hair dancing in the light beckoning me to chase her through the fields of rare flowers her laughter filling the air warming my heart, our bare feet pressing into the soft grass as I chased her across the fields, I could see her white summer dress that ended at her knee's billowing in the breeze her hand wrapped around mine leading me further into the field "I'm coming Cass" I mumbled closing my eyes and waiting for the end.

I could sense the axe lowering towards my neck and my friends screaming my name, Jen could drop him with an arrow if she had the chance to aim but even if she did the momentum of the axe would still separate my head from my shoulders. This was it and I was ready to go in peace … but the end didn't come.
The only sound I heard was the sound of steel hitting steel "What the …?" the demon mumbled before screaming and bursting into ash.

I thought that Jen had managed to fire off a shot at the last second but if that was the case then how come the axe hadn't met my neck, I slowly opened my eyes to see a bright glow beckoning down at me "Am I dead?" I mumbled believing that this was the afterlife come to collect me. "Not yet kid, Now get up, we've got a war to win" the voice commanded lowering a hand and raising me up, the man stood before me almost made my jaw drop to the ground.

His hair was neat and styled perfectly to the right not a single hair out of place, he was dressed in a long white robe a suit of leather armour placed over it like an ancient warrior. A bright glow surrounded his entire body illuminating his already shining skin and his blue eyes glistened like the summer sky, but the thing that truly surprised me were the two wings protruding from his back "You're an Angel" I mumbled unable to say anything else.

"That I am kid, the names Castiel … now let's kill some demons, shall we?" Castiel asked spinning the Divine steel sword in his hand grinding his sandalled feet into the ground.

## Chapter 50
### I fight alongside an Angel

So far, I'd been surprised many times on this assignment. I'd found out my heritage, I'd been introduced to the academy and told my responsibilities as a Protector for the rest of my life, been attacked by a Chimera, a Fallen Angel, An Arch-demon, A pack of werewolves and found the Gates of Hell but standing alongside an angel ready for combat took the grand prize.

"What are you doing here? Last time I checked Angel's don't help Protectors" I mumbled standing back-to-back (Wing to wing?) with Castiel. "Yeah, I know kid, but I was bored and I really don't want the universe to come to an end so I figured I'd join in the battle and help win, if you really want to, we can kill each other later, okay?" Castiel asked spinning in a circle deciding our best point of attack "Here, drink this, it'll help with the exhaustion" Castiel added passing me a small vial.

For some inexplicable reason I decided to trust Castiel and the fact that if I died right now from the poison that may be in this vial then at least he won't be far behind, I un-popped the cork in the bottle using my teeth and drank down the cool liquid within. My senses went into overdrive and my heart beat with incredible speed at the sour liquid tickling my taste buds, "Holy water" I mumbled grinning at the demons who now looked utterly terrified. "You're welcome ... now what do you say? I go left, you go right?" Castiel replied looking over at his shoulder and winking at me, "Let's do this" I replied driving Divine Fury through the demon closest to my right spinning on my heels and Castiel spinning to his left driving his sword through the demon to his left.

We thought like a finely tuned machine spinning in a perfect circle stabbing and slashing our way through the crowd, any demon that got too close found itself trapped in our tornado of Fury and attacks. Every few moments Castiel would let out a burst of heavenly light and fry a few of the demons who approached, at one moment I leapt backwards and rolled over Castiel's wings stabbing the demon in front of him, I ducked lower to the ground at Castiel's nod and rolled before drove he his sword through an approaching demon (Think, buddy cop action movie and you'll know what I mean).

I glanced over to the rock outcropping where Jen was stood firing arrows out into the army full of the confidence from the beginning of the battle dropping any demons before they were within twenty feet from her, Will and Katie were stood at the bottom of her pillar slaying any demons who got too close to Jen's pillar thinning the crowd with each kill.

"DUCK!" Castiel shouted to me driving his sword towards my head, sensing the movement I ducked under his stab and slid on my knee driving Divine Fury through the demon behind Castiel and he used his sword to separate the demons head from his shoulders behind me, both demons screamed and burst into ash as the battlefield went silent.

The army had been wiped out entirely, not a single demon remained leaving us on a sandy battlefield covered in ash and black demon blood, "Thanks for the backup" I spoke smoothing my hair ignoring the disgusting black blood was stuck there. "Glad to have joined in on the fun, just to be sure we're not going to kill each other, right? Because I really don't want to have to fight you and your friends too" Castiel replied holding his hands upright in surrender as Jen, Will and Katie ran up towards us.

"Like you said, if we need to … we can kill each other later" I replied stumbling when Jen grabbed me in a tight hug "Thought we'd lost you there for a second" Jen mumbled breaking the hug that had begun to feel awkward before softly punching me in the shoulder playfully.

Katie stood in front of me now and smiled … right before slapping me across the cheek as hard as she could, "OW!" I shouted rubbing the slowly growing large red hand print on my cheek "If you ever do anything that stupid again, I'll kill you myself" Katie spoke crossing her arms looking at Castiel behind me.

"I like her" Castiel added nodding his head at Katie, "Right, sorry, Katie, Jen, Will this is Castiel, Castiel these are my friends" I replied gesturing in that awkward motion you make when you're introducing strangers to each other.

"An actual angel … awesome" Will spoke first spawning a victory cigar between his teeth chewing on the end of it. "Why are you here?" Jen asked coldly crossing her arms "To help, that's all, now let's figure out a way to build a kill zone before …" Castiel replied stopping abruptly when a loud horn pierced the air.

We all turned and stared as the last Brazier lit and the Gates began to slowly creek open, "Damn" I mumbled watching as the large Gates slowly separated an inch at a time, the planets had aligned and the Gates had opened with the setting sun back on the surface, an army of demons ten times the size we'd fought a few moments ago were waiting ready to begin their destruction on the mortal realm.

"Oh hell" Will spoke spitting the cigar from his mouth shuffling nervously preparing for another battle. "Hello, Protectors" a voice called out from the entrance to the Gate, a voice I'd heard only in my nightmares, darkness enveloped the gate as a figure slowly walked through the small gap the black tendrils of darkness stabbing the ground around him, the temperature seemed to drop by a hundred degrees and his cold red eyes examined each of us one by one. Slowly the shadows closed in on him revealing what appeared to be an ordinary man in his early 30's with Jet black hair slicked backwards like a 60's greaser, he was dressed in a sharp black suit with a black shirt and red tie giving him the appearance of an old school mafia boss but the same wave of cold and misery still emanated from him.

"Welcome to Hell" Galadriel spoke opening his arms outwards in welcome as the crowd behind him roared.

## Chapter 51
## Protectors vs. Galadriel

I'd been seeing this vision of Galadriel every time I closed my eyes ever since that first dream when I'd seen him stood proud behind the Gates of Hell and the second vision when he was sat on his throne kicking a demon to death, but now that I was stood actually in front of him ... I was shaking from head to toe.

My soul felt as though someone had placed a ten-thousand-pound weight on my chest while trying to suck it out of my body with a straw (Weird explanation but the best one I have), his cold red eyes burned into my very soul and made me shiver, I looked at Will, Jen and Katie for support but even they seemed as terrified as I was.

The Gates ahead of us were still opening slowly allowing the odd demon to squeeze through one at a time and place himself behind their loyal commander. "If we don't shut the Gates soon it will be too late" Jen whispered into my ear, "Agreed ... I've got an idea" I whispered back walking ahead and standing my ground in between Galadriel, my friends and Castiel.

"Galadriel I'm presuming? I'm guessing it's you ever since you decided to pop into my mind" I spoke sarcastically placing one hand behind my back, "You must be Jason, I've heard many a tale of you from my loyal subjects, slaying Samuel Blake ... an impressive accomplishment to say the least" Galadriel replied. I signalled in American sign language (I learned it when I was twelve in Boston from a deaf homeless guy who was short with strange pointy ears?) with the hand behind my back to signal for Jen to go left to cast her binding spell, I heard the crunch of sand and hoped that Jen had understood me.

I couldn't turn around because then Galadriel would see my plan unfolding. "Well, Blake was a challenge but driving my sword through his heart sure felt good" I replied edging slowly towards Galadriel praying and hoping that the gate's would close soon when Jen cast her spell.

"Yes, well, I'm afraid that he will be the last Arch-demon you kill" Galadriel replied the shadows emanating around him covering him in a veil of darkness once more, "Sorry, Galadriel but I didn't come all this way just to let the gates open and for this world to come to an end, so I guess I'll be adding one more Arch-demon to my list" I replied glancing over at the Gate which had now opened enough for four demons at a time to squeeze through, over fifty demons now stood behind Galadriel of various sizes.

"And how do you plan on doing that when the Gates are already opening? There's only you out on this battlefield and your three friends and that angel back there" Galadriel mocked spawning a large demonic obsidian blade into his right and left hand duel wielding them both, I smiled my wicked grin and outstretched my wings in a display of power like a proud peacock (Damn it, I can hear you laughing).
"Simple my demon friend, because you made one fatal mistake" I replied spinning Divine Fury in my hand,
"And what is that?"
"You said you counted three of my friends behind me … but there's only two" I replied, Galadriel looked over my shoulder and his jaw dropped in shock.

I dared to look over and smiled at the sight of Katie, Will and Castiel stood grinding their feet into the ground ready for battle with their wings unfurled ready to launch themselves forward like a rocket, "NOW JEN!" I shouted looking over to my left where Jen was stood with a protective shield around her. "*RESTRINGO*!" Jen shouted sending out two white tendrils from her fingertips, the tendrils latched themselves onto the two Gates and slowly began to draw them back to closing position, "NOOO!!" Galadriel shouted sending a fireball towards Jen which crashed against her shield and disappeared in a puff of smoke.

"Sorry Galadriel but never underestimate the will of a Protector" I spoke launching myself forwards at Galadriel when his guard was down, at the last second Galadriel moved back slightly leaving only slash a small blade strike across Galadriel's chest.
 "That was foolish" Galadriel grunted placing his palm against the black blood slowly oozing from the wound, "Then it's a good thing I'm the king of fools" I replied launching back towards Galadriel locking blades with him.

I could only glance over as I duelled with Galadriel, Will and Castiel were fighting in the middle of the demon army cutting them down as fast as they could, I spotted Katie stood guarding Jen and cutting down any demons who tried to break their way through her shield.
"Looks like it's just you and me Galadriel" I spoke dodging a dual blade strike from Galadriel feeling the cold steel brush against my skin almost breaking through, "I'LL KILL YOU WHERE YOU STAND HALF BREED!" Galadriel screamed attacking with utter fury leaving his guard down and allowing me to deliver another slash blow to the back of his thigh, Galadriel howled in agony and used the shadows to pull himself ten feet away.

I looked over Galadriel's shoulder to the gates which were now almost closed completely allowing the odd one or two demons to squeeze through but I could also see the pain on Jen's face from the pressure of using so much magic in one time span after a big battle. The shield that was guarding her had begun to fade and flicker and I knew that soon it would collapse completely leaving her vulnerable to any attack, if the shield dropped and she had to stop the binding spell then the Gates would reopen and we'd be back at square one.

"If I can kill Galadriel now then the rest of the army should be easy" I thought charging towards Galadriel with Divine Fury raised high. "Enough of this!" Galadriel shouted spreading two demonic scaled wings from his back and flapped them both, I was launched backwards rolling from the blast of the wind until I came to a stop when I hit a large black rock with a heavy Thud, "You may be powerful Half Breed but this battle must end, the Commander told me about your lack of the ability to fly, so I'm taking this battle to the air" Galadriel announced launching himself upwards at least fifty feet from the sandy surface.

"Commander?" I wondered hearing that same title yet again, "JASON!" Katie shouted surrounded by at least ten demons and then I saw why she had shouted for me, Jen's shield was gone and Katie was struggling to hold them back, I pumped my wings flapped them occasionally to launch myself forwards. "*COMPADIRE*!" I shouted stretching out my arm sliding across the dirt, a large orange shield appeared in front of Jen as I slid behind her and stood upright and Katie jumped into the shield with us. I used my willpower and magic to bring the shield around us all forming a protective bubble that kept the demon army at bay.

The sweat was pouring down my brow and my breathing became heavier from the intense pressure of the massive battle, already the shield was beginning to weaken and Jen's tendrils from her binding spell had begun to lose their grip on the gates, Will and Castiel backed up from the army until they were stood against the shield doing their best to keep the army at bay.
 "If we don't do something soon, the gates will open again" Castiel shouted over the battle cutting down a demon in front of him, "I can't hold it much longer" Jen mumbled through gritted teeth, one of her eyes was completely bloodshot from a capillary burst from the intense pressure and her nose was slowly bleeding her blue blood running across her lips.

"Castiel" I spoke grabbing his attention "Can you take my place and bring up a shield around you all?" I added, "Yes but why?" Castiel replied kicking back a large demon in his chest using his wings to launch him up a few feet spinning around and separating the demons head from its shoulder. "I'm going to run past the army and push the Gates closed" I explained planning my route through the army, "But you can't push the Gates closed, you'd have to be on the other side and then you'd be stuck" Katie mumbled resting on my shoulder gasping for breath from the battle.

I took one look at Katie without saying a word conveying all my emotions into my stare, Katie studied me for a moment and seemed to read my mind "No ... Jason, you can't do this!" Katie said taking a step back from me "I have to" I replied nodding over at Castiel and lowering the shield.
 Castiel sensing the danger jumped in between Katie and Jen creating a glowing white energy bubble around them, "I love you guys and it was an honour serving alongside you" I mumbled nodding at all my friends inside the bubble and turned to face Will "I love you too man ... which is why I'm doing this" Will replied, before I had a chance to react Will punched me in my nose and grabbed me by my collar using the momentum and my own weight to throw me towards the energy bubble, Castiel dropped the shield just long enough for me to land inside before closing it again.

"Will ... WHAT ARE YOU DOING?!" I shouted wiping away the small amount of blue blood dripping from my nostril, "You've sacrificed enough on this mission, your entire life has been a struggle and full of sacrifices, now it's my turn" Will replied using his wings to launch him five feet off the ground and out of the demons' reach. "WILL ... NO!" I screamed but Will simply smiled and spawned another cigar into his mouth between his teeth, "See you around" Will spoke with the same wicked grin he always had before turning and flying across the battlefield towards the Gate's.

I tried my best to break through the shield screaming at Castiel to "Lower it!" but he refused ignoring my pleas leaving me to watch as Will reached the Gates and jack-knifed through the gap in the Gates. Will winked at us one last time and placed a hand on either side of the Gate fifty foot in the air and pushed with all his strength, "NOOO!!!" both Galadriel and I screamed as the Gate's slammed together.

I could barely breathe from the pain in my heart, Jen had collapsed to the ground panting heavily from the use of her magic almost passing out from exhaustion with tears rolling down her cheeks, Katie had her head placed in her hands weeping heavily at the loss of Will and Castiel was still keeping the shield in place a single glowing tear rolling down his cheek, my best friend … my brother, was trapped in Hell for all eternity left at the mercy of every demon and monster on the other side, I knew in my heart that he was alive but I wondered how long that would last before his luck ran out.

The pain in my heart intensified from the loss I'd faced on this mission and throughout my life, I'd lost Cassie when Blake had shot her, I'd lost Will in battle, my parents had died when I was a child and my grandmother, my only relative and connection to my past had died when I was six before she could tell me about this world, I'd lost foster homes, kind and loving foster parents, so much in sixteen years and all I could feel was pain "Wait" I thought to myself feeling a shift in my body.

I remembered something in that moment that Katie had taught me back at the motel in what seemed like an eternity ago, *"Your angelic abilities are connected to your emotions, find you emotion and your powers will activate"* the words echoed in my mind as I felt the pressure building in the muscles in my wings.
 I closed my mind and meditated slowly feeling the rhythmic beating of my battle ready heart and slowed my breathing finding that deep seated emotion in my very soul.
 Katie used joy to use her angelic abilities, Will used confidence to activate his demonic powers and finally I realised what my emotion was … it was pain.

Some may claim that the most powerful emotion is love, but in that moment, I knew that pain was infinitely more powerful. Pain was connected to grief, anger, hatred, revenge, love and every emotion in between, it was the emotion that could cripple you and if the pain was too much possibly even kill you, pain was the thing that kept us alive, made us who we are and it was my trigger, I slowly opened my eyes feeling the steady beating of my heart connecting to the pain within.

The ground seemed to shift underneath my feet and I felt a warmth path its way through every nerve ending in my mind and body, "Jason?" Katie questioned a confused look on her face, I stared up at Galadriel who was flying high above the ground glaring down at us in anger at his foiled plan. My wings tensed and pulled themselves tight against my back, the sand underneath me shifted and span like a small tornado bringing tiny chunks of rock into the air that floated around me in a steady cyclone.

I looked down at my hands which were now glowing with heavenly light and Divine Fury in the palm of my hand, the divine steel side of my blade was glowing with the same intensity as the rest of my body. "Your abilities" Jen whispered seeing the determination on my face, I simply smiled at Jen and nodded at Castiel who smiled back at me lowering the top of the shield above me, with a strong and heavy flap I beat my wings and launched myself into the sky like a rocket with my wings outstretched.

I was flying, for the first time since I gained my angelic abilities I was flying and I'd never felt freer, I hovered fifty feet in the air occasionally beating my wings to keep me level "It's not possible" Galadriel mumbled a look of shock across his face. "I'm a Protector Galadriel, my life is the impossible ... this is for Will and all the lives you've taken" I spoke pointing Divine Fury directly at his heart ...

 "You should have stayed in Hell" I added propelling myself forwards at Galadriel.

## Chapter 52
## I believe I can fly

I slammed my blade against Galadriel's double blade's sending out a loud deafening shockwave of metal slamming against metal fifty feet up in the air as we battled. For the first time since receiving my abilities I had never felt more fulfilled or powerful, I could understand now why Katie loved flying so much because even now in the midst of a battle for my life and high above a battlefield of demons and the Gates of Hell … I felt free.

I dodged a blade strike from Galadriel and swung my sword leaving a larger gash wound across Galadriel's chest who launched himself backwards a few feet groaning in agony, "Damn you!" Galadriel growled black blood oozing between his fingers after placing his hand against his chest to keep his internal organs in. "The only one damned around here is you Galadriel" I replied spinning Divine Fury in my hand with a wicked grin spread across my face.

I glanced down at the battlefield where Katie and Castiel had grabbed Jen and moved to a higher vantage point to fight off any demons on the ground, they were holding them off well but I needed to come down and give them a hand which meant I needed to get rid of Galadriel and fast.
 "Do you know the old saying for stopping an army?" I asked Galadriel my body pulsating with heavenly light.
 "Enlighten me" Galadriel growled,
"Cut off the head of the snake and the body will die" I replied letting out a burst of heavenly light.

Galadriel covered his eyes and growled in pain the light burning his skin lowering the level of shadows around him, sensing my opportunity I launched myself back at Galadriel at impossible speed over his head and then grabbed him by the back of his collar. With a heavy swing of my sword I drove it down and removed both of Galadriel's wings from his back in one momentum, Galadriel howled in rage and dangled in my grasp, if I dropped him now he'd fall to the desert sand and be finished but staring to my right I had a better idea, I flapped both of my angelic wings heavily and flew towards the Gates of Hell as fast as my wings could take me.

Galadriel kicked and screamed like a child throwing a tantrum until we were hovering high above the top of the Gates, the spikes protruded upwards towards us razor sharp and deadly. I spun Galadriel round and wrapped one of my hands tight around his throat squeezing it tight, I pulled Galadriel in close and smiled at the fearful luck in his eyes "Galadriel" I whispered "Go to Hell" I added loosening my grip on Galadriel's throat.

Galadriel seemed to freeze mid-air in terror like a cartoon before he plummeted down towards the Gate screaming in rage and terror. I watched smiling as the distance closed in and Galadriel slammed onto of one of the spikes on top of the Gates spearing him through his chest, Galadriel placed his hands on the wound and stared up at me in shock before bursting into ash his essence scattered across the Gates, his army once proud and strong looked up at their fallen boss and his destroyer floating high above the Gates with a smile on my face at the look of terror in their eyes.

The army was still vast in number but their confidence had dropped at Galadriel's defeat so sensing my moment I flew back down and landed next to Castiel, Jen and Katie "Jen cover your eyes!" I shouted, Jen looked at me and nodded her head covering her face in the crook of her elbow. "Ready guys?" I asked standing by Castiel and Katie "Let's shine" Katie replied with a nod grasping a tight hold of my right hand sharing our strength, "Once more unto the breach" Castiel added grabbing a tight hold of my left hand and sharing his strength with me.

I stared down one demon who had stopped mid-attack at our expression "Uh-oh" the demon mumbled as I flooded the emotional power of pain throughout my body and pushed every inch of heavenly light within me out of every pore on my body, Katie flooded her system and released her heavenly light and Castiel did the same resulting in an atom bomb level shockwave carrying itself across the battlefield vaporizing any demon in its path. I watched as the demons one by one burst into ash a few trying to run back to the Gates and back into their pits in hell but it was too late, the Gates were closed and there was no way out, the last bit of heavenly light hit any remaining demons by the Gate turning their bodies to ash and slamming into the Gates.

"Nice job" I mumbled to Katie drawing my heavenly light back into my body, "Thanks, not too bad yourself" Katie replied with a smile before her eyes rolled into the back of her head and she fell backwards, I caught her moments before she hit the ground and lowered her down gently onto the ground.
Katie was absolutely exhausted from the battle and was slowly snoring from the strength she had used, I looked over at Jen who smiled at our victory and laid down backwards before passing out in sleep as well from the relief.

"Thank you Castiel" I mumbled my eyelids feeling like ten-ton weights my body screaming at me to rest, I collapsed down onto my butt and clenched my knees together struggling for breath "Any time Kid, good work, do you need to rest?" Castiel asked me lowering himself down onto one knee and looking me in the eye "Maybe … just, five minutes" I replied collapsing onto my back. My wings redrew back into my body and I laid staring up at the black stalactite ceiling every ounce of energy in body completely spent, "Rest up kid, don't worry … I'll get you all somewhere safe" Castiel whispered softly as my eyes shut and I drifted off into slumber.

# Chapter 53
## Rise and Shine

The sound of the city coming to life slowly rose me from my slumber and forced me to open my sandbag heavy eyelids. The sun beaming through the windows was excruciating, "Wait … the sun?" I thought to myself sitting bolt upright my head throbbing from the pain, I held my hand up in front of my eyes to try and reduce the sun rays while my vision refocused and when it finally did, I was looking out on the Las Vegas strip skyline.

The strip below was alive with traffic, mortals, tourists and shows all throughout the city, the sound of casino's blasting out heavy music and the blaring of car horns in traffic was a totally different sound to what I'd been expecting.

I climbed out of the king size bed I had somehow found myself in and walked over to the window feeling the comfortable rug underneath my bare feet pressing in between the gaps in my toes, I realised that I was currently dressed in a pair of loose-fitting tracksuit bottoms and pressed my hands against the few new scars on my body from stray stab and scratch wounds from the demons' that hadn't healed after the battle. I pressed my fingertips against my Hunter marking on my chest where a new shape had appeared "That's new" I thought to myself running my index finger along the tattoo.

Behind the shield that symbolised my accomplishment in combat magic and the "H" that symbolised me as a Hunter was a small sword hidden behind the shield, the hilt stood proud at the top of the shield and the tip of the blade was protruding from the bottom, "You're awake" a voice spoke from behind me, I spun on the spot ready for battle despite the ringing in my head and noticed Castiel stood in the doorway holding a glass of water.

His appearance of a white robe with leather armour and sandals had shifted into a white shirt and blue jeans with white trainers "New look?" I asked perched on the edge of the bed on shaky legs. "Do you honestly think I walk around in my battle uniform all day? Do you have any idea how uncomfortable it is?" he replied passing me the glass and sitting down alongside me,

"Holy Water?" I questioned

"Just filtered I'm afraid, can't give you too much of the good stuff after all" Castiel replied as I drank the ice-cold liquid feeling the chill run down my throat and hydrate my body, "Thank you" I replied placing the now empty glass onto the bedside table.

"Wait … where is everyone?" I asked my instincts kicking in once my brain function had returned slightly, "They're fine, your friend Jennifer is in the next room sleeping still and your other friend Katie woke up shortly before you did, she's recovering in the room across the hall" Castiel replied placing his hand on my back and gesturing to the door.

"How did we get here? The last thing I remember is passing out in front of the Gates?" I asked breathing a sigh of relief at the comforting thought of knowing my friends were safe.

"After you and your friends fell unconscious I transported you up here, a little manipulation of the Haze was enough to convince the mortals to give you all this room for two days" Castiel replied,

"TWO DAYS?! How long have I been out?"

"About twenty-one hours, checkout is tomorrow at eleven" Castiel replied. I knew that big injuries and battles for Protectors could leave us unconscious for a long time but twenty-one hours was unbelievable, "Thank you Castiel I just wish …" I replied feeling the tugging sensation of grief in my heart.

My mind kept drifting to the thoughts of Will stuck in Hell with no way out constantly running from demons, I knew that he was still alive somewhere he had to be, Will and I were practically brothers and if he was dead then I would know it (Or at least I wanted to believe it).

"Are the Gates still shut?" I asked trying to bring my mind back to reality,

"Yes, your assignment was a success, they should stay shut now for the foreseeable future or at least until the planets align again in another two thousand years"

"That's good, I just wish Will was here to celebrate that with us" I mumbled brushing a tear off my cheek.

"Ah yes, William, do you want to know something truly incredible that we angels can do?" Castiel asked me, I looked back over at him and nodded staring into his kind eyes. "We have the ability to travel between all the realms for wherever we may be needed and if the circumstances are valid … well, we can bring people back with us" Castiel added as the sound of the toilet flushing in the bathroom rang throughout the room.

"Ooohhh boy …" the all too familiar voice spoke "You do not want to go in there" Will added standing in the doorway in his usual gear reattaching his belt stood with a cigar between his teeth, "WILL!" I screamed running over to my friend and embracing him in a tight brotherly hug.

"You're alive!" I mumbled stunned hugging my best friend, my brother who I thought I would never see again feeling the tears run down my cheeks, "You didn't think you'd get rid of me that easily did you" Will joked patting me on the back and laughing in joy, I broke the hug and placed both my hands on his shoulder, I smiled up at him and then punched him as hard as I could with what little strength I had.

"OW! What was that for?" Will questioned rubbing his arm where I had punched him "Next time you plan on doing something that incredibly stupid, let me try first" I replied before bursting into laughter and hugging him again.

"Will … is that you?" I heard Katie ask, I stood smiling still as I turned to face her, Katie was dressed in a white tank top with grey tracksuit bottoms and barefoot like me, she had a new scar on her right arm just above the elbow from a demons' three clawed scratch and her eyes stressed the amount of exhaustion she was feeling also.

"The one and only" Will replied opening up his arms for Katie who ran over … and punched him in the stomach. "Damn it!" Will spoke through laboured breaths "What is it with you guys? Next time I'm going to have Castiel leave me in hell" Will added before being tackled by Katie in a strong hug similar to the one I'd given him shortly before.

"Thank you Castiel … truly, I owe you big time" I spoke turning to face the angel who'd helped us and reached out to shake his hand, "Any time kid, happy to help some Protectors for once, the Arch-Angels may not like your kind but I've always thought you were spectacular" Castiel replied turning his head as though a sudden sound had caught his attention.

"Everything okay?" I questioned
"Yeah, boss is calling so I've got to go, best of luck to all of you, stay safe" Castiel replied spreading his large angelic wings.

"Wait before you go, I need to ask you something?" Will spoke stepping forwards, Castiel turned to face him with a quizzical expression on his face and smiled, "Castiel is an interesting name but last time I checked it was used on a little show called Supernatural, did you steal it?" Will questioned.
"Honestly …" Castiel replied shaking his head in frustration, "You show up to one Hollywood set for fun and the next thing you know your names on Prime-time television" Castiel added winking at Will and laughing before disappearing in a burst of light leaving us alone in our hotel room.

We decided now that we were all back together to go into the next room to check on Jen and how she was healing after the battle, Katie entered first knocking lightly on the door and pressing finger to her lips for us to be quiet tiptoeing over to Jen who was snoring loudly into her pillow.

 Jen's hair was plastered all over the pillows in every direction like someone had thrown an octopus onto the bed, her three braids left untangled in the mess of hair, she was pale from exhaustion and snored so loud that for a brief moment I wondered if there was a warthog hidden somewhere in the room with us "Jen?" Katie whispered kneeling down in front of her.

Jen slowly roused from her slumber and looked directly at Katie before shifting her gaze to me and the finally settling it on Will, "Oh … Will's here? I'm dead, aren't I?" Jen mumbled slowly sitting upright.
"Not quite yet I'm afraid" Will replied
"WILL!" Jen shouted jumping upright on shaky legs and crushing Will in a hug similar to how Katie and I had hugged him … before slapping him across the face. "Stupid idiot doing something like that!" Jen shouted before stumbling back and collapsing down into a seating position on the edge of the bed, "That's it! I'm going back to Hell" Will complained rubbing his cheek and throwing the cigar into the trash can in the corner.

"I see that you've earned your sword mastery tattoo also" Jen spoke pointing to the sword shaped symbol on my chest, "Wondered what that meant" I replied smiling down at her, "You sure you're okay?" I added
 "Tired but I'll be okay" Jen mumbled her eyelids slowly shutting and opening from exhaustion.

 "Well then, I suggest we order room service, have a decent meal for the first time in days and then sleep till check out tomorrow" I suggested, "I could go for a cheeseburger" Will spoke up throwing himself onto the bed and grabbing the menu from the side table. "Glad to see your appetite hasn't' changed" I spoke landing down next to Will with Jen on my right grabbing the TV remote.
 "Oh no, my room, my TV" Jen added stealing the remote from my hand sitting upright on the bed her shoulder pressed against mine, "Move over I'm not getting left out" Katie shouted jumping through the air and landing across mine, Jen's and Will's legs with her entire body, we all let out a loud grunt of pain and burst out laughing in joy at our reunion and friendship.

## Chapter 54
## Back Home

You may be wondering how we got back to the academy from Las Vegas to the outskirts of Chicago, well the answer to that is simple, when you're a Half Angel and your friends are the children of a Demon and an Angel it's easy to dodge downtown traffic by simply flying to the nearest train station, although I had to carry Jen since she was the only one of us without wings.

Several long train rides later we arrived back in Chicago but due to a lack of funds in our wallet (Being a Protector doesn't pay well) we decided to fly back to the Academy with Katie and Will leading the way, "Glad to see you finally got your wings" Jen shouted over the wind blowing through my hair and feathers (That sounded weird right?).

"What can I say? Guess someone must have rang a bell" I joked smiling down at her, in truth I'd never felt freer and more connected to my heritage that when my angelic abilities had activated. Being a Hunter with the gift of combat abilities, agility, enhanced eyesight and magic was incredible but the feeling of flying through the air with the wind flowing through my hair making my feathers dance felt beyond amazing, it felt ... angelic.

We arrived back at the academy a few hours later descending through the magical barrier and landing in front of the main hall of the academy to the thunderous applause of the audience who had seen us flying in, we barely had space to land as the crowds gathered around us shouting our names in joy and clapping us on the back for a job well done.

Katie found herself surrounded by her fellow Angel children being lifted high into the air and thrown up and down, Will disappeared amongst his fellow Demon children pushed into a celebratory mosh pit and having a large bucket of ice cold water dumped over him like players would to a coach at the end of a winning football match and Jen and I were pulled into the Hunter crowd being clapped so many times on the back that I thought I would end up covered in bruises again.

"Well done Young Protectors" Isaac shouted descending from the stairs of the main hall clapping his hands together surrounded by the rest of the council who were all smiling at us with pride. I looked over at Coach Jones who had led us to the needle to Dante's compass and was confused at what appeared to be a fake smile, but then again, he was always grumpy so maybe I was just reading him wrong.

"The Gates of Hell are closed and the mortal world is safe from threats for another day" Isaac continued, the crowd dulled their joyous roar in congratulation's and simply stood around us each of us in turn stood in front of the council smiling back at them.

"Thank you, Council members" Jen replied bowing her head in respect, "Please Miss Wilson, we are the ones who should be bowing to you" Isaac replied dismissing her with a hand and bowing over in respect, the rest of the council members also bowed and all students and anyone else who surrounded us and for the first time in a long time I felt as though I truly belonged, I felt at home.

After the bow the council asked us to follow them into the hall to discuss the mission in private, we told them the entire story from start to finish the council simply nodding their heads in agreement at each step of our journey, when we finished we found ourselves staring up at them waiting to see what would happen next.
"Your bravery on this mission for all of you is outstanding and as such deserves a reward, ask and you shall receive" Isaac spoke holding his arms out to us, we all stood in silence feeling incredibly awkward trying to decide which one of us would dare to go first.

"Actually, council I do have a request" I spoke choosing to go first, "On the mission a life was lost, her name was Cassandra and I ..." I spoke pausing at the pain in my heart, "I loved her more than words can explain, without her this mission may have failed because I wouldn't be here today, I wish to bring her here so I can give her the funeral she deserves ... the funeral of a Protector" I added looking up at the council who were all staring at each other and whispering.

"Was she mortal?" Madam Rosemerta asked an elderly council member who was the daughter of a Deinonychus, "Yes, she was, but she had the heart of a Protector, without her we would have failed there is no doubt in the matter ... she deserves this right" Jen defended standing by my side.
The council continued their whispers and then looked down at me, "Very well Jason, you have the council's permission but if you wish to perform the burial on the lake then you will need Nimue's permission also" Isaac spoke, "Thank you Council members" I replied bowing my head and turning to walk out of the hall leaving my friends behind to receive whatever reward their heart desired from the council but I had two things that I needed to do.

I walked down the hill from the main hall and across the walkway until I was stood in the main Blacksmith classroom in the middle of the Lake, "Nimue? Are you here?" I shouted out onto the Lake's reflective surface, "Hello Jason, how can I help?" Nimue asked floating upwards from the lake and walking across the classroom till she was stood facing me her blonde hair cascading down her shoulders.
 "I have a favour to ask of you" I replied rubbing my hands together nervously,
"Of course, but may I ask first, you look sorrowed, as if you have lost someone dear to you" Nimue stated staring deep into my eyes almost boring into my soul.

"You're good" I replied wiping away the tear that was rolling down my cheek, "Her name was Cassandra, I called her Cassie, she was killed on the mission" I added, Nimue took a deep sigh and then raised her hand softly wiping away another tear on my cheek resting the palm of her soft hand on my cheek.
 "I am truly sorry for your loss Jason, there is no pain than that of a broken heart" Nimue replied smiling at me a small drop of lake water rolling from the corner of her eye (I don't technically know if it was a tear).

"Thank you, I wish to perform a true funeral right for her and to push her body onto your lake in a raft and set it alight, I know that's what she would want" I asked "Of course Jason, you may use my lake for your goodbye" Nimue replied a kind smile across her face, "Thank you my Lady, I also have something for you" I spoke reaching into my pocket and removing the now slightly damaged and burnt item I had found in Dagon's safe in what seemed like years ago.

"I found this in a safe in St. Louis and I think it's something you may want to see" I added passing her the photograph I had stolen from the safe. Nimue slowly took the photograph from me and her face suddenly changed from one of confusion to shock (I told you I'd reveal what was on the photograph), "It's him isn't it?" I asked, Nimue nodded her head and held the photograph close to her chest.

You see the photo I'd found all those days ago was that of Merlin stood in a train station from a security camera dated less than a year ago, "He's still alive" Nimue mumbled wiping a tear away.
 "I promised you that I'd find him, this is a clue and my promise continues, one day I will find him and bring him home to you"
"Thank you, Jason" Nimue spoke softly turning back to the edge of the dock and slowly sinking beneath the gentle waves of her lake still clutching the precious photograph.

# Chapter 55
## A Funeral for a love

When I returned to my friends I discovered that Jen had requested for her reward to have someone travel to Dallas and retrieve Cassie's body from the authorities so that she could be given a true burial, she would be arriving the next day thanks to a little council sorcery. The news had she had given me caused me to hug her thanking her repeatedly and sighing in relief that I would be able to grant her peace at last once she arrived.
Katie and Will had also asked for something from the council but had refused to tell me what they had asked for simply stating "You'll find out when the time is right".

The next day Cassie's body arrived in a wooden casket and was escorted to the Funeral building dedicated for last rites of any Protectors to be prepared for burial on the lake. At sunset we headed down to the Lake and stood on the shore alongside Cassie's body which had been laid in a wooden raft surrounded by lavender and Iris petals, her favourite flowers.

She seemed totally and utterly at peace, a smile was spread across her face simple and pure, her scarlet hair had been braided into a long braid that rested onto her shoulder wrapped in flower petals holding it in place like bands, she was wearing a long white robe that made her whole appearance look like an Angel more than she had been in life and her arms were folded across her chest holding a bouquet of white roses.

"Goodbye my love" I whispered softly kissing Cassie on her forehead laying down a single white rose on her chest, "Bye Cassie, thank you for being my sister" Jen spoke next clasping Cassie's hand while placing another white rose onto her chest, "Bye Cass" Katie whispered placing her rose on Cassie's chest and softly touching her cheek. "*Puissiez-vous trouver la paix éternelle dans le Royaume des Protecteurs*" Will spoke placing the rose on her chest and kissing her on the forehead,
"What did that mean?" I asked Will curiously
"May you find Eternal peace in the Realm of Protectors" Will translated, "She may have been mortal but no one deserves a place there more than her" Will added placing his hand on my shoulder, "Thank you" I replied placing my hand on his.

"There's also one last thing I arranged … it was my request to the council" Will spoke looking down at the edge of the lake, I followed his gaze to see a flash of scarlet hair slowly appear from the surface of the lake, "Alexa?" I asked curiously spying the first mermaid that I had ever met when I arrived at the academy, "You asked and we shall answer, push her onto the lake and we can start" Alexa replied a kind smile on her face, with the help of my friends we pushed the boat further out onto the lake setting the tides slowly carry her out onto the lake.

"*If I die young, bury me in satin*" Alexa began to sing softly mesmerising me in her tone, "Will?" I asked turning to face him,

"It was her favourite song ... it's only fair it's how she's said goodbye to it" Will replied looking over at Alexa who continued to sing Cassie's favourite song as four more mermaids appeared out of the water and continued to sing floating softly idly on the surface of the lake.

"It looks like my surprise is here too" Katie spoke looking up at the hillside that led down to the lake and my jaw almost hit the floor in wonder, the tears that were already running down my cheeks were now falling even more.

Coming down the hill was every, single, student in the academy and any families that lived on the grounds and the council all carrying a single candle in respect lighting up the hillside in a soft orange glow, "Katie" I mumbled walking over to her and hugging her tight "Thank you" I added trying my best not to cry like a child as the council approached.

Isaac came up first and stood before me holding the candle in front of him, "Thank you for coming" I spoke to him softly, "It's like you and your friends said Jason, Cassandra was worthy of being a Protector and she deserves the true respect of one" Isaac replied looking over at the lake where Cassie had drifted almost into the middle of it with the Mermaids continuing her favourite song.

I looked over to her and knew at last it was time, "*Ignis*" I whispered casting a small ball of fire to appear in my hand before casting it outwards and onto the lake watching as it soared over the surface before colliding with the boat the flames softly tickling at the edges.

The boat continued to burn as small embers rose into the air disappearing into the night sky and combining with the stars, somewhere deep in my heart I hoped and believed that Cassie's sacrifice had been accepted and that one day I would be reunited with her in the Realm of the Protectors. The Mermaids finished Cassie's song as the boat finally cracked from the heat and Cassie and the boat sank beneath Nimue's Lake to rest in peace for eternity ... "Goodbye" I whispered for the final time.

## Chapter 56
## Coach Jones wants to talk

It had been two days since Cassie's funeral on the lake and life at the academy had been pretty much returned to normal, well, at least as normal as you can get for the children of supernatural beings who spend most of their time training to prevent the Rapture from taking place and using the little free time we had to laugh and joke with each other and just enjoy life in general the way any normal teenager would.

Every night we agreed to have a movie night and I introduced Katie, Jen and Will to the marvellous films such as It's a wonderful life (Katie had a good laugh at that one) and Indiana Jones which after watching Will decided he was going to buy a whip (I didn't want to ask why).

On my third day I was walking through the Academy streets finally feeling free from stress and preparing for the upcoming Sunday when I would find myself back out in the mortal world defending it from any supernatural threats that may seek to harm the world. "Jason!" I heard a voice shout from my right, a student came running up and passed me a small note, "Thanks" I replied as the student smiled and continued on his merry way heading into the market for supplies for his room, I unfolded the note breaking the wax seal and quickly read what was inside:

*Jason my boy,*

*Meet me in the main Hall at your earliest convenience,*

*We have much to discuss,*

*Sincerely,*

*Coach Jones*

Following the instruction, I headed straight to the Main Hall and pushed open the creaking heavy oak door, "Hello? Coach Jones?" I asked heading down the main aisle "Thank you for coming Jason" Coach Jones replied suddenly appearing from the shadows on the right side of the hall almost making me jump out of my skin.

"You scared me for a second" I laughed clutching my chest "I got your letter" I added holding the note in my hand and slowly approaching him.

"Yes, I wished to talk to you about your assignment, there were some questions I wished to ask you but I never found the time during the briefing, please sit" Coach Jones replied taking a seat at one of the tables beckoning me to sit down next to him which I slowly did. For some unexplained reason my Hunter instincts at the back of my mind seemed to be screaming in red alert but then again those few times I was in school as a kid they did the same thing when I was called in to see the teacher.

"What would you like to know?" I asked placing my hands on my knees,
"Not so much as ask you, as tell you my opinion of you" Coach Jones replied cracking the tension in his neck with a loud pop.
"You know Jason, I was truly impressed with the work you and your friends did on this assignment, I was pleasantly surprised when I learned that you'd found the case of Dante's compass and defeated Dagon I must admit, the Chimera in the train station was definitely a surprise" Coach Jones spoke.

"Making it all the way to Valentine with a bounty on you head and retrieving the magnet from Isaiah, that truly was an impressive accomplishment I must admit, defeating an Arch-demon with broken ribs? I mean wow" Coach Jones continued laughing at his statements.

"Of course, Blake was a total disappointment, had he succeeded in wiping your memory then this mission would have gone entirely differently but sadly even he can't follow simple instructions" Coach Jones grumbled rubbing the stubble on his chin with his thumb and index finger,
"Killing young Cassandra was foolish, I did tell him to aim for Miss Wilson but clearly he made the wrong decision" Coach Jones added and in that instant moment all the alarm bells that had been screaming quickly shot to Def-con 1.

"Coach?" I asked confused slowly tensing the muscles in my body, "Ah yes, the title given to me by the students, I do love teaching the agility teaching sessions but I never did like the nickname, I always preferred to be called by my true title that I was worthy of, you may have heard of it on your assignment" Coach Jones replied.
"You and your friends and the rest of these Protectors call me Coach … but my true title is Commander" Coach Jones spoke and instantly my mind went into overdrive.

I had heard the title throughout the mission from almost every enemy we had faced from Isaiah to Blake to Galadriel, the commander had given them all instructions on how their task should go and their instructions. "You … it's you … you're the one who was trying to get us killed" I mumbled in shock "And clearly they failed, it truly is hard to find good help these days" Coach Jones complained, I went to clench my fists ready to bring Divine Fury to life "*Impediendum*" Coach Jones spoke.

## Chapter 57
## Bet you didn't see that coming


Suddenly, I couldn't move, my body was completely frozen in place and Coach Jones or I suppose as I should call him now Commander Jones slowly stood clapping his hands, "Fine effort Jason, truly fine effort, Impediendum … you haven't learned that yet but it is nothing more than a simple paralysis spell, you'll be able to move once I leave but for now I need you to listen" Commander Jones spoke twirling his hand. I was still trying my best to clench my hands and bring Divine Fury to life so I could stop him but my hands were frozen, I couldn't even scream for help from the paralysis of my vocal chords.

"Do you know the biggest problem with this academy?" Commander Jones asked me "You all hold yourselves so high and mighty above the mortals but we're no better, do you know what an undeclared is?" Commander Jones asked me despite the fact that I couldn't answer him.

"An undeclared is the name of a child who has supernatural parents but no supernatural abilities, basically they're mortal but with the knowledge of knowing the academy exists" Commander Jones continued. "When they go through the identification ceremony and receive no powers then they are banished from the academy grounds and sent out into the mortal world, my son is one of them and I'm sure you can understand the resentment he holds" Commander Jones explained as I felt a slight twitch in my fingertips.

"Well, I decided that I should do something about that, the council is old and flawed and should be run by someone worthy of the power, a man of true knowledge and value, a man … like me" Commander Jones continued his rant pacing back and forth like a mad dictator. "So, here is my plan … now I am telling you this because once I leave I want you to deliver this message to the council" Commander Jones spoke, I could feel it again the twitch in my fingertips now spreading to my right hand, his focus was slipping.

"I want you to tell them that I will be returning one day with an army and when I do the academy will fall and the council will be killed, I will take their place and any students and families who wish to survive this attack are welcome to join me, so long as they vow to leave the grounds and declare their undying loyalty to me and my cause" Commander Jones ranted turning to face me as the feeling returned to my right hand, I kept my focus locked on his eyes so that he wouldn't notice the attention I'd shifted to my now usable hand.

"This is my cause Jason and it is a good one, you can join me too of course after you've delivered my message, a soldier like you would be the perfect weapon, so my boy … what do you say?" Commander Jones asked me loosening the paralysis around my lips. My feeling had fully returned to my right hand and lower arm so with one quick movement when his guard was down, I brought Divine Fury to life and stabbed forwards aiming for his head.

Unfortunately, Commander Jones was faster so all I left was a large gash wound across his cheek cutting into his demonic skin with the Divine steel side of my blade. "Go to hell" I growled spitting onto the floor my body now paralysed once again, "YOU FILTHY MONGREL!" Commander Jones growled pressing his hand against the wound taking away some of the blue blood that was running down his cheek, the wound would never heal no matter how much sulphur he drank which made me smile at the thought of leaving him with a nasty scar, "That was impressive I'll admit but clearly you need to be taught a lesson" Commander Jones added taking a Demonic obsidian dagger from his belt and slowly approaching me.

"Deliver the message Jason … but try not to bleed out before anyone arrives" Commander Jones whispered into my ear before driving his dagger into my lower abdomen. The cold blade lodged into the muscle in my stomach and I tried to scream in pain but my lips were paralysed once again, I could feel the blood oozing into my shirt and running down to the floor, Jones left the blade in my abdomen and stepped away from me pressing a napkin from the table against the wound on his cheek.

"Goodbye Jason, I'll see you soon" Commander Jones chuckled opening a dark portal with the flick of his hand in the middle of the hall stepping through it leaving no trace of him being there behind.
The paralysis spell wore off a few seconds after he left and I collapsed onto the cold stone floor, my blue blood spilling out into the stones, "I think he's in here hey Jason!" I heard Jen announce as the door behind me opened, "OH MY GOD JASON!" Jen shouted running over and flipping me onto my back.

"SOMEBODY GET HELP!" Jen screamed, I could hear the frantic movement of students running into the hall to see the commotion and spotted Katie suddenly appearing and kneeling alongside me, "Hang on Jason, you're going to be okay" Katie mumbled removing the dagger with a quick pull which would have made me scream in pain had it not been for the blood in my mouth before beginning her healing magic, "Jones …. Jones …" I mumbled spitting a clot of blood out of my mouth and onto the stone floor.

"What about Jones?" Jen asked me placing my shoulders against her knee leaning me up slightly, "Stabbed me … traitor … Jones is …. Commander" I stammered looking up at Jen who was staring down at me in shock. "It can't be" I heard Jen mumble, "The dagger … it's the Coach's" I heard a student speak who had picked up the dagger that had been previously lodged in my stomach.

"Katie … why isn't it working?" Jen questioned frantically her hands coated in my blood from pressing her palm against the wound, "There's so much blood, we need to get him to the Infirmary now!" Katie ordered "Hang on Jason … just hang on …" I barely heard Jen speak as my vision started to blur and my hearing disappeared before everything went black.

# **The End**

Authors note

To all my readers, I want to thank you all for reading this tale and following Jason on his journey to close the Gates of Hell. There are many people to thank for help in creating this first book in my first attempt at a series, thanks as always to my mom for listening patiently as I bounced ideas off her and regaled her with countless ideas and thoughts.
Special thanks to T. G. Willis an amazing author for proof reading my first draft of Jason Parker and the Gates of Hell reminding me of how terrible I truly am at grammar. And to you, the readers who without you, none of this would be possible.

 When Jason approached me and passed me this journal expressing his exploits and asked me to share it with you all so that you would be welcomed to his confusing and amazing world I decided that I could hardly say no to him. The inspiration from this book has come from my fascination and love of fantasy books and series and was heavily inspired by the Percy Jackson series by Rick Riordan who I cannot possibly recommend in words.

 Rick is an amazing author and I have read almost every single one of his books and look forward to the Disney plus series coming out soon. If there are any Percy Jackson fans that have read this book then you may have noticed a few easter eggs dropped into the tale, rest assured that this tale is one of many that will come in the future as soon as Jason gets back to me providing, he survived the cruel betrayal and attack by Commander Jones.

If you enjoyed this book then please leave a review and recommend it to any of your friends and family so that they too can enjoy this tale, Jason, his friends and I all look forward to seeing you again soon.

You can reach me with any comments or queries on:

Facebook – J. Boardman Author
Email – j.boardman.author@gmail.com